CURRENTS
of WILL

BOOK TWO OF THE ATLANTIS CHRONICLES

SUSAN MACIVER

Copyright © 2017 by Susan MacIver
All rights reserved.

Cover Design by Monica Haynes; thethatchery.com
Interior Graphic Design by Colleen Sheehan; wdrbookdesign.com

No part of this book may be reproduced in any form or by any electronic or mechanical means including information storage and retrieval systems, without permission in writing from the author. The only exception is by a reviewer, who may quote short excerpts in a review.

Susan MacIver
Visit my website at www.susanmaciver.com
FaceBook.com/SusanMaciverAuthor
Instagram@susan.maciver
Twitter@SusanMaciver

Printed in the United States of America
First Printing: 2017
Published by MacIver Publishing, LLC

ISBN: 978-0-9991782-0-1
Ebook ISBN: 978-0-9991782-1-8
Library of Congress Control Number: 2017911158

DEDICATION

TO MY SON, Eric MacIver, a beautiful gift of tremendous joy, eternal wisdom, and infinite kindness. These attributes, coupled with your dry, fall-on–the-floor-laughing sense of humor, have kept me going through times the tunnel seemed never-ending. Thank you for coming into my life.

Always and forever.

ACKNOWLEDGMENTS

I HAVE SAID BEFORE that no one writes a book by themselves; our family, our experiences and friends, all play a part. However, by virtue of the incredible women who have stepped into my life when I didn't know where to turn, the truth of that statement has never proven more true. Their talents are as big as their hearts and each of you have made my vision and my words take flight.

Monica Haynes of The Thatchery, your cover designs are more beautiful than anything I could ever have imagined. The covers alone have beckoned readers that might never have given my story a second look.

Colleen Sheehan at WDR Design, your humor is infectious and the emails we've shared have provided many moments of LMAO! Your graphics have given the interiors of my books the feel needed to artfully reflect the stories.

Tammi Labrecque with Larks and Katydids, your editing skills are kind, thoughtful and write on! You have elevated my words to a much higher level, (dare I say it?) to rival the beauty of the lark song.

To each of you, thank you from the bottom of my heart.

And finally, once again, to the one man, the alchemist, who has turned my dreams into reality. My Duke, you have always made me feel like your Duchess. I love you with all that I am or ever will be.

Susan
9/17/17

PRONUNCIATION

ARIS – AIR/iss
CLEITO – klee/ATE/o
DARIA CAIDEN – DAR/ee/uh KY/den
ENNAEL – uh/NEEL
EUMELUS – Yoo/mue/les
KAI-DAN – KY/dan
KALLI-KAN – KAL/ee/dan
KYLA – Ky/la
MARIK – MAIR/ik
NA-KAI EVA EVENOR – na/KY ee/va ev/uh/nor
NI-CIO EVAW AZAES – NEE/shee/o ee/va UH/zays
OIA – EE/ya
OOMI – OO/me
PELTOR – PEL/tor
POSEIDON – PO/sy/den
ROGERT – RO/jer
TRAVLOR – TRAV/lor
YLNO – IL/no

Synopsis for Tides of Change

TIDES OF CHANGE, Book One of *The Atlantis Chronicles* trilogy, takes place beneath the Aegean Sea where a band of one thousand Atlanteans survived the cataclysmic wrath unleashed by Poseidon thousands of years ago. Through the ages, remarkable evolutionary gifts have appeared in the offspring of the original colony and in present day, the small community thrives in their hidden underwater sanctuary.

Na-Kai, Atlantis's Most Sovereign Healer, has kept her people in health and by doing so, extends their lifespans to the specific age of four hundred and eight. At that special moment, the Atlanteans do not taste physical death, but their bodies begin to give way to the spirit, until, in the blink of an eye, they transcend to the other side of life.

To her disappointment, Na-Kai has found no one in Atlantis who exhibits the healing gift necessary to inherit her position. If another healer is not named before Na-Kai transcends, her people will face another extinction event. With no other choice, she unleashes a terrible thought-form; a powerful telekinetic energy the use of which was forbidden by the ancients. Na-Kai's thought-form rises to the Greek island of Santorini and traps a "topsider."

Daria Caiden, against her will, is forced from the jagged cliffs into the depths of the Aegean Sea. As she releases her last breath she is rescued by an Atlantean. Bringing her safely to Atlantis, Ni-Cio is horrified to learn that an emergency council meeting has voted unanimously to eject the topsider at depth, ensuring her death and their continued anonymity. As the angry mob gathers, Na-Kai intervenes revealing the true reason Daria was brought to Atlantis. Daria is the only person who has the gifts that will enable her to become Atlantis's Most Sovereign Healer.

Accepted as one of their own, Daria, taught by Na-Kai, awakens her healing powers. Finding her place in Atlantis, Daria is irresistibly drawn to Ni-Cio. Both topsider and Atlantean fall in love and take each other as lifemates.

When Daria meets the reclusive and mysterious Travlor, he gives her a deadly potion supposedly designed to help her acclimate to the strange Atlantean food. With each surreptitious sip, Daria ingests a poison meant to kill her as it is absorbed into her system.

Daria and Na-Kai are thrust into a critical healing session when a mortally wounded Atlantean is brought to them. Weakened by the poison she has ingested, Daria falls into a coma as the healing nears its conclusion. Na-Kai orders Daria taken to her quarters. Depleting her own precious reserves of energy, Na-Kai finishes the healing. Once the Atlantean is out of danger, she asks to be carried to Daria's side.

Severely weakened, Na-Kai sacrifices her life in order to heal Daria. In their last exchange, Na-Kai teaches Daria everything

she must know in order to become a Most Sovereign Healer. She also reveals that Travlor has been imprisoned in Atlantis for many years and is responsible for her poisoning.

As Na-Kai transcends, Daria is too weak to keep Travlor in Atlantis.

Fleeing to Santorini with the aid of his son, Evan Gaddes, Travlor is determined to wreak vengeance. His aims are to destroy Atlantis, but his ultimate goal is world domination. Repulsed by his father's maniacal schemes, Evan undergoes a change of heart and decides to help the Atlanteans.

In the horrific aftermath of Travlor's invasion, Ni-Cio realizes that Travlor has kidnaped Daria and again disappeared. Poisonous gas, released by Travlor's mercenaries, causes the immediate evacuation of the remaining Atlanteans. Ni-Cio and Evan lead the small band of survivors to Travlor's abandoned compound. There, they must teach the Atlanteans how to survive in the strange topside world, locate Travlor's whereabouts so that they can initiate Daria's rescue, rebuild Atlantis and avoid another Travlor-inspired war in which the entire planet could be annihilated.

And so begins *Currents of Will*, Book Two of *The Atlantis Chronicles*

The Canons

⊰ I ⊱
As children of Poseidon you are granted the paradise that is Atlantis
In the purity of your actions will it remain thus

⊰ II ⊱
The healing power descends through my lineage
Live that you flourish
Attend not and you will surely weaken

⊰ III ⊱
No matter the form
All life is held sacred

⊰ IV ⊱
Whether in the heavens or the earth
We are bound by the same essence that creates life
Hurt another and you ultimately hurt yourself

⊰ V ⊱
Behold the miracle that is You
Cherish this offering

⊰ VI ⊱
The sacrament of love is inviolate
Written in the heavens before your time
Heart, mind and soul will bring you into awareness of your life mate
Act not until they speak as one

⊰ VII ⊱
Love is manifested within the smallest detail
Living thus will your life be enriched

⊰ VIII ⊱
Let your essence be filled with the joy of life
And spread that joy to those you touch

Chapter 1

BREATHE IN, BREATHE OUT. He could not talk; his heart still beat and blood still pulsed through his veins, but the words would not come. With each contraction, a band of grief constricted around his heart, strangling it, so that Evan didn't think it could expand again, and yet it did. Heartbeat, eye blink. Still, no words.

With practiced skill, Kyla piloted the craft through the turbulent water. Behind her, Evan watched her movements. They had not spoken since their evacuation of Atlantis, but he felt the breaking of her heart as if it were his own.

Kyla set course for his deserted compound, then navigated the biosphere with mechanical detachment. Her normally fluid motions were too quiet, too contained. She moved as though the weight of the dead, like remora, had attached themselves to her limbs and might never leave.

Evan reached to stroke her hair, then hesitated. He had no right; her life had been shattered because of his father. And though he had tried to thwart Travlor's invasion, he had been stunningly unsuccessful by every standard. He dropped his hand and, worried about her physical wellbeing, spoke instead. "Kyla, when we are clear of this vessel, grab handfuls of sand and scrub it over yourself and your bioskin as hard as you can. It will help neutralize the gas."

A slight tilt of her head was the only acknowledgment he received. At last she spoke, but her voice was thick. She cleared her throat. "Evan, are you all right? You must have inhaled some of the gas. Do you feel any effects?"

He didn't answer. The ocean floor had risen to meet them and he braced himself as the craft decelerated. In the shallows, Kyla halted the biosphere and Evan clambered out as soon as the hatch dematerialized.

He gasped from the sudden blast of frigid saltwater. An incoming surge washed over his chest while he helped Kyla out of the craft, and though he tried to shield her body from the worst waves, she was already soaked. He ducked underwater, grabbing handfuls of sand. He scoured her back and shoulders with the abrasive grains, then gave her a nudge, prompting her to move. "Do this all over your body, and keep scrubbing until I tell you to quit!"

Kyla followed Evan's lead and scrubbed her body with the sand. "What about you?"

Evan did not break rhythm. "Ni-Cio reacted so quickly that I'll be all right, but I don't want you to take any chances."

During their ascent Evan had searched his memories for anything he knew about nerve gas. Although he wasn't sure what agent had been released, he knew that copious amounts of soap, water, and vigorous scrubbing helped neutralize most poisons. He continued to scour Kyla's back, hoping the saltwater and sand would stave off any immediate effects. He needed to get everyone to the compound as soon as possible; the ominous skies threatened storms and it would be dark soon.

"Kyla, I think the saltwater will be enough to neutralize the outsides of the biospheres, but your people don't have much time. As soon as they start surfacing, get them out of the vehicles and out of their bioskins. Show them how to scrub each other down."

He stopped and looked at her. Sadness and fear dulled her beautiful topaz eyes. More than anything he wanted to take her in his arms and hold her until her grief subsided and she was able to smile again. Instead, he blinked hard and raised his voice over the sounds of the surf. "The saltwater and sand should be enough for initial decontamination, but I have to go to the compound for extra clothes. Once the bioskins are off don't let anyone touch them. Use a stick to put them into a pile, then wait for me!"

He turned to leave, but couldn't help himself. He cupped her beloved face in both of his hands and kissed her full lips. He tasted salt and tears and longing, and was astonished to feel her arms wrap tightly around his shoulders. Kyla clung to him and her body trembled—whether from shock or cold or grief, he didn't know, but it took every ounce of his willpower to pull away. Evan held her quivering chin and used his other hand to brush the wet hair from her eyes. "I'll be back as soon as I can."

Kyla nodded and dropped her gaze. Though Evan would have given his heart to stay, he turned and grabbed the biosphere, then slogged through the surf and carried the craft onto the beach beyond the high water mark. Once he had secured the biosphere, he allowed himself a backward glance.

Kyla stood alone, watching him from shore break. He couldn't leave her, but when he started back, Kyla's thoughts poured into him. *"Go, Evan ... Please, we must help the others ... I will wait here for you ..."*

Evan turned and sprinted up the rocky, cliffside trail.

At the summit, he stopped and sucked in a few lungfuls of sea-tinged air, then raced toward the compound in an all-out run. He leapt over the withered branches of the defunct vineyard and slid down the hillside until he pounded into the courtyard in a cloud of dry, red dust.

Rounding a corner, he flew past the kitchens, where he sighted the sagging, faded red truck that had been used to ferry supplies. He skidded to a halt beside the vehicle and yanked the door open. He jumped into the cab and, fumbling blindly, heaved a sigh of relief to find the key still in the ignition. The starter ground and he pumped the accelerator, praying that the old relic still had some kick. But the truck was stubborn and tired. A string of curses gathered force, but Evan refrained and tried yet again to cajole the vehicle to life, rubbing the dashboard and pleading. He ground the reluctant starter once more and it faltered. Cursing, Evan cranked the key again. The truck hesitated, belched blue smoke, and rattled to life.

Rusty gears protested when he rammed it into reverse, but Evan backed the truck into the lifeless courtyard without another problem. He swerved toward a set of cabins, jumped out of the cab and was through the door of the closest cabin before the old vehicle jittered to a stop.

Searching the empty room, he found exactly what he had suspected: two army-issued duffels lay abandoned in a corner. He crossed the cabin's squealing floorboards and hoisted the bags over to the beds, then upended the contents onto the lowest bunk. Seizing all of the clothes, he crammed them back into one of the duffels, slung both bags over his shoulder, and bolted from the room. He repeated the process until he had ransacked all the cabins and commandeered every article of clothing.

At last, he rested against the side of the antiquated clunker and pulled massive amounts of air into his lungs as he surveyed the mountain of duffels he had launched into the truck bed.

Ragged gusts of frigid wind whipped through the compound and Evan eyed the black clouds roiling overhead. Their bloated underbellies warned of the ominous birth of a monster storm. He had to move.

With one final glance at the skies, he vaulted into the cab and slammed the truck into gear. He urged it forward, alternating between vitriolic threats of destruction and promises of resurrection, and the old jalopy bounced its way through the vineyard. It wheezed to a stop at the edge of the cliff and Evan pushed the door open, jumped out, and ran around to the back of the truck. Without breaking stride, he grabbed an armful of bags, reached the edge of the cliff, and hurled them over the side. His thoughts roared through Kyla. *"Grab the closest bag and get out of that bioskin!"*

Drenched in an icy prelude of the approaching storm, Kyla shivered. Her life had turned surreal and Evan felt like her last link to reality. His strong arms tightened protectively around her and she could tell that he did his best to shield her from the stinging nettles of ocean spray.

Currents of Will

They stood, arms around each other, long after Evan returned with the supplies. The wind had whipped the surf into a frenzy and they struggled to remain upright. Evan urged her to go ashore, but Kyla refused. She had a terrible feeling that if she did, she would never again see any of her family or friends. She would be the last and only survivor of the horrific holocaust that had been visited upon her people. That, she would not be able stand. So, she remained. The surf battered her as she desperately scrutinized the horizon for any indication that someone—anyone—from Atlantis had followed them topside.

"I'm so sorry, Kyla . . . I couldn't stop him . . ." Evan's thoughts were heavy with remorse as his words faded away, echoing a lifetime of unshed tears.

Rivulets of water coursed down Kyla's cheeks and spilled over her lips. She tasted the salt and neither knew nor cared whether they came from within, caused by her own searing sense of loss, or were merely trails of unremitting sea spray. She swiped her eyes and continued to search the mammoth line of swells that rolled across the empty horizon.

The genocidal rage that Travlor had unleashed upon her people had taken a catastrophic toll. She knew that the cavern floors of Atlantis were littered with the bodies and blood of Atlanteans and mercenaries alike; however, she knew the lengths to which Evan had gone to protect her and her people. Her thoughts brushed his with infinite tenderness. *"I do not know anyone who could have withstood the choices you have had to make . . . We have both lost so much, yet your safety alleviates a measure of my grief . . ."*

It seemed as though her compassion broke the very heart of heaven. Winds that had sung a mournful dirge escalated to an earsplitting keen and an explosive blast of thunder shook the ground.

Jagged shards of lightning ripped through the rain-engorged clouds, and Evan and Kyla held each other before an onslaught that seemed as though every element of heaven and earth had joined in a vast primal wake.

Blinded by the storm's ferocious display, Kyla almost missed the faint shimmer of light. A biosphere broke from beneath the weight of the sea, and hammered by wild surface waves, labored to reach shore.

"Evan, over there!" Kyla tore herself from Evan's arms and bounded through the surging tides into deeper water. Followed closely by the topsider, they grasped the slippery sides of the biosphere and steadied the craft as the canopy dematerialized.

Mer-An, cloaked in dark glasses and earplugs, dragged herself from the vehicle. She willed the canopy closed and clung tenaciously to the stern. Her thoughts found Kyla. *"Nine children inside ... terrified ... more are on their way!"*

They strained against the inexhaustible undertow and wrestled the biosphere to shore. The hatch dematerialized, opening a new world to some of the last children of Atlantis. Even though their goggles and earplugs shielded them, they were terrified to move when they were lifted from the biosphere. Seeing them lined up in a passive, silent row, Kyla's heart wept. *"Come to me ... We must get you out of your bioskins and into topside clothes ... Mer-An is here and we will take care of you ..."*

Mer-An and Kyla helped the children out of their bioskins and guided them into the surf. They scrubbed their tiny bodies with sand while Evan threw the 'skins into the empty duffels and found clothing for them.

Currents of Will

The storm raged even as Kyla helped the children to shore and into the ill-fitting topside garments. Mer-An stood alone in the surf, listlessly scrubbing her bioskin. The woodenness of her motions revealed her exhaustion. Evan waded out to help. *"Mer-An! Let's move!"* His sharp command seemed to re-energize her. Together they scrubbed her skin while Kyla found clothes for her.

Once Mer-An was dressed, they huddled around the children in silence, their voices and thoughts muted by the might of the storm and the cataclysmic events of the day. Tension began to ease as weary thoughts from beyond their numbers began to penetrate the blanket of numbness that had crept into their minds.

"We are almost there..."
"I am behind you..."
"I think I see shore break..."
"There are others that follow..."

Through the driving sheets of rain, several dim beams of light appeared at random intervals as biospheres breached the surface. Evan and Kyla battled their way back into the crashing surf, leaving Mer-An to safeguard the children.

Exhausted beyond thought, everyone worked mechanically, repeating the same process as biospheres made it to shore. Each one was intercepted, dragged to shore, emptied of passengers and secured well past the high-water mark. Everyone helped each other decontaminate as best they could.

As the storm shrieked to its furious apex, the final vessel emerged from the bitter depths. To Kyla, it looked as though Ni-Cio had lost control of his craft. The biosphere careened through the high seas and hurtled toward a lethal outcropping of volcanic rock. Evan bellowed loud enough to be heard over the storm. "They're not going to make it!"

He broke from the group and leapt frantically through the incoming surf. Twenty spent Atlanteans followed his lead. Kyla watched in horror as the men struggled to gain purchase on the slippery vehicle. They swarmed the craft and, through their combined strength, they were able to alter the deadly trajectory of the storm-driven vessel. At last, stabilizing the biosphere, the canopy disappeared.

Ni-Cio evaw Azaes rose from inside and jumped with weary grace into the storm surge. Even from her vantage point, Kyla could see that fatigue had carved tight, grim lines into his handsome face. And the tired, encumbered movements with which he strained against the violent blows of the surf spoke of the tremendous ordeal he had endured. She held her breath and watched as, in agonizing degrees, he raised one muscular arm to offer aid to his best friend. Aris thrust his body from the biosphere.

Surrounded by Evan and the others, Ni-Cio and Aris were scrubbed down and divested of their bioskins. At last, they waded through the waist-high water and stumbled upon the rocky beach. Kyla had their clothes ready, and once they were outfitted, they trudged over the sand-covered rocks to stand before the shattered remnants of Atlantis.

Kyla moved next to her brother and took his hand to comfort him. She saw the questioning looks that lay beneath the shock and sorrow on the defeated faces of her people. She knew that Marik had bequeathed a terrible task to Ni-Cio, a task that he had never wanted.

His entire adult life, Ni-Cio had resisted the fact that he was next in line to succeed Marik as council leader. He had never wanted to be tied down by such an obligation and its inherent responsibilities. He gratified his need for something different with his job collecting samples. Wandering the seas and surreptitiously stealing glimpses of topside life helped offset his desire for adventure.

Ni-Cio never suspected that Kyla knew his deepest secret: with his unquenchable wanderlust, Ni-Cio had been bored with life in Atlantis.

When Daria had come into his life, Ni-Cio's restless soul had found peace and fulfillment. His wanderings had ceased and he had felt secure enough in the new healer's love that he had accepted his ascendency with less reluctance.

Now, everything had changed. Travlor had taken Daria, only the gods knew where, and Ni-Cio was the default leader of a displaced group of people who had no idea how to survive topside. As the existent council leader, everyone looked to him for guidance and deliverance. And it was clear that Ni-Cio struggled with his own grief. *"Kyla, how am I to guide the needs of others when I could not even help Daria? I am not prepared for this ... What can I possibly say that will help? What am I supposed to do?"*

Kyla raised the back of his hand to her lips. *"Marik chose you, Ni-Cio—no one else. I know it seems unbearable, but he died defending our freedom. His last words were, 'Lead them well' ... he knew that you would ..."*

The storm began to play itself out and Kyla watched as Ni-Cio slowly raised his head. His violet eyes blazed with an inner light and he tenderly released her hand. Stepping into the midst of their people, his deep voice broke the stillness. It came, low and strong, with confident reassurance. His words were a soothing balm that imparted hope and comfort. "You fought well and bravely this day. That any of us remain is a testament to your courage and the strength of your spirits."

Hot, silent tears slid down Kyla's cheeks and mixed with the cooling caress of rain. She bowed her head in mourning. The wind subsided to a refreshing breeze and Ni-Cio's voice rose with conviction. "We will find rest within the walls of Evan's home. And we will stay until we regain our strength. When we are ready, we will leave to rebuild our home … but it is here and it is now that we begin to heal our grief."

Kyla felt the raw ache of his soul. Ni-Cio's voice trembled. "We cannot and we will not let our sorrow dishonor the memories of those who gave their lives that we might continue."

Ni-Cio lifted his face to the night sky. Drops of rain glistened on his cheeks and lingered upon his lips. Kyla, too, savored the sweet, pure taste of the fresh water. When her brother began to intone the first tremulous notes of the sacred *Song of Passing*, she let the water christen her parched mouth. One by one, Atlantean voices joined in a mystical, loving tribute, and the grief in every heart found an outlet in the ethereal song.

Blanketed by soft mist, Evan stood apart from the group, his somber gray eyes closed and his head bowed. Kyla knew his anguish and she left the solemn proximity of her people to stand next to the solitary topsider. She gently took his hand in hers. Her touch, and the haunting voices echoing across the sea, must have stirred depths of remembrance in Evan, for together, they lifted their voices as one.

Chapter 2

CHURNING AT FULL SPEED, the immense freighter sliced effortlessly through the relentless rise and fall of the ink-black swells. Dark waves thundered over the bow and crashed onto the slippery steel decking, trailing clots of gray foam. Deep inside the bowels of Travlor's ship, in a cramped, locked room, Daria sat alone. Hour after agonizing hour, she desperately repeated the same thought-form in an endless stream as she rocked back and forth on the hard bunk. *"Ni-Cio, I am here ... please answer! Ni-Cio, I am here ... please answer!"*

Over and over Daria intoned the single plea until her control finally slipped. Beyond all endurance, she could deny her exhaustion no longer. Her cries faded as heavy lids closed over red-rimmed eyes, and her head nodded forward. A heart-rending sob escaped her lips, the forlorn sound echoing off the cabin's hard, gray walls.

Wrapped within the utter silence of sleep that comes before dreaming, Daria's body drifted down to settle on top of a scratchy, woolen blanket. Even in sleep, the comfort of oblivion eluded her; almost immediately, haunted dreams flickered in foggy, disjointed patches.

Daria mumbled and twitched in her sleep, blindly chasing scores of elusive shadow people who were impossible to catch, impossible to reach. The horror and grief that had descended upon her waking world found their frightening counterparts in the nightmare illusions of her dreams.

On the bridge, Travlor swept a black gaze over the rolling vista. His ragged voice ripped through the night sounds, startling the man hired to captain the ship. "How long before we make port?"

Fear was not a familiar companion to the weather-worn seaman, but the commanding figure standing next to him inspired a healthy dose of caution, so he carefully weighed his answer before replying. "Barring any more weather, and maintaining this speed, we should dock late Saturday afternoon." Studying Travlor's brooding countenance, the captain longed for that day as the next set of waves washed over the bow of the ship.

"See that we do."

Satisfied that his orders would be executed fully and without hesitation, Travlor turned from the horizontal line of watch windows and quietly exited the bridge. Winding through the narrow hallways and spiraling downward, the Atlantean glided silently past several decks until he came to a stop in front of the door to his prisoner's makeshift cell.

Listening intently for any sounds of activity within the cabin, he leaned a hardened shoulder against the cold, sweating steel and placed a bony forefinger above the door. Slowly he traced a line through the beads of moisture. A symbol so ancient as to be lost to any but this one Atlantean flared briefly, then was lost again amid the encroaching condensation.

He parted his thin lips in the ghost of a grisly smile—one that never quite reached the corners of his mouth. Then, as silently as he had come, Travlor slipped away, melting into the nighttime shadows of his ship.

Chapter 3

THE FREIGHTER WAS nowhere in sight. Nothing but a vast, endless, barren sea stretched beyond the limits of his anxious gaze. In the desperate rush to vacate Atlantis and usher everyone to shelter, it had not even occurred to Evan to look for signs of Travlor's command ship.

Disgusted, he dropped the heavy binoculars back into their place against his chest. Briskly rubbing the back of his neck, his mind slid back to the previous night.

Having expended the last of its might, the storm had scuttled into trailing wispy clouds and disappeared into the fabric of the night. The landscape had lain exposed in an eerie white glow emanating from the dispassionate face of the full moon.

He had reluctantly released Kyla's hand, along with the fleeting peace that had settled into his heart, as the echoing tones of their poignant lamentation mixed with traces of the cool night breeze. At last, everything had faded to stillness. Walking the short distance, he stood before Ni-Cio, and the hushed tones of his voice broke the reverent silence, bringing with it the necessary intrusion of reality. "We should get to the compound; this day has already been too long in the making."

A slight nod was the only indication he received that Ni-Cio had heard. Falling behind Evan's sluggish lead, everyone picked their way cautiously over the rocky terrain. Not a sound was uttered as, in single file, the group carefully ascended the hazardous, rain-slick trail.

The worn out band of survivors finally approached the abandoned compound and Evan shuddered with revulsion. The thought of occupying the same space that had so recently sheltered the savage mercenaries of Travlor's army caused him to reconsider. But whatever aversions he felt, the needs of his friends took precedence; with no other options to offer the displaced Atlanteans, Evan clamped down on his feelings of repugnance.

Once inside, he organized another round of decontamination and separated people into groups, giving detailed instructions on the use of the soap and rags. After assuring himself that everyone could operate the showers, Evan opened the kitchens. He scrounged through the pots and pans and grabbed a stack of the largest ones. He quickly located a huge box of detergent. Kicking the screen door open, he dumped everything outside, filled each pot with soap and water, then used a stick to stir in the bioskins before leaving them to soak overnight.

He returned to find Ni-Cio and Aris raiding the pantries. Aris had uncovered a cache of stout Greek beer and was filling mugs for those arriving from their showers. Evan grabbed one of the nearest tankards and took a huge swig; it was the best beer he had ever tasted. "Aris, you just saved my life," he declared, as the ghost of a smile played over his lips.

His comment was met with murmurs of assent by others who had already sampled the potent brew. With the beer flowing, the three men cobbled together a simple yet filling meal. They handed out steaming bowls of thick vegetable soup and placed a huge wheel of peasant cheese along with warm pita bread on the main table. Everyone helped themselves and the hearty fare was gratefully consumed in fatigued silence.

During the meal, the tattered remnants of Atlantis's families quietly bonded, merging into new clans. After they had finished eating, they trudged toward the rundown cabins. Ni-Cio sent a final thought to his departing friends. *"Find your rest ... Though we have been through the very fires of hell on this grisly day, we will mend our grievous hurt ... Know that all will be well ..."*

Hearing the last door groan shut, Evan yielded to his own bone-deep exhaustion. He found his cabin and lurched through the doorway, barely making it to the sagging bunk before his body collapsed onto the naked mattress. Sleep consumed him before his eyes were even closed.

Morning's first light had pushed roughly through the dingy, dirt-crusted window and jerked Evan from his dreamless slumber. He hadn't yet registered a breath when he remembered the enormous freighter that he and Travlor had purchased. A sudden rush of adrenaline pushed him to his feet and sent him out the door.

Currents of Will

Near the precipitous edge of the cliff they had skirted the night before, Ni-Cio and Aris stared in the direction Evan pointed. "It was anchored right there. But I was so intent on getting everyone to safety that it never even crossed my mind." Evan shook his head. "I have absolutely no idea where he could have gone, which means we have no clue how to find Daria."

Ocean breezes tugged at Ni-Cio's raven hair, loosening several strands from its binding. With an anxious swipe of his hand, he batted the hair away and his steely, violet eyes glinted from behind his protective glasses. They were all wound tight as razor wire, but Ni-Cio's gaze was riveted on the location Evan had indicated; if sheer strength of will could bring the ship back, Evan believed that Ni-Cio would have already brought her to shore.

"Travlor is blocking her thoughts. By the gods, I should have taken that man when he first set foot on this accursed island!" The sliver-thin strand of will that Ni-Cio was hanging onto was about to snap.

Aris knew his friend well and sensed how close Ni-Cio was to breaking. He approached his friend and placed a hand on his arm. The volatile Atlantean's posture reflected a depth of calm that Evan knew he didn't feel. "The point is moot, Ni-Cio. What has passed is done. Daria will find a way to break through his constraint. When she does, we will be ready."

Evan nodded. "My father grows older with each breath; although he is still strong, he cannot continue to block her thoughts forever."

Shaking Aris away, Ni-Cio lifted his arms in a wild gesture that took in the limitless scope of the vacant horizon. "Do you not understand? Daria has no way of knowing *any* of us have survived. He could have taken her anywhere. And if he compels her to attend his health, it could *be* forever!"

Outraged, he turned and stomped to the edge of the crumbling precipice. A stiff, salt-laden wind raced up the rocky heights and swirled through his loose clothing, lifting them in a maniacal dance. Fleeing its tie, his hair rose like black whips, angrily lashing a countenance writhing with fiery stripes of red and black.

In a startling transformation, the formidable Atlantean took on the appearance of a wrath-filled god, and Aris blanched at the deadly calm in Ni-Cio's voice. "This round is over Travlor. Count it as your only win. By every blessed life we have had to sacrifice, I will not let it happen again."

With purpose fueled by rage, Ni-Cio turned his back on the empty seascape and summoned his friends. "Follow me. There is much to attend before we begin the hunt."

Aris and Evan sprinted down the dusty trail toward the compound after the departing figure. Evan was afraid to ask what ideas churned through the Atlantean's mind.

Chapter 4

THE MEN CAREENED AROUND the corner of an outlying cabin and thundered toward the middle of the deserted courtyard. Their feet pounded the scorched earth and sent choking clouds of red dust billowing into the air.

As though speed alone could hasten the progression of time and events, Ni-Cio shouted orders even before sliding to a halt in front of the hastily assembled group. "Someone on this island must have seen the direction Travlor's freighter headed. I need that information! And gasses, I need to know how long before we can return to our home!"

Men, women, and even children, faces drenched in the dark blue hues of mourning, rushed to volunteer. Anything to divert their hearts from the losses they suffered. However, before Ni-Cio could issue more commands, Evan stepped in front of him. "I will get you that information."

Dust drifted over the unsettled gathering as Ni-Cio considered the man before him, then nodded once. "Find out how long the effects of the gas remain. The bioskins protected us, but I am not prepared to risk anyone in prolonged exposure."

He gazed at the small vestiges of his family and friends and tamped down on the sorrow that threatened to bring him to his knees. He was almost grateful to be the leader now—it helped him focus on something other than his own rage and grief. As much as it pained him, Ni-Cio knew what was necessary. Solemnly, he announced, "Until I know the gas has been rendered inert, no one is to return to Atlantis."

He forced himself to ignore the silent pleas on the shocked faces that surrounded him and he bent his head toward Evan. "My friend, do you think the decontamination worked?"

Evan shrugged. "The bioskins obviously protected everyone from the worst, and since no one has become symptomatic, my best judgment is that we're clear. Even so the 'skins should soak for the rest of the day. The water and soap will need to be changed and the clothing stirred."

Mer-An cautiously approached the topsider. "Evan, the children need to be kept busy, but more importantly, they need to feel needed. If I take responsibility for that duty will they be at risk?"

Evan carefully considered the children. He struggled to keep his composure in the face of their obvious desire to belong somewhere, even if that somewhere was in a foreign topside environment. He ran a hand over his face then squinted at Mer-An. "No, the clothing is decontaminated; it's just an added precaution. But give each of them another good scrubbing in the showers once the sun goes down."

Mer-An nodded her thanks and stepped back among the crowd of youngsters.

Ni-Cio moved to the assembly of children. Seeing such sadness in their young faces was almost more than he could bear. Refusing to give in to the grief that threatened to explode into a never-ending rage, he took a deep breath, steadied himself, and dropped to a crouch, nestling two of the youngest children into each arm.

Once they were settled, he glanced at the others. "I am assigning a duty that is very important. You will see to the bioskins. We must have them ready for the time we can go home. I am asking Mer-An to be in charge and you must promise to follow her instructions carefully."

Most of the older children held tight to the hands of their younger siblings, their heartache and fear reflected in their silence. Still, Ni-Cio could see that they were anxious to help.

The children stared back at him with such adult sorrow coloring their beautiful faces that without thinking about it, he wrinkled his nose and pulled a funny face. He was grateful to hear a few soft giggles and for a moment his heart lightened. He signaled the children to come closer and lowered his voice to a conspiratorial whisper, "Don't worry, I will see to it that Mer-An introduces plenty of playtime."

When the whole group of children giggled, Ni-Cio's heart lifted. He gently released the youngsters and stood, kissing the tops of their heads, then watched them melt back into the group. He wasn't sure if he was just wishing it so, but it seemed that each child stood a little straighter and their faces looked a little brighter.

Somewhat heartened, Ni-Cio turned back to Evan, and the business of moving forward. "What about contamination of the biospheres?"

"The salt water was enough to clean the outsides and the potency of any residue lessens with time, but just to be safe the interiors should be scrubbed with a solution of bleach and water."

Rogert stepped forward. "My men and I will see to that."

Ni-Cio studied the stalwart Atlantean. The man had fought like a risen Hercules and had been a magnificent force against Travlor's soldiers. However, he had lost both his beloved wife Sann, and his vivacious fourteen-year-old daughter, Na-Sann. Rogert had such a tight rein on his grief that Ni-Cio was not certain how he still drew breath. He touched Rogert's shoulder. "Thank you, my friend."

Turning back to the others, Ni-Cio continued to organize his people into work details, singling out the leaders of each group. They were all ready to have something to do. "You are to be responsible for replenishing the food supply ... take your group to the cabins, they must be brought into some semblance of order ... those of you in this group ..." And on it went until everyone had been given something to do and some way to help.

At last, Ni-Cio turned to Evan. "And, my friend, it falls upon your shoulders to help us find a way to blend into this new world."

Evan's gray eyes narrowed in thought. "I can mask our presence at the compound and whoever accompanies me can be masked as well."

The doubt in Aris's voice carried throughout the courtyard. "Would you care to explain how *that* is a possibility?"

The skeptical look in Evan's eyes told Ni-Cio that he and Aris should've already known the "how" of it. "Travlor taught me."

Ni-Cio was as nonplussed as Aris and they simultaneously released a torrent of questions. "How close do we have to be? Are you able to mask individuals as they move about? Are we invisible or can our presence be detected? How many of us can you mask at once? How far does this power extend?"

Evan held up his hands. "Hold on! First of all I'm not sure about anything. I've never had to do more than maintain the mirage of a deserted compound."

Lost in the enormous possibilities that Evan's talent presented, Ni-Cio beckoned to several children. "Then we will experiment." He indicated various directions to each child. "Run until you reach the area I have shown you. Then, turn around and stand very still. Do you understand?"

Adventure tinged the air and the children quickly nodded their heads. "All right ... show me!"

In a sudden burst, young arms and legs pumped furiously. When each child had reached their designated site, they stopped in anxious expectation.

Ni-Cio looked at the topsider and nodded, "Let us see what is possible."

Evan scanned the assembled Atlanteans and then looked uncertainly at the scattered youngsters. Ni-Cio watched the topsider's sudden inward concentration, then quickly shifted his gaze to the waiting children. It was as though a shimmering wave passed before the body of each child, and then they were no more.

Barely able to believe what he had seen, Ni-Cio heard the shocked exclamations, and strangled gasps of his people. Some of the Atlanteans took off, heightened colors of purple writhing over their features, to find and collect their beloved child.

Ni-Cio touched Evan reverently on his shoulder, "By the gods, you continue to amaze me."

Evan gave a sharp shake of his head, telling Ni-Cio he was still unsure of his ability. "I know the illusion of the vineyard can be maintained even as far away as Fira, but as for masking people as they spread out ... well, I've no idea."

Ni-Cio slapped Evan's back. "Then we will find out."

Once his people quieted, Ni-Cio sent the different groups to their tasks, then he and Aris helped Evan lay out a course of experimentation. With remaining volunteers on standby, testing began to determine the parameters of Evan's masking ability.

Chapter 5

"It would be nice to be a saint, but truly, who wants to do the work?" Travlor turned from the miniscule porthole. "No, I intend to utilize the shortcut you represent."

"You can't possibly be serious." Daria rubbed her eyes and rose from the bunk. She needed a moment to think, so she poured a glass of water from a nearby pitcher. Tasting tin, she swallowed hard and set the glass down, then crossed the small space and stood before her brutal kidnapper. "I won't do it."

The look of a ravenous bird of prey settled over Travlor's face and his eyes pierced her very soul. Her insides shook. "Mark my words young woman—I am deadly serious and you would do well to consider that, and the safety of your unborn, before attempting a mutiny."

Daria stepped closer with a look that she hoped was defiant. "Maybe it would be well for you to remember that without my intervention, your bones will become dust sooner rather than later."

Their eyes locked, unblinking. Daria held her ground until she could no longer look into that lifeless void. Yielding, she felt weak and pulled a chair from the table. She sat down and fought the urge to start screaming because she knew if she did it would be the end of her. She was proud that her voice remained steady. "You say you want nothing less than world domination, so, where do you propose starting this so-called … religion?"

"My dear that is no business of yours. Suffice it to say, the less clothing the better, as the climate will be rather warm."

Daria couldn't hide her surprise and something masquerading as a chuckle slipped from between Travlor's lips. "Don't worry, we are decidedly *not* going to hell."

When she refused to respond, the Atlantean briskly rubbed his hands together. "We will be arriving in port in the next few days and unless you want to remain in these rather grim surroundings, I suggest you relax and enjoy the trip. I have had my man prepare a sumptuous meal with which to break your fast. All that is required is your presence."

Daria's stomach had been rumbling ever since Travlor had abruptly entered the cabin and unceremoniously begun outlining his egomaniacal schemes. She knew there was no way she could break through the stranglehold he had on her thoughts, so for the time being, she let need overcome valor. "Lead the way." She heaved a sigh and stood.

Travlor opened the door with a flourish. "Oh please; you act as though I am accompanying you to the gallows. At least humor me with a show of lighter spirits."

"Said the spider to the fly."

"Don't mumble. I can't abide people who don't speak up."

She almost rolled her eyes at the egotistical bastard, but thought better and stepped over the threshold. She waited for

Travlor to lead the way, then followed the Atlantean through narrow passageways and up steel stairways until she found that she had been escorted to the bridge. When Daria walked over the steel decking to stand beside the finely laid table, she had the unshakable feeling that she had just stepped onto a gangplank.

Without a doubt, the compound was showing signs of life. The physical release of manual labor kept minds and hearts occupied and everyone worked with focused care. The small families of Atlantis worked to fulfill their designated obligations. The decrepit wasteland that had been Travlor's compound began to show renewed signs of life, and as the compound began to heal, so too did Atlantean hearts.

Island breezes twirled through the open doors of the busy kitchen and wafted out carrying the mouth-watering aroma of freshly baked cookies.

Each cabin was given a thorough cleaning until the weight of years of dust and neglect were thoroughly swept away. Windows that had been blackened with grime slowly began to gleam in the morning sun, and tattered angles and sagging porches began to look less forlorn. The grounds were raked and any leftover signs of Travlor's encampment were deposited into garbage bags. An air of quaintness settled over the entire area.

However, it wasn't until the sounds of children at play could be heard that any signs of Travlor's presence were truly expunged. When the blessed noise of childish laughter and tuneless rhymes rose with the morning sun, a feeling of normalcy and a sense of home stirred the hearts and minds of the newest inhabitants of the old vineyard. The outward signs of grief began to yield to the need to move forward and once again embrace life.

While this small transformation was not lost on Evan, when he entered the front gates, he was mired in thought. The others of his group trailed behind, their attention sharply focused on him, oblivious to the fact that he wanted to be alone; he didn't need them to witness his failure.

That he had failed was abysmally clear. He shoved his hands deep into his pockets, hunched his shoulders, and clenched his jaw. Walking to escape the others, his muscles felt stiff and disjointed and he grumbled, "I cannot believe I won't be any more useful than that! What good is this stuff if that's the extent of it?"

He heard steps quicken and felt a hand on his arm. He just about shook it off when he realized that it was Ni-Cio. He signaled the others to catch up, then looked at the Atlantean. "Don't start."

"Topsider, cease your rumblings!" Evan was momentarily stunned into silence because the curt command was issued with the full authority of a true council leader. The Atlantean fixed him with a perplexed stare. "The powers you have exhibited are extraordinary, yet your discouragement refutes those very gifts." Ni-Cio turned his palms up and rushed on. "So they are finite and not as far reaching as you would have them. That you have come this far is nothing short of miraculous!"

Evan ground his teeth and looked away. They needed so much help and time was running out. Travlor was proceeding with his agenda and there was no one to stop him. His escape, as far as he knew, had gone unnoticed and Evan was scared. He was scared for all of them and he could only imagine how

Ni-Cio felt. He took a deep breath. "Ni-Cio, believe me, I'm not trying to refute anything. But the longer it takes to find Travlor, the harder it will be to get Daria back. Knowing him, he will be in such a fortified position that it might just *be* impossible to get her back. He won't rest until he has total control of this topside world!"

"My friend, you run ahead of yourself. Do not get so far into the future that you cannot work the present."

Aris stepped between the two men. "Evan, one step at a time. Until we have some idea of Travlor's whereabouts, it is of no use to worry about his plans ... no matter his aims. We must focus on what we *can* do and what we know."

Aris motioned toward the other men. "We are in awe of the abilities you exhibit. It is a wonder that whoever is within two hundred yards of you can be masked while at the same time you can keep the compound disguised from as far away as the main town. That ability alone keeps our presence hidden and therefore keeps us safe. Travlor will feel he has more time to work his goals if he believes we have been exterminated. In the meantime, if any of us leave the compound without you, we will just have to try the same disguises that Daria used for Kyla. Certainly that tactic is not without risks, but it can be done."

Aris's seriousness melted into a smile, "I am with Ni-Cio, do not let yourself become discouraged; why, you have become our most formidable asset!" Aris rubbed his stomach. "Come, the sun has yet to reach its zenith. The kitchens are open and if my nose does not deceive me, a fine meal awaits and I am ravenous."

When his friend clapped him on the back, Evan couldn't help that his mouth quirked into a small grin. He liked the hot-headed Atlantean and couldn't resist baiting him. "I'm fairly certain your nose will still be working when other parts of you aren't."

The laughter that followed his remark made Evan feel more a part of this Atlantean family than he had ever felt among topsiders. Together, the men made their way to the kitchens.

Chapter 6

"THE PLANS ARE set then," Ni-Cio nodded at Evan, "You and Kyla take the truck into town and try to find information as to the direction Travlor's ship is headed. In the meantime, as the biospheres have been cleaned, I will accompany Rogert's group. It is time to restock the larders."

Ni-Cio's glance took in Aris and Mer-An. "It is up to you to design a workable disguise. I am not comfortable being completely dependent upon Evan's close proximity. Therefore, it is imperative that we have the capability to move about the island without being masked."

It was then that Evan set some of the lunch dishes aside and solemnly propped his elbows on the table. Ni-Cio waited. "Kyla and I will research the different gasses that Travlor could have possibly used. However, once released, most gasses dissipate fairly quickly. Worst case, three days should be enough for whatever they used to have completely broken down. Even so, the entirety of Atlantis needs to be scrubbed as an added precaution."

Currents of Will

When the topsider hesitated, Ni-Cio instinctively knew he was not going to like what he was about to hear. Slate gray eyes looked across the table and Evan quietly resumed. "Ni-Cio, it is the bodies that concern me. They have to be taken care of or there will *be* no Atlantis to return to."

Ni-Cio sat back, speechless. He had refused to allow the hideous remains awaiting his return to enter his thoughts. Somehow, he had known that any acknowledgment, however slight, would cause his mind to follow the path toward the madness they represented. And now, Evan had flung that door wide open.

He shuddered as the grisly images poured through his mind's eye and Ni-Cio slipped toward the dark cover of insanity. Nothing he had ever known had prepared him for the devastation he had survived. Now, dancing seductively before him, blackness beckoned with whispered intimations of a final release. Oblivious to everyone and everything around him, Ni-Cio sank into a somnolent dream state.

Raising his arms to embrace the endless void, Ni-Cio prepared to surrender his burden. Twitching at an unexpected touch, he felt steady hands gently take hold of his shoulders. By degrees, Ni-Cio felt himself being pulled back from the yawning abyss. He blinked to clear his vision and turned around. He recognized the intruder. Dully, he acknowledged the topsider. It occurred to him that he should be surprised to see Evan in this place. But he was not. A moment passed.

"*You are needed elsewhere...*" Compassion felt rather than heard.

A halting sigh laced with fathomless sorrow. "*I cannot...*"

"*The choice is not yours...*" An implacable statement.

That inescapable truth produced the ghost of a smile. "So, you are prepared to stay until I accompany you?"

The image of an immovable force spoke volumes and Ni-Cio stifled a gruff laugh. "*I truly do not want you around that much...*"

The quiet lengthened. Finally, Ni-Cio took a deep breath. "*Thank you...*"

A slight lift of the topsider's broad shoulders was the only reply, and it was done.

Even though it seemed as if no time had passed, everyone was aware that something highly unusual had just taken place, and they were relieved when the conversation picked up where it had suddenly left off.

In an unwavering voice Ni-Cio addressed Evan's earlier statement. "The bodies. Yes. Once you have determined that it is safe to return, we will see to your request."

With a curt nod of his head, Evan let the subject drop and the small group turned to other matters.

Kyla watched Evan cajole the old truck around the worst of the potholes as they bounced over the rough gravel road that wound through the countryside. With the shock absorbers no longer in existence, the antiquated vehicle bucked its way toward town like a sway-backed mule. Although a shimmer of anticipation had run through Kyla when she had learned she was to accompany the handsome topsider, she could hardly keep from laughing as Evan fought the ornery gears and muscled the steering wheel through the winding curves.

She studied the lines of his determined features and the shock of their first encounter played through her memory.

The topsider had resembled Travlor so closely, that to her untrained eyes, the two had seemed one and the same. Poised to attack, it had taken all of Daria's assurance to convince Kyla that Evan was not Travlor.

Over a lunch that now seemed so long ago, Kyla had listened as Daria and Evan reached an understanding of each other as friends rather than lovers. Irresistibly drawn to the mysterious man, Kyla could feel her guard dropping, and the fears and misconceptions she had entertained regarding the Terran world crumbled. Through her quivering new awareness, she came to the realization that Evan Gaddes was one of the loneliest people she had ever met. She remembered impulsively taking his hands in a gesture of comfort, but both she and the topsider had felt a sudden shift in their perceptions as skin touched skin. She had wanted to stay with him; however, their undeniable infatuation had been put on hold when events thrust them onto opposing sides of a horrific war.

Now, sitting beside him, Kyla was overcome with awe. Denying his father, this man had risked everything to help her people. That any of them had survived was due in large part to his heroic efforts. An unforeseen desire to protect him from further hurt flooded her heart with such intensity that her breath caught in her throat.

Evan must have sensed the sudden change, but he mistook Kyla's reaction as one of fear. Though he powered the truck through the tractor-sized ruts, his voice flowed over her like warm silk. "Don't be afraid; I have you masked. No one will see you."

"It is not that." Her voice quavered. She swallowed hard and blinked her eyes in an effort to regain control of her reeling thoughts.

Evan glanced at her and time stopped. He looked entranced and Kyla could feel warmth rising from her collarbone. Faint tendrils of rose coloring wound over her mouth and traced the outer corners of her eyes. She couldn't hide her emotions. Her feelings were laid open before him.

Evan brought the old truck to a miraculously quiet stop and opened his door. Kyla watched him slide from behind the wheel and step down to red earth. He rounded the cab and slowly opened her door. The suppressed emotion of an entire lifetime smoldered behind gray eyes burning silver. The raw need of his desire ignited a response within Kyla that could no longer be denied. Their bodies collided in a crushing consummation of unspoken passion. Mouths explored each other ravenously.

He lifted her out of the truck and carried her across the empty, windswept field. The tumultuous sounds of breaking surf created a symphony with the crashing thunder of her heart as he settled her tenderly on a cushion of wild grass. The feel of Evan's mouth on hers erased every sound on earth but the breath they shared as one.

Chapter 7

STROLLING IN A lover's embrace, Evan and Kyla threaded their way through Fira's crowded square. Masked to resemble tourists, they listened intently for any hint of innuendo, rumor, or gossip. The freighter, since it had not been hidden, should have piqued someone's curiosity. And if anybody had noticed the direction of its departure, it would help narrow the scope of their search. They desperately needed some idea of the course heading.

They waded through boisterous throngs of locals displaying their colorful wares and meticulously scanned the busy thoroughfare. They were about to pass an outdoor café when Evan noticed a beefy man seated nonchalantly under the cool shade of an open umbrella. He pulled Kyla around so that she partially blocked his frame, his eyes fastened on the unsuspecting patron. "Love, do not look around, but I recognize the man in that café."

Tremors raced through his body, and to Kyla, he felt like a wild stallion on the verge of a murderous stampede. Though she spoke to him in gentle tones, it took him awhile to concentrate on her words. He realized that she was attempting to reign in his flaring temper.

"Evan, I am with you. We will do this together." She willed him to look at her.

He wrenched his gaze from the man to meet hers. She lovingly kissed his mouth, letting her lips trail over his closed lids, and she pulled him closer. With her cheek resting against his, she held him until the trembling in his muscles began to subside. Her voice was like a cooling breeze on a hot day. "When you are ready, we will do this together."

She waited a beat, then Evan heard the delicate release of her sorrowful sigh. "I know he is the soldier Travlor sent to execute you."

Astounded, he raised his head to look at her. "How did you know?"

"Oh, Evan, in my eyes you are such an open book. I have loved you from our very first meeting and when our bodies finally joined, your heart and mind were known to me."

The crowds flowed around them in relaxed eddies and the years of loneliness and the outrage of unspeakable loss dimmed in the light of this new beginning. Unable to voice his feelings, Evan simply nodded. Kyla took his hand and led him into the cool shadows of a nearby veranda. "Come, we will wait. When he leaves, we will see where he takes us."

Regardless of Travlor's ability to block her thoughts, Daria still tried to reach Ni-Cio. At intermittent intervals she released thought-forms into the ozone and even as she waited, without hope of a reply, her heart refused to believe that he was truly gone.

Before the loathsome Atlantean had burst into her cabin and requested her appearance at breakfast, Daria's mind had calmed and logic had resumed. As she assessed her situation, a singular deduction had fueled her desire to continue trying to contact Ni-Cio. *If Travlor were certain of Ni-Cio's death, he wouldn't need to block my thoughts!*

Now, after having endured Travlor's presence throughout what seemed like an endless breakfast, Daria lay resting in her cabin. She wracked her mind for a way to escape, but finally had to admit that she was stuck.

Without seafaring abilities and a navigational aptitude that precluded the use of anything but a GPS, even if she were to get off the ship, she wouldn't have the slightest idea where she was or where to go.

She rolled over and touched the sweating gray wall. "It's your game until we reach dry land; after that, all bets are off."

She traced the outline of a heart and watched as glistening beads of moisture slid like tears from the soft edges of her drawing. The unutterable sorrow of Travlor's actions once again took hold. Her thoughts were thrust back to the harrowing recollections of death and destruction visited upon her Atlantean family, and she felt she could die from the grief. But as she wound through the scenes of grotesque horror, a shared memory floated to the surface, bringing with it a promise of release.

From deep within her soul, the haunting refrain of an ethereal melody poured into her aching heart. Rising from her bunk, she crossed the cramped space and stood before the misted porthole. Accompanied by the peaceful swaying of the ship, Daria's voice found an outlet for her pain as the eerily beautiful *Song of Passing* wrapped around her in comforting waves.

The final glimmering intonation had risen through the tepid air when someone pounded frantically on her cabin door. Her heart leapt to her throat and Daria hurried to open the heavy steel door. An anxious seaman stood before her, wringing his cap. "You are to follow me! There has been an accident!"

He didn't wait for a response, but turned and sprinted down the corridor. Daria bolted from her room and tried to catch up to the fleeing figure. She couldn't imagine what had necessitated such panic. She scurried to follow the seaman down an adjacent passageway when the alarming cries of someone in acute pain assaulted her ears.

She saw a crowd of men held motionless by shock. She pushed her way through the group and burst into a room that she dimly recognized as the ship's galley. Noticing one of the stoves covered in white powder, she halted in confusion. She didn't see anyone and she tried to make sense of why she was needed. Suddenly, Travlor rose like the grim reaper from behind the furthest stainless steel table. "Get everyone out and close that door," he sneered.

She stumbled to obey the terse command and quickly herded the stragglers out of the room. The steel clang of the door resounded in her ears and her heart raced in fear.

"Over here—now!" The strong compulsion in Travlor's voice almost worked. Instead, she braced herself and stepped cautiously around the other tables until she had an unobstructed view of a man splayed face-down on the floor. Wisps of smoke curled into the air. Her mind slowly absorbed the spectacle and she realized with mounting horror that the smoke emanated from the man. Her voice sounded like it was weighted with anchors. "Is he dead?"

"Unless you prefer to delay until that moment occurs I would surmise … not yet." The dripping scorn that colored Travlor's statement galvanized her as his compulsion could not. She moved quickly to kneel by the unmoving figure and helped Travlor roll him over. She gasped. Third degree burns covered the upper half of the man's body and his melted face was unrecognizable.

Daria immediately began the unearthly healing tones that would move the man from unconsciousness into a sedated sleep. With Travlor's remorseless eyes watching her every move, she ran her hands lightly over the worst of the trauma. The atonal sounds she emitted worked in tandem with the broad sweeping motions of her hands. She introduced a strong antibiotic into his system. With unerring precision and the utmost concentration, she focused on the cells of unmarred skin. Her healing tones deepened and lengthened until, reproducing at an unnaturally accelerated pace, the healthy tissue began growing by imperceptible degrees. As it did, the charred skin gradually started to flake away.

After a time, the young cook's scorched features were entirely replaced so that he looked much as he had before the terrible grease fire. Daria reinforced a suggestion that he would awake refreshed with no memory of the agony he had suffered.

Once the skin on the seaman's torso had been restored, Daria sank against the back of a table leg. Her voice shook and she wasn't sure if her words reached Travlor's ears. She was too tired to care. "He is well. But he'll sleep throughout the day and the rest of the night. Have some of the men take him to his quarters."

Travlor squatted next to her. "You have done well, topsider. Better even than I had hoped. This little foray into all things miraculous will do much to help fuel the religious fervor I require."

Travlor's cynical gloating grated on her nerves. Even so, an abrupt cause for distress rose within her. "Is my baby all right?"

She searched Travlor's face, afraid to hear his reply. She thought she saw something like concern pass over his features, but it was gone too quickly to be certain. "Not to worry, the health of your baby is irrevocably tied to the state of my own health. Unless you disobey me, nothing I ask of you will endanger her." He offered his hand and helped her from the floor. She hated that she couldn't walk without leaning a bit on him as he escorted her across the galley. "I will have my chef bring you a proper meal to help restore your energy."

Daria could barely nod her grudging thanks as Travlor reached for the door. When the men realized they were coming out, they made way for what they thought would be a body. However, Travlor stepped through the doorway first and sagged dramatically against the frame. The men immediately crowded around the Atlantean to offer aid, and ignored the young woman who had been summoned.

Daria wanted to lie down and sleep forever. She started to shuffle back to her cabin when she heard the hard rasp of Travlor's melodramatic voice. His words caused a tremor to run up her spine.

"He will live. I have done all that I can."

Chapter
8

EVAN AND KYLA OBSERVED their target from beneath the dark shadows of the veranda. They watched the bullet-headed mercenary slurp down a third espresso. He finished his morning paper and glanced at his watch, then tilted back in his chair with a self-satisfied air and let out a loud, jaw-cracking yawn. Reptilian eyes flicked lazily over the wandering crowds. At last, he pushed away from the table and rifled heavily through the pockets of his dirty camos. Without bothering to count, he flipped a pile of loose change onto the table, and like an ungainly beast, began pushing his way out of the café.

The man entered the square and lurched into the wake of a young girl. The smirk on his square face said everything about the sordid fantasies that ran gleefully through his lizard brain. He picked up speed and lumbered after her.

Evan clenched his hands and his breath accelerated as he and Kyla gave chase. He was about to break into a run, but Kyla restrained him. He inhaled and let his breath out, reaching for some semblance of inner calm, but he was light years from nirvana. "I'd like to hit *him* with a Taser about now."

They sidestepped a family of picture-snapping tourists, then Kyla settled into him. "It would be no more than he deserves; however, there is a certain irony in the fact that his love of wielding a Taser is what unlocked the powers you now possess."

She smiled at his smoldering reluctance. He quirked an eyebrow and with a shallow snort, gave a quick nod.

Done with his leerfest, the mercenary abandoned the object of his perversion and abruptly darted into a narrow alleyway. Evan grabbed Kyla's hand. "Come on!"

They rounded a corner to the alley and Kyla heard Evan's hurried thought.

"We're entirely masked now; don't worry about making noise..."

They trotted up a winding incline. Their target was moving rapidly in and out of the overhanging shadows so Evan and Kyla picked up their speed.

They had narrowed the gap when the man stopped to hitch up his pants. He investigated the area quickly before he ducked inside a seedy, run-down motel.

"Evan, do you think we should go in?"

Before he could reply, the musclebound figure reappeared with a brown paper sack tucked securely under one arm. With a quick, furtive glance, he decided that he hadn't elicited any undue attention. Tramping uphill for another block he angled left onto a constricted one-lane road before winding through a twisted maze of centuries-old housing. He stopped before a termite-riddled stairway, checked the surrounding area once more, and then ascended. The dilapidated stairs sagged under his weight and groaned beneath the rhythm of his step.

The soldier inserted a key and sidled through the door, slamming it shut against the intrusion of any outside light. Waiting for something to indicate that the man was getting settled, Kyla anxiously whispered. "What should we do now?"

He squeezed her hand. "*We* do nothing. I'm going to get in that room and find out what he knows."

Before Evan started across the cramped street, Kyla nailed him with a look. "You go nowhere without me, Evan Gaddes."

"Kyla, this is no time to argue!"

"So, do not!"

He was surprised at her vehemence, but he tried one more time. He took her into his arms. "I don't want you to get hurt."

She shook him off. "Do not try that on me. You know I am a master of *Last Strike*, I think you do not want me to see what you will do to him."

He closed his eyes against the truth of her statement and relented with a heavy sigh. "All right, but at least stay behind me until I know what we're dealing with."

She brusquely nodded her consent and they crossed the street.

"We're still hidden, but take the stairs as quickly as possible…"

With that thought, they charged up the worn stairway and rammed through the decrepit door.

Caught completely off guard, the mercenary spun around from his laptop, gun in hand, prepared to fire. His surprise ratcheted into shock and then to outright fear when an invisible force grabbed him from behind and slammed him to the ground. Evan drove his knee into the back of the beefy neck, cutting off the man's terrified scream.

Panic pooled in the mercenary's eyes, sweat poured off him in waves, and he struggled to breathe. "I will kill you right now unless you keep your mouth shut. Understood?" The deliberate blink of a heavy lid signified compliance.

Evan's hurried thought found Kyla, *"Grab the sheets, wet them down and spread them out on the floor..."*

The sound of footsteps disconnected from anybody sent a new wave of terror through the mercenary. Evan could feel his muscles bunch, so he pressed the nozzle of the gun into his cheek. "Don't even."

Kyla returned with the dripping sheets and she worked to flatten them across the floor. Evan dug the gun in harder. "I'm going to lift my weight off you. When I do, I want you to crawl over to the edge of that first sheet and lie down on top of it, arms at your sides. Got it?"

Again, the slow blink of a lid. Carefully, Evan pushed off the man and moved away. The soldier, shaking like he was hypothermic, crawled across the floor and collapsed onto the sheet. He whimpered, but held his arms tight to his sides and clamped his eyes shut.

"Roll him up tight in that first sheet."

She rolled him up until he was securely cocooned inside, then Evan set the gun aside and helped her roll him into the next set of sheets. When the man was secured, Evan unmasked himself, keeping Kyla hidden.

He kicked a chair over to the prone figure and hoisted the man to the seat, then peeled the sheets from around his head. Shock clouded his beady little eyes, but when the soldier eventually recognized Evan, his eyes bugged and he struggled to get the words out. "Wh—where'd you come from?"

Evan took in the room and eyed the computer. "Not your concern." He approached the laptop and saw the white powder laid out in nice even lines. He touched the keypad and turned back to the mercenary before the screen jumped to life. "I need to know where Travlor went."

The man frowned and anger bubbled up in a snarl. "How'd I know? In case you didn't notice, I got left behind. And the bastard still owes me money."

"*That* doesn't concern me." Evan glanced over his shoulder and what he saw glowing on the screen almost made him retch. He clamped down on a violent urge to kill the son of a bitch and closed the lid, hoping Kyla hadn't seen anything. He faced the immobilized man and saturated his words with an intense compulsion. "Tell me where Travlor went."

The man's expression blanked and his voice fell to a flat monotone. "Travlor never told us anything. It was a need-to-know basis. I was left behind to take care of you. When I woke up after you Tasered me, I was the last one in the compound."

"Where did you go after that?"

"Down to the beach to see if anyone was waiting for me."

"Was the freighter in sight?"

"There was a ship on the horizon, but when I looked again, it was gone."

"Course heading?"

"Due west."

Evan thought for a moment. "You had no indication of any plans following the attack on Atlantis?"

"No."

"All right, what kind of gas was used?"

"Nerve agent GD."

"Lasting affects?"

"Breaks down after two days."

Evan glanced at Kyla. "Can you think of anything else?" She shook her head.

Evan batted the soldier on his head and left him with a Travlor-worthy compulsion. "You will tell the authorities everything they need to know regarding the drugs and your … website, but not until after several hours of very heavy persuasion." Evan knew that the Greek authorities never took it easy on a monster with his type of perversion.

Evan picked up the handset to an antiquated black phone and signaled Kyla to take the receiver. He scribbled the address on the back of a piece of paper. "What little Greek I know leans toward the food industry, since you're fluent, ask to be connected to the local authorities. When you get an officer, tell him the man at this address is dealing drugs and that more specifically, the proclivities exhibited on his website will warrant a full scale investigation."

Kyla reached for the phone while Evan dialed "0" for her.

Chapter 9

"That is not much to go on." Ni-Cio shook his head. He lifted the goggles from his face and threw them towards the pile that had grown as Atlanteans acclimated to the Terran environment. He rubbed his eyes and blinked from the harsh glare of the overhead lights. He sighed and concentrated on Evan. "There is no doubt that Travlor is moving toward a prearranged destination, but the world is almost limitless. Without any other information …" He shrugged, there was no need to state the obvious.

Although the evening meal had been cleared, most everyone remained. Kyla, Rogert, Aris, Mer-An and Evan sat at the table with Ni-Cio.

Aris thumped a fist on the table and leveled his gaze at Evan. "I don't understand. Can we not locate this ship through some kind of recordkeeping? Surely you have the ownership papers?"

"Of course I have the registration, but I never filed with the port authority. Even if I had, it wouldn't matter because Travlor masked the ship once they were underway. Radar won't even be able to pick them up. Believe me when I say that no one—and I mean absolutely no one—will know that ship is out there."

Mer-An touched the back of Aris's hand. "Once he reaches his destination, will he not have to unmask in order to make port?"

Evan regarded Mer-An and shook his head. "Assuming he doesn't scuttle the ship. Even so, there are how many ports? Once through the Straits of Gibraltar, there are four continents that are easily accessible." His gaze took in the others. "I doubt he would need the ship if he chooses Africa or Europe, but that still leaves the entire eastern seaboard of North and South America."

A brooding silence settled over the gathering; Ni-Cio studied his topside friend then pushed his chair back and stood. "It is not within the man's nature to remain hidden, especially since you have indicated that his sole ambition is to dominate the Terran world."

Ni-Cio looked around the table and shrugged, "We can almost understand his need for revenge against Atlantis, but why the Terran world? His wealth is beyond imagination, so what could he possibly gain?"

Evan couldn't keep from wincing. Travlor's maniacal ambition was so vast that he wasn't sure he even understood what drove his father. He tried to explain. "His thoughts have always been blocked from me and he's never shared anything. So, his history's hidden. It's just a theory but I think he suffered the loss of a deep love before my mother, but again, it's nothing I really know—more like a feeling."

Evan slowly rose from his chair and went to Kyla, gently placing his hand on her shoulder. "About the only thing I'm sure of is that the love he had for my mother was as immense as the love you have for Daria, or the feelings that bind me to your sister." He stroked the back of Kyla's neck, "When my mother died, what remained of Travlor's heart died, too."

Evan gazed around the table, "The years spent imprisoned in Atlantis caused his wrath to morph until it spiraled out of control. Because of an insatiable desire for power, his bitterness has been honed to a fine edge. For the misery he believes he has suffered, he will extract vengeance upon the entire world.

Aris turned red as fire and jumped up, toppling his chair. "That is just crazy!"

A derisive laugh escaped Evan. "What do you think I've been trying to tell you?"

"But, we cannot just sit here and wait! We have to find him!"

Ni-Cio walked over to Aris and motioned for him to take his seat. Aris grumbled under his breath, eyeing Evan as he righted his chair. Ni-Cio looked at his friends. "We have reached a dead end and as much as I had hoped for a quick resolution, I cannot waste any more time pondering Travlor's whereabouts. Sooner or later, he will make his presence known and when he does, I swear before all of you—as long as I have breath in my body—I will hunt him down! I *will* bring Daria back!"

Ni-Cio closed his eyes, taking a moment to regain his equilibrium. When his anger diffused somewhat, he looked at his friends. "Until other information is forthcoming, we will refocus our efforts. Our underwater home must be made habitable again. I will lead a recovery team and once we have seen to the bodies, the entirety of Atlantis must be scrubbed and the debris cleared."

Rogert spread his big hands out on the table, he looked glum. "I would remind everyone that we are without an energy source."

Ni-Cio felt the high bronze coloring of his skin fade.

Evan straightened in his chair. "Generators, air, and water filters will work until we can think of something else, but … why would Atlantis be without power?"

Ni-Cio couldn't speak and motioned for Rogert to explain. The unflappable Atlantean looked wretched. "Poseidon created Atlantis to receive and reproduce energy from transcendence. Na-Kai's transcendence was not enough to overcome the energy that was expended defending our home."

Evan looked baffled. "I still don't follow."

Rogert cleared his throat, his voice unsettled. "When an Atlantean reaches the age of four hundred and eight, the physical aspect transitions into spirit. At that precise moment, a tremendous amount of energy is released. That singular release powers all of our energy requirements until the next transcendence occurs."

Rogert leaned across the table and stared at Evan. "The premature deaths brought about by your father have precluded anyone from transcending. Of those left, no one is near the age of that event. However, when someone does come of age, it will be impossible for the energy from that one transcendence to restart Atlantis." He lowered his head to within inches of Evan's face. "It will take nothing short of a miracle to recreate the energy necessary to sustain our lives."

That bleak statement hung between them like an iron curtain and Evan felt his heart squeeze. He turned to Ni-Cio. "I … I don't know what to say. It seems the hurt I've caused has no end."

Kyla slid from her chair, gently brushed Rogert aside, and knelt before Evan. She took his face in both hands and smoothed his hair. "You must hear me: the sins of the father are not yours. If not for you, none of us would have survived! And now, you are the only one who *can* help us." She glanced around the room and then back at Evan. "My love, look upon these faces; do you not know that you are among people who count you as family?"

When Evan refused to look at her, she rose to stand over him and shook his shoulders. He didn't respond, just kept staring into space. Exasperated, Kyla threw her hands in the air. "Guilt is such a useless emotion! It can render one incapable of action. Your refusal to forgive yourself becomes a burden. One that we can do without."

Her bluntness caught Evan by surprise. Different emotions chased each other across his handsome features and Kyla playfully tagged his shoulder. "I believe topsiders say it best and so I would encourage you as well … 'Get under it!'"

A grin split Evan's face. "I think you mean 'Get over it?'"

"Exactly!" Kyla beamed and wrapped him in such a bear hug that the air leaving his lungs sounded like a bellows.

Everybody chuckled and the atmosphere lightened considerably. Everyone scooted their chairs back and made ready to return to their cabins. Ni-Cio concluded the meeting. "All right, we will utilize the equipment Evan spoke of until the time we can think of a way for Atlantis to be restarted under her own power.

"Aris, I am counting on you and Mer-An to get me those disguises."

Aris managed a terse nod before Mer-An shoved him toward the door. She looked over her shoulder. "Tomorrow, Ni-Cio. Time enough tomorrow."

"Well said, Mer-An." Ni-Cio winked at Aris. "Enjoy your rest."

Aris shrugged in an overblown display of helplessness and raised his arms in surrender. He grinned at Ni-Cio and allowed himself to be ushered through the door.

Chapter 10

THE HARDENED MEN ON Travlor's ship were accustomed to performing the duties requisite to an accepted assignment. But, as mercenaries, their motivation was always and only about the monetary reward waiting at the completion of a successful mission. They focused on their jobs with a single-minded, almost fanatical, determination: watch your back, stay alive, collect the money. It was never about making friends or influencing people.

However, there was not a soul on board who didn't realize the young cook should have died from his grievous burns, and the comportment of everyone had undergone a radical transformation. The miracle they had witnessed went far beyond their immediate comprehension and was credited to a man they had bound themselves to in a fervid religious awe.

In their minds, God and Travlor had merged to become one and the same. So much so, that some of the men no longer dared look upon the man that commanded their ship. Men who had only ever spoken God's name in vain now offered up quiet prayers. Uttered in the privacy of cramped bunks, darkened corners, or under night skies, their lips moved in worshipful wonder and always their supplications ceased in a flurry of devoted amen's to the Almighty Travlor.

Because the rapid spread of his religious crusade needed an inciting incident, Travlor had no compunction about creating one. The unsuspecting cook had provided the perfect opportunity and now his overall plan was proceeding even faster than he had originally forecast.

As God-In-The-Making, Travlor no longer needed to underscore his orders with a compulsion. Like starving children fighting for a scrap of bread, the men clamored for the smallest chance to carry out his will. And as the fever of their maniacal worship grew, Travlor greedily hoarded the reserves of his precious energy. But, upon waking and through every single second of every hour, an excruciating, anticipatory anguish never left him. It was an irrefutable fact, known only Travlor, that the energy he guarded with such miserly care continued to leach away in slow, frightening degrees.

And so, in tyrannical desperation, he drove his men mercilessly. He knew that once they docked it would be easier, for word of "his" healing would spread like wildfire. And the country he had chosen as his staging area was rife with the poor, the downtrodden and the sublimely ignorant.

Indeed, it was a country full of dark dealings, ancient superstitions, and frantic prayers for divine intervention. A savior would be hailed with such messianic devotion that the ambitions Travlor had set forth would bear orchards of fruit in no time at all.

Meanwhile, as the Atlantean protracted every ounce of speed from his men and thus from his ship, Daria was free to move about. After the healing, her strength had returned quickly and she took that as a sign that she was managing the energy transfers more proficiently. She knew that there was much she could learn from Travlor, but his earlier garrulity had been replaced with a furtive reclusion. And she had neither seen nor heard from him since the healing. However, he still maintained the iron vise blocking telepathic communication, for there was not the slightest indication that her thoughts had traveled anywhere but through her own mind.

Walking on deck, she savored the sharp tang of salt air and reveled in the whipping caress of stiff trade winds. It was the only time her thoughts quieted. Because of that she was able to derive some small shred of enjoyment from her confinement.

She rounded a corner and nearly ran into one of the older sailors. He had been leaning on the rails and in his hands he held what looked to Daria like prayer beads. His grizzled, sun-creased face cracked into the semblance of a rusty smile and his whiskey voice, heavy with years of hard living, labored to reach her. "What a time to be alive!"

His eyes glittered with the fevered light of fanaticism. "My old man used to recite scripture while he beat me. He'd scream that on the final, fateful day, the righteous sword of the risen Lord would smite all sinners!" His remembrance brought a grimace. "I guess by not sparing the rod he believed he was saving me from hellfire and eternal damnation."

His expression was confounded before he turned back to the sea.

"Humph, who'd've believed the old man was right?"

Daria shivered and quietly backtracked until the old seaman was out of sight. Her thoughts churned. *He's going to do it! I never thought it would work, but God help me, he's going to succeed.*

Killing him is out of the question, but there has to be something I can do!

She took the nearest set of stairs and wound her way to the upper portion of the ship. She stepped onto the bridge and was glad to see that the portly captain was alone. She approached him, eyed the barrage of instrumentation, and gave a nervous laugh. "How long did it take for you to learn to use all this?"

The man's dark, suspicious eyes raked over her with the intensity of an x-ray. She felt like he could see right through her, but Daria saw a slight shift of facial muscles, and underneath a bristling black mustache, the corner of his upper lip twitched into a derisive grin of masculine superiority. "I have worked ships since before you were born." His eyes scoured the horizon as if another vessel would suddenly appear off their port bow.

"I'm sure you have, but boats didn't always have such advanced technology."

The surly captain actually puffed his chest with pride and it took a great deal of control for Daria to keep from smiling.

"First, this is not a boat, it is a ship. Second, I worked my way up. I learned through hard work." His thick accent conjured up visions of migrant workers struggling to adapt their musical tongues to a difficult and harsh language.

"Where are you from?"

The question, innocuous in itself, set the man on edge and he quickly grabbed a set of binoculars and turned to the watch windows. He adjusted the glasses and did a silent sweep of the horizon. Daria realized that she would not receive an answer. So, she tried again. "What are you looking for?"

He took his eyes from the glasses and glared. "You ask too many questions. What do you want?"

Daria knew she was on the edge of being dismissed. "I've never been in the middle of the ocean before and all this water makes me nervous." She pointed at the bevy of blinking lights and intermittent readouts. "I just thought if I knew a little bit of how this all works, I wouldn't be so worried."

The mercenary looked down his aquiline nose. "I do not depend on technology. If something should happen, I steer by the stars."

"But, if we lose the ship how would we be found?"

The captain ground his teeth together so hard his jaw popped. She thought he would order her from the bridge. "A beacon box would signal our position—similar to the black box on an airplane. Now, no more questions. Go."

Daria thanked him and retraced her steps from the bridge.

Chapter 11

WRAPPED IN EVAN'S ARMS, Kyla lay dreaming. His warmth surrounded her like a down comforter. Misty rays of dawn slipped through the windows and touched the sleeping lovers in a tentative caress. Drowsily, Evan opened his eyes as a cascade of pastel light drifted over Kyla's luxurious curves and bathed her in a shower of morning rainbows; he smiled.

Mesmerized by her gossamer beauty, he traced the swirls of color, gliding over her silken skin with a whisper touch. Kyla stirred and moved out of sleep with a contented sigh.

Topaz eyes flicked opened and when she beheld Evan's face, her generous lips curved into a rapturous smile. "It was a short night my love." She stretched languidly and reached for him. Her alluring bronze skin pulsed amber. "But, oh so memorable."

Evan was drowning. Their kiss deepened and he was overcome with such a profound sense of joy that his heart hurt. He no longer possessed the capacity for speech.

Kyla raised her head and Evan saw the intense reflection of her feelings. "Our ways are new to you, but once a mate has been chosen, it is customary to share thoughts." She sat up. Her look was solemn as she took his hand. "I would have you as my life mate, if you would have me. By virtue of thought-touch, we will be joined, one to the other, as long as we draw breath."

Evan swallowed hard to get past the lump in his throat. "I don't know how it's possible, but it feels as though I've known you forever. I can't imagine living without you." He folded her into his arms and kissed her. "You were always mine and I will forever be yours. Show me what we need to do."

As their thoughts flowed from one to another, the morning air glistened with sunlight. Beams of yellow light danced around them, enveloping them in a soft golden glow.

Daria hadn't slept well. Her mind refused to rest. Agitated thoughts looped around her fear of Travlor and the sheer lunacy of his plans. Like buzzards circling dying prey, thoughts continually bombarded her. *I could kill him before this goes too far!*

The counter argument rose like a whip. *Killing betrays everything Na-Kai taught me.*

The stealthy return, *He is weakening; eventually the opportunity would present itself. Think of the people you would save!*

An adamant counter, *That singular act makes a mockery of all that I know.*

A sly thought slithered forward, offering the ultimate bargaining chip. *No one will ever know.*

Daria slammed her fists down on the bunk. "*I* would know!" The empty room reverberated with her anger. She sat up, "My God, I'm not ambiguous about this. I can't and I won't insert my will! There's a reason and purpose for everything, even this madman. If I kill him, even to save other lives, I could initiate a worse reaction." Daria rubbed her eyes and ran her hands through her hair, muttering, "Not only that, the healing gift would desert me and that's a consequence I'm not willing to suffer ... for any reason."

Though the sun had yet to rise over the watery horizon, she left the minimal comfort of her bunk and dressed. She thought about finding the young cook. He should have suffered no ill effects from his horrible accident and would be back on duty. As midnight black relaxed into early morning sapphire, she decided to talk to him.

Stepping out of her room, she shivered from the damp cold and hurried through the dingy, narrow passages. Upon entering the galley, she saw the lone figure of Javier hard at work preparing the morning meal. His back was to her. Not wanting to startle him, she cleared her throat. "Good morning."

The rapid chopping motions ceased and the young Hispanic turned around to greet his visitor. "Ah, senorita! Buenos Dias, but I would say for you, is an early Dias indeed." He grinned and motioned for her to join him as he continued his task.

She approached the table and the sweet/spicy smell of onions, red peppers, chilies and freshly baked biscuits wafted through the air, making her mouth water. Her stomach woke with a sleepy rumble. "What are you making?"

"Today I make my specialty: scrambled eggs with green chilies and chorizo." He grinned shyly but kept chopping. "Do I make you hungry?"

"It smells delicious and I feel like I could eat my weight!"

Their shared laughter illuminated a curious bond that she felt for the young man. Javier dropped the knife onto the chopping block, ran his hands over his apron and grabbed an oven mitt. He loped to one of the ovens and pulled out a huge pan filled with steaming biscuits baked to a scrumptious golden brown. The smell of hot bread filled the air.

He lowered the tray and popped one of the rolls onto a plate, sliced it open, and slathered a thick layer of butter on each side. Gallantly, he proffered the plate to Daria. "To ease the hunger."

Daria accepted his offer and settled on one of the tall stools. She took a bite and closed her eyes. The warm bread melted in her mouth. "Javier, I've never tasted better! This is wonderful!"

The chef in Javier basked in the warmth of her high praise. He acknowledged her words with a brief bow, but hastened to return to the work at hand. He began his high-speed chopping again. Daria wanted to draw him out. "I was talking to the captain yesterday and he told me that all ships have a black box … you know, something to help find us if the ship goes down."

"Yes, is true."

She took another bite and finished the other half of her biscuit before she continued. "Do you know where the box is?"

That innocuous question sounded decidedly false even to her. Javier paused momentarily and his gaze slid across the space separating them. He regarded her carefully then regained his rhythm. "No, but I know only the captain has the key."

Daria stifled her disappointment. "So, what if we sink and he's too hurt to reach the box?"

Javier shrugged. "Do not worry, senorita. I have made a few voyages with this captain and I am still here. Besides, we should make port in another day or so." Javier shifted on his feet, looking uncomfortable. "If you are through, I must finish preparing breakfast or the crew will throw me overboard."

Daria stood up and nonchalantly brushed a few crumbs from her lap. "Well, thank you for your help, I've never been on the ocean before, and believe it or not, I was feeling a bit claustrophobic."

Good humor returned, Javier grinned in understanding. "It takes some getting used to."

Hoping she had allayed any reservations he might have regarding her intentions, she thanked him again for the biscuit and left him to his galley.

As she stepped through the bulkhead, a flicker of movement caught her attention. She studied the area, but saw only an empty passageway. Still, a feeling of unease crept over her and although she couldn't say why, she no longer felt like she was alone.

The small community was already up and getting the day underway when Evan and Kyla entered the kitchen. The thought-touch they shared had left Evan in such a state of unabashed wonder that he was finding it almost impossible to regain a sense of reality. Throughout his solitary life, he had dimly hoped for the possibility of love. But even when he had tried to open his heart to Daria, the lonely void at the core of his being had remained untouched.

Currents of Will

His wildest imaginings could never have prepared him for the power of the intimacy he and Kyla shared. The physical aspect of his love had been elevated to such an emotional and spiritual level that it defied description.

They had dallied in each other's arms and Evan felt as though his entire being had been filled. The essence that was Kyla had become part of his very soul. He had gazed upon her in undisguised rapture and her smile was blissful. "And it will always be thus."

Arm in arm, they entered the dining hall. Ni-Cio looked up from his table and waved them over. "Rogert, if you would organize the men in teams, we start recovery efforts today. Most everybody should be able to help, but I want the women and children to stay here. Once we get underway, we must finish the project as quickly as possible."

Murmurs of assent rippled throughout the hall.

Evan held a chair out for Kyla and waited for the question he knew Ni-Cio needed to ask.

"Evan, we look to you for advice. Within our memories, we have not had to dispose of many bodies due to our gift of transcendence. Those who actually tasted physical death were placed in hidden cairns at depth. In this manner, their remains became part of the ocean we love. Now, however, the numbers left in Atlantis are far too great for that type of burial. Is there another method you would suggest?"

Evan took a moment to ponder Ni-Cio's dilemma as he seated himself next to Kyla. "The problem is the time that has passed since the attack. There will be varying degrees of decomposition, so I don't think the remains could or should be transported out of Atlantis. If there is a room or tunnel that can be spared, the bodies should be sequestered there and the whole area sealed off."

Ni-Cio's face was grim. "By sealed, do you mean with the aid of explosives?"

"Yes, I'll help Rogert and Peltor ready the C4 and detonators and explain how to deploy them."

The Atlantean hesitated only slightly. "Very well, we will locate the appropriate space. Do you foresee any more complications with contamination?"

Evan shook his head. "Until I can gather the necessary equipment, you'll need full 'skins to provide air while you're down there, and they've proven to be effective barriers. But upon your return, I will have you repeat decontamination procedures for the 'skins as well as yourselves."

"Understood." Ni-Cio faced the others. "I do not know how long this will take. However, we still need to be able to move about the island without Evan's aid. Those not directly involved with the kitchens get together with Aris, Mer-An, Kyla and Evan and get those disguises."

Aris stood. "We will come up with something."

Ni-Cio wrapped his knuckles on the table. "All right … in the words of our favorite topsider, let's move. We have much to accomplish."

Daria wanted to run but she deliberately slowed her pace. In an effort to determine the source of her dread, she willed her mind to quiet and sent her awareness into the surrounding space. She wasn't sure if it was due to her pregnancy, but her instincts were on high alert.

She paused in order to scan more thoroughly, and the certainty that she was no longer alone could only mean one thing, "Travlor, I know you're here."

The vague outline of a figure began to appear and as she watched, color eventually penetrated his whole form, bringing the Atlantean into focus. He cocked an eyebrow and stepped toward her. "My, my, your abilities are quite astounding. Why, even your beloved Na-Kai showed no cognitive awareness of my presence once I was masked."

"Well, for whatever reason, it's become patently obvious to me and I don't appreciate your sneaking around and spying on me."

"Ah, it is rather tiresome I must say. However, in light of your recent inquiries, I would suggest that being masked presents a definite benefit."

Daria's anger peaked. She closed the distance between them and shoved a finger in his face. Her voice shook with escalating fury. "I refuse to be the instrument by which you attain godhood! You're a monster and I won't be a party to your ..."

Reaching the limits of his tolerance, Travlor grabbed her wrist in a grip as sure as death itself. Daria yelped with pain and struggled to escape his hold. But the brunt of a venomous rage had finally been released. Spittle sparked from Travlor's mouth and his words erupted like a volcano. "YOU WILL DO WHAT I *TELL* YOU TO DO!"

Like a red hot knife, cramping began low in her back and seared its way into her abdomen. Through a haze of nightmare red and indescribable pain, Daria recognized that she was about to lose her baby. Her knees gave way and she went down gasping for breath. "Stop! You're killing her!"

With the storm that rampaged through Travlor's mind, she knew her plea hadn't registered. She gathered her breath and screamed. "Please!"

Just as suddenly as it had appeared, the pain ceased. She curled into a fetal position at the base of Travlor's feet. She heard the scrape of uncertain footsteps and a labored voice as the Atlantean turned to go. "Do not try me again."

Daria did not rise even after the sounds of Travlor's shuffling exit faded to silence.

Chapter 12

"Well, in theory, your description of a burka-type covering might work." Aris tossed his writing tablet onto the table. Several hastily designed disguises covered the page, each one crossed out. "The problem with that idea is that the locals might view us as a religious sect. If that were to happen, I think they would be more wary of us than if they saw our normal skin fluctuations."

Evan considered the Atlanteans seated around him and was hard pressed to figure out a disguise that would work. At this moment, they were glowing a peaceful bronze and certainly looked harmless enough. But the first time any kind of emotion took hold, that would be the end of it. He only had to remember his reaction upon meeting Kyla for the first time to know they had to think of something.

"What if we painted our faces with tattoos?"

Kyla laughed out loud and patted Mer-An's hand. "I do not think that quite meets the requisite of "fitting in." The locals are simple people. If the island is suddenly inundated with tattooed strangers they might take exception."

However, Mer-An's proposal caused an idea to form in Evan's mind. "Maybe not paint or tattoos, but what about makeup?"

No one commented. It was evident that they had no idea what he had suggested. Their blank looks begged for an explanation.

"Terran women use it on their faces to hide irregularities of the skin. If we get wide brimmed hats, large sunglasses and heavy duty coveralls, it just might suffice."

Aris caught the idea and fielded a question. "It certainly is worth a try. How do we acquire these things?"

"I would say we go to town and procure the items."

Mer-An wrinkled her nose at Kyla. "This should be interesting."

"Just wait until you see the square." Kyla glowed with anticipation.

The recovery teams had just begun their descent down the dusty trail leading to the beach. Every man carried a duffel loaded with the tools necessary for the job. The explosives had been portioned out, and the men that carried them walked with extreme care.

Bringing up the rear, Ni-Cio paused for a moment and haphazardly swiped at the stinging trickles of sweat that pooled in his eyes. Lightheaded, his first thought was that it was too early in the morning for the heat to have affected him. His insides seized in the grip of a powerful cramp and he dropped his burden. The dim thought that he was glad he wasn't carrying a bag with explosives flitted through his mind before another cramp hit. It felt as though a hot lance had ripped through his stomach and he fell to his knees with a low moan. He teetered on the edge of the cliff.

"Ni-Cio!" Rogert threw down his pack and ran back up the trail. He grabbed Ni-Cio's shoulders and dragged his friend away from the steep precipice. Ni-Cio heard a hint of panic in Rogert's order. "Bring some water!"

But Ni-Cio shook his head and sat up. Whatever had crippled him had passed as rapidly as it assailed him. Rogert helped him stand. "Are you all right?"

Ni-Cio dusted his knees and when he looked up he could see the apprehensive faces of his friends. "I feel fine."

"Should I get Evan?"

Still baffled as to the cause of such a swift cramp, he shook his head and stood. "No, truly, I am fine now. Let us continue."

Rogert picked up the packs and followed his friend down the trail. Ni-Cio tried to imagine any reason that would help explain the sudden cramping. But all that came to mind was the same overpowering need to reach Daria. With her absence, a physical ache was lodged so deeply inside his heart that he struggled every waking moment just to keep moving forward. There were times the pain was so acute that it almost bent him in half. So, Ni-Cio drove himself and his men because he knew the only way for him to be rid of the pain was to have Daria in his arms again, safe and well. *"Ah, love, you are my heart . . . Stay strong I will find you . . ."*

Ni-Cio's thoughts flashed through the atmosphere. He poured the strength of his love out to Daria, wherever she was.

Daria stirred and through the haze of mortal terror she had experienced for the safety of her daughter, a feeling of courage flowed into her soul and gave her the will to rise. When she found the baby unharmed, she stood and took a tentative step, and as she did, she knew with every fiber of her being that her beloved Ni-Cio had somehow breached the Travlor-imposed silence.

Chapter 13

A TUGBOAT HAD PULLED Travlor's ship into the teeming harbor of Barranquilla, Columbia. Moored alongside one of the docks, Travlor, with a firm grip on his hostage, led his men down the gangplank. A soldier dressed in fatigues met him once he stepped onto the cement pier, saluted smartly, then offered his hand. Ignoring the overture, Travlor growled, "Where are the rest of your men?"

Embarrassed, the Columbian quickly withdrew his hand and stood a little straighter. "Standing by. I was uncertain of the number of vehicles we would need." He raised a radio to his lips. "Tres." He waved for Travlor and his party to follow. "If you will come with me, the trucks will not be long."

Travlor waded into a quagmire of humanity that parted as easily as the Red Sea. His soldiers followed closely in his wake. Since he couldn't compel the topsider, he maintained a vicelike grip on Daria's wrist even though she twisted around like an injured snake. "Cease your efforts!"

She tried to pry his fingers away. "You're hurting me!"

Currents of Will

He dragged the topsider to his side. "Cease your efforts and it will hurt less!" He wasn't about to risk losing his prize. Should she escape, all his efforts would be in vain.

Three military trucks pulled up and his men separated into groups of twenty, climbing aboard. Travlor shoved Daria into the cab of the first truck and pushed in next to her, barking a command at the driver. "Go! You know the route."

The gnarled driver looked neither left nor right. With dreary eyes pinned to the road, his arthritic hand threw the truck in gear. He guided the vehicle smoothly into traffic and the other trucks closed in behind.

Daria scooted as far from Travlor as she dared and massaged her wrist. His touch was repugnant. She couldn't remember ever feeling so miserable. She wrinkled her nose and sniffed. "This truck's disgusting and smells like dirty feet. How long do we have to be in this thing?"

Travlor stared out the window. "It is a good drive. I would suggest that you relax and enjoy the scenery."

"Where are we?"

"The less you know, the better. Should you somehow break my constriction, I do not want you informing anyone of our whereabouts."

Daria squeezed her eyes shut. A slow burn ignited in her chest and heat rose up her neck and into her cheeks. *The man is a risen demon!* She tried to calm herself by taking some slow, deep breaths. It didn't help much. *I should know better; he's always trying to bait me.* She tried breathing again and felt the tightness in her chest ease. She sighed and shook her head. *If I don't learn a sense of calm, I'm going to burst a blood vessel!*

Her anger receded, helping her think more objectively. She opened her eyes. Signs! There had to be road signs. *Surely I'll see something that will give me an idea as to where we are.* She craned her neck to find anything she could comprehend.

The city was obviously a major port. As they wound further away from the docks, high-rises towered overhead and buildings sprawled in either direction as far as Daria could see. Old buildings were tangled in with the new, and traffic was thick. The city's flavor retained a deep sense of its Spanish heritage, yet modern buildings soared into the air with typical Latin flair. Palms and tropical vegetation grew thick and lush and splashes of vibrant color caught and held her attention.

Daria remembered Travlor had described the place as warm, but this was tropical, hot. As she settled herself and concentrated more intently, she noticed people dressed in vivid colors, colors as appealing as the bright flowers growing haphazardly throughout the city. It truly was a dazzling place. If she had not been brought here against her will, she might have liked to visit.

She was discouraged to find that all the signs she could see were in Spanish. She had such a limited grasp of that language that she couldn't make sense of any of them. *I might as well be in Timbuktu.* She continued to look for anything in English; however, it was a lost cause.

She shivered. Even with the air conditioning cranking full blast, the air felt humid and close. She angled the vent more in her direction. It helped a little. "I'm thirsty. Can we stop for water somewhere?"

Travlor reached under the seat and pulled out a cooler, producing a couple of bottles of water. He handed one to Daria. She twisted the seal and nearly drank the whole thing. *Seems I'm always thirsty now.* She grinned in spite of herself and a warm glow spread through her heart. *A girl, a beautiful baby girl.*

She hugged herself and when she felt like she received an answering hug, she smiled, *That wasn't my imagination!*

Ever since she had learned that she carried a girl, she had felt glimmerings of that sacred life growing within. *Is it possible that a heightened awareness already exists between us?* It didn't matter; impossible or not, Daria felt her love returned and that was all she needed.

It took forever to get outside the city limits, and though she had tried to understand some of the signs and advertisements, Daria had become confused. Giving up, she concentrated on the sights, hoping she might be able to describe the area so well that it would give Ni-Cio a clue as to her destination. Her guess was South America. *We have to be somewhere in Central or South America. It couldn't be Spain. The trip from Greece was too long.*

However, until she knew something concrete, she wasn't going to fall prey to false hope and mistaken assumptions.

The driver finally turned off the interstate and the roads started to narrow. The countryside was verdant with unfamiliar trees and plants. They passed smaller towns and with each turn, the road conditions deteriorated and the towns dwindled. Daria was feeling the need for a break. "Aren't we ever going to stop for gas?"

Travlor rolled his shoulders and spoke to the driver in Spanish, then looked at Daria. "We will take a break in the next town. But be quick."

The stop came sooner than she expected. The driver pulled into a crumbling gas station that hardly looked occupied. However, as Travlor escorted her from the truck, an attendant greeted them from inside the ramshackle doorway. Travlor held up a hand, replied in Spanish, and they were quickly shown inside to a single bathroom. Daria hesitated; the place looked ready to collapse around her feet. Travlor sighed, "Go on. You asked for the stop."

She didn't need to be told to hurry. She tried not to cringe as she reached for the crusty iron knob. Inside the tiny room, there was not one window and only one way in and one way out. Disappointed, Daria abandoned her hope for an easy escape, and didn't waste any more time than she had to in the moldering toilet.

Back in the truck, after what seemed like hours of driving, the road began climbing. Vegetation shouldered the sides of the two-lane road so that sunlight barely penetrated the wall of green. Daria inspected Travlor. "Aren't you tired yet? It seems to me that the energy you expended destroying Atlantis has taken a toll on you. You're even more gray than usual."

Travlor stared straight ahead, but Daria thought she saw one eye twitch. "Do not worry about my energy. I have all that I require. You just maintain your calm so that the child may grow in health and tranquility."

Daria stifled a laugh. "Well, you've given her a hell of a start."

Travlor didn't respond, so she reclined against the hard seat back and tried to get comfortable. She crossed her arms and closed her eyes. As always, her thoughts and her heart went straight to Ni-Cio. She tried to see him in her mind's eye. Where was he now? What was he doing? How were the survivors faring? She shifted and unintentionally jostled the driver. She sighed and resigned herself to enduring to the end of the journey. *My love, does your heart continue to beat after the deaths of so many?*

She knew Ni-Cio would let nothing stop him from finding her, but she wanted his heart to heal. She needed his smile to shine again. She wanted his smile to be the first thing their daughter saw. He would be so proud! She gasped and jerked up. "He's a father!"

The sarcasm in Travlor's voice was more suffocating than the humid air. "Yes, as so many of us are."

Daria ground her teeth together to keep from snarling like a dog. However, before she could respond, the driver interrupted, "The next turnoff will be the road to the complex."

She studied what little she could see of their clogged surroundings. The jungle hovered so close it was stifling, and Daria felt discouraged. *It's impenetrable. If Travlor clapped me in irons and left me to rot in a dungeon, it couldn't be much worse!*

Glancing at her captor, she hardened. *I'm patient. There'll come a time you won't be so observant and when that happens, I'll break your stranglehold.* That thought was followed quickly by a gleeful taunt. *Unless that man dies, you're here forever, FOREVER!*

Daria clamped down on an insane desire to giggle. She forced herself to think logically. *He's been kept in health for so long one would think he would be ready to go.* Stealing a glance at the man to her right, she admitted, *Right, he's never been willing to step through death's door.* She rubbed her tired eyes when an unbelievable thought occurred to her. *There's something other than death he fears.*

She looked at Travlor, then laid her head back against the seat and closed her eyes. *An interesting thought; one that might provide a small wedge to shake his unflappable demeanor.*

Chapter 14

NI-CIO AND HIS CREW descended the trail without another incident. Rocks clapped sharply beneath the weight of Rogert's determined tread as Ni-Cio and the rest of the group brought up the rear.

The biospheres, invisible to any but the Atlanteans, were lined up in neatly ordered rows. The men separated into their designated groups grabbed the 'spheres, and carried them over the rocky shore and into waist deep water. The hatches dissolved and the teams entered their crafts.

Before his hatch materialized, Ni-Cio warned his men, *"Do not let yourselves dwell on the remains of our home ... we will finish our duty as quickly and efficiently as possible; however, should anyone need a break, do not hesitate. Our ocean is there for us and her beauty will help soothe you . . ."* Arcing with the grace of dolphins, both biospheres slipped silently beneath the crystal blue waters.

Descending toward their home, Ni-Cio steeled himself. No matter what advice he gave to his men, none of them were ready to witness the remains of a carnage they never thought to behold.

Thankfully, when those memories had flooded his mind, Evan had kept him from the madness that threatened to devour him. The topsider had helped him more than he would ever know, and Ni-Cio had come to love him like he loved Aris. It felt as if the two friends were his brothers.

When Evan had pitted himself against his rapacious father, the dispossessed son had been instrumental in defending Atlantis. Evan had placed himself in mortal jeopardy with no regard for his own safety. Ni-Cio shook his head sadly, *The son has a strength of character that reflects the best part of the father.*

How Evan could ever reconcile himself to the knowledge that Travlor was his sire, Ni-Cio didn't know. *If he can live with that knowledge, then our task ahead is made less horrific by the example he has set forth.*

Ni-Cio glanced over his shoulder. "Rogert, is everyone clear on procedures? And do you have any suggestions as to how we can make this easier or faster?"

He felt rather than saw the immutable shrug that was just as much a part of Rogert's character as his careful speech. He waited patiently for his reply. The silence continued until the taciturn Atlantean put a hand on Ni-Cio's right shoulder and squeezed. "My friend, try as you might, there is only one way through this odious task, and that is to put our heads down and place one foot in front of the other.

"We have determined the tunnel in which we will place the bodies. Right now, that must be our only focus. When that is complete, we will be ready to seal off access. Only then will the souls that have been lost find rest.

"Once that rite is complete, we must ensure that our home is free of contamination. That will involve nothing but muscle. When that is finished, and we rebuild the structural integrity, there will be no trace of the degradation we suffered. There will be nothing left to mark the passing of so many lives except our memories. The only memorial will be the wall that seals the tomb."

Ni-Cio was surprised; it was more than he ever remembered Rogert saying at one time, but the man wasn't through. "We must also be cognizant of our air supply. While the 'skins can last indefinitely, we do not want to tax ourselves beyond our limits. My friend, we will do what we can, then we will leave. There is always tomorrow."

Ni-Cio smiled; it was comforting to have this man at his side. Rogert was always willing to share his strength and his wisdom. "I have never known you to give bad advice." Ni-Cio turned his attention back to their descent. "We are almost there."

He steered the craft toward the only remaining portal. As the portal's entry lights no longer worked, Ni-Cio entered the tunnel at quarter-speed. The biosphere's lights only illuminated a scant twenty feet ahead and as Ni-Cio carefully navigated the tunnel, an oppressive black veil blanketed them. Ni-Cio squinted into the dark and frowned. He couldn't help thinking, *The opening of our home is as hidden from me as Daria's thoughts.*

Chapter 15

EVAN, KYLA, AND MER-AN approached the marketplace in Fira. Kyla and Evan heard the quick intake of Mer-An's breath with her first real glimpse of Terran life.

Kyla laughed. She remembered her first time in the Terran world and decided that Mer-An was handling the transition much better than she had. She took her hand. "I think you are adjusting quickly. Wait until you see some of the wares. You will love it!"

Mer-An smiled through gritted teeth. "I am doing my best."

"We should be able to find everything we need over there." Evan took both their arms and led them to a nearby drug store.

Upon entering, Evan quickly found the rows of makeup. He grabbed the first thing he saw and, after scouring the contents, realized it was a blusher. "Hmm, this is harder than I thought. Wait here."

He was only gone a short while before he returned with a stout Greek woman. "Show them what they need, please."

The woman's English was halting but quite understandable. She looked Kyla and Mer-An over so thoroughly that they both began to feel uneasy under her scrutiny. Before their skin started to reflect a change, Kyla plunged in. "We are in a hurry. If you could just show us what we need."

The woman's bushy eyebrows rose almost to her hairline. "You do not be in such a rush. You are beautiful women and I must find the right shades for you."

She took one of the bottles, opened it and signaled for Mer-An to hold her hand out. Mer-An was startled and unsure of what was wanted; she glanced nervously at Kyla. Her friend nodded and her soft thought found Mer-An, *'Just hold your hand out to her . . .'*

Slowly, Mer-An offered her arm. Grabbing the Atlantean's wrist, the woman dabbed a spot of color onto her arm and rubbed it around. Mer-An watched with timid curiosity. The woman held Mer-An's wrist up and scowled, shook her head and grabbed another bottle. Shaking the contents rapidly, she unscrewed the cap and repeated the procedure on Mer-An's other wrist.

She measured her work. "This is closer, I think. It is the nearest I can do." She looked at Kyla. "Hmm, you are different."

She rummaged through the merchandise locating the one she wanted. Handing the bottle to Kyla she nodded. "Try yourself."

Kyla was very glad that Evan had used such a generous amount of talc on their faces. As uncomfortable as she felt under the woman's watchful eye, their emotional coloring would have given her the shock of her life. Obviously, Evan's efforts were working as the sales lady detected nothing out of the ordinary. Kyla mimicked the actions Mer-An had submitted to and held her wrist to the light.

"That is good. Now, you pay." The woman's face split into a huge smile.

Evan took Kyla's hand. She could tell something was worrying him. *"What is it, love?"*

"She's not going to believe me when I tell her how many bottles we're going to need…"

He cleared his throat. "Before we go, we'll need twenty-four bottles of each color."

The lady's mouth dropped open, her eyebrows bristled, and her eyes bulged. Evan sent a gentle compulsion and she closed her mouth, lifted a finger and turned around. "I'll be back."

Escorting the ladies to the counter, Evan handed Kyla some money. "Here, pay her, then take the stuff back to the truck. I'm going to locate those supplies we need."

Kyla nodded. "We will be there when you get back. But hurry, love."

"As quick as I can."

He exited the store and Kyla whispered to her friend. "How are you doing?"

Mer-An's gaze had not stopped roving since they entered the store. "I am fascinated by so many items. It is a mystery what they do with everything."

"And this is just a small part of what you will find. Terros is truly marvelous."

An obdurate look crossed Mer-An's face. "I would never want to live here. It is simply too much. How do people pick anything from so many choices?"

"Do not worry. As soon as Evan and Ni-Cio repair Atlantis, we will be back in our home safe and sound and with stories to share," Kyla turned around, looking for the saleslady.

Mer-An hung her head, "Kyla, I do not think I will ever feel safe again."

Surprised by Mer-An's whispered confession, Kyla was afraid to admit that she felt the same way. Gently, she covered Mer-An's hand with her own. "I doubt any of us will ever again feel safe. But I think it will help to be in familiar surroundings. There is comfort in that." She gave Mer-An a loving hug and when she released her, Kyla saw the tears sparkling in her friend's sad eyes. She placed a finger under Mer-An's chin, encouraging her to look up. "You have Aris to keep you safe. I am not certain where Evan and I will end up, but I would follow him to the ends of Terros and beyond if needed. Just as I trust his love, his strength, and his heart, *you* can trust Aris. As long as we have that, then we are as safe as we will ever be."

Mer-An nodded. "You are right. No one is ever truly safe." She sniffed and blinked her eyes. "So, we must embrace the moments when we feel that we are."

A rattling of wheels and the huffing of the saleslady interrupted their conversation as the woman returned with a cartful of product. She went to the register and rang up their purchase, then held out her hand. "It is not a small purchase."

Kyla carefully counted the money into the woman's outstretched hand. The saleslady helped them put everything into bags and eyed them as they turned to leave. "I do not know who would require such an amount of makeup." Jolted, Kyla almost broke into a run. "But, if you need more, please come back."

Perspiration tickled her hairline and Kyla pushed Mer-An out the door before they had to engage in any more conversation. Leading her back to the truck, she tried to take her friend's mind off her first topside encounter. "You did well. You did not even let your emotions surface when she held your wrist."

Mer-An's mood lifted and a shy smile played across her lips. "I replayed one of the night's Aris and I were alone." She laughed, "It took me to another place, but I had to halt that line of thinking as I could feel my temperature start to rise and I did not want to risk embarrassing myself."

Delighted, Kyla joined her gentle laughter. "We are going to be fine, just fine." Arm in arm, they wound their way back to the truck. "Have you contacted Aris?"

A curt nod. "He says that the compound is coming along nicely and the food supplies are rapidly being restocked. I am ready to be back there. I do not think I can take much more today."

"I agree. Let us hope Evan finds what he needs quickly."

They hoisted the bags over the side of the truck and placed them in the bed. Sliding into the cab, Kyla tried the ignition, and surprisingly, the truck roared to life. She turned on the radio and spun the dial so that it ran through the stations. When she found what she was looking for, she smiled at her friend, "Listen, Mer-An, topside music."

Mer-An scrunched her face and covered her ears. "It is just a terrible noise to me."

Good-naturedly, Kyla let her be, content to lose herself in the vibrant Greek music. Her foot tapped a beat and she sat back and crossed her arms. "Evan will be back soon. Try to enjoy yourself."

Mer-An made a sound that Kyla considered rude. She shook her head and let her mind take her where it would.

Evan hurried back to the truck, a big smile on his face. He excitedly got behind the wheel and was amazed to find that, not only had Kyla been able to start the old relic, she was rocking out to some pretty fast music. He laughed out loud. "You are extraordinary! How did you figure all this out? And do you really like that noise?"

Mer-An grumpily added, "Thank you; I am glad someone else agrees with me. Can we not have some peace and quiet?"

Resigned, Kyla turned the radio off and hugged Evan as hard as she could. She looked into his eyes. "I love this music. I want you to teach me more of these Terran ways because I am finding everything to be quite wondrous!" Her eyes shone with a sense of adventure.

Even through the talc covering, Evan could see the color striations that wound over her countenance indicating how happy she was at this particular moment. He lifted his hands to her face and planted a passionate kiss on her luscious lips.

He sat back and put the truck in drive. "That should keep you until we get back to the compound. But I'm not sure it'll keep me."

Mer-An snickered. "Ah, love! A tender moment enjoyed by … me! Evan, punish this truck and get us home. You make me long for my Aris!"

Complying with a bit of difficulty, Evan ground the gears and took off.

Kyla changed the subject. "How did your hunt for the equipment fare? Were you successful?"

Evan glanced at her and nodded. "Easier than I thought. The man at the hardware store has supplies shipped in regularly. We're going to need at least ten generators and probably twenty-odd filters and purifiers. He ordered the equipment and it'll arrive on tomorrow's ship. With those items secured in Atlantis, it should be enough to get the air and water supply working and will allow everybody a rest from their bioskins."

Kyla quirked her head. "How much more equipment do you think it will take?"

"By the time we've finished rebuilding, we'll probably have thirty units functioning around the clock. I'll also order extras as backups in case one of the machines breaks down."

"That is a lot, love. How are these things supposed to work?"

Evan concentrated on the road as he wound through traffic and considered the extent of the toxic air that had been dispelled during the attack. Given the two day shelf-life of the gas, and the time that had passed, he didn't think the air was still contaminated. However, he was still worried about the safety of the salvage crew as well as the returning families. He wasn't willing to gamble anyone's health on the hope that the gas had been rendered inert.

When he had cleared traffic and was headed back to the compound, he explained, "The generators run on gas. Travlor installed a huge storage tank on property so that the soldiers could keep their vehicles gassed. I'll see that it's filled up for our purposes. The generators and fuel bladders will ensure sufficient power. I think around twenty air purification systems will be enough to scrub any residual poison from the air and we'll probably need the same amount for the water."

Mer-An was surprised at the amount of fuel needed to run one of the topside machines. "I do not think the Terrans have been very thoughtful about the way they power their machines. Do they not have alternative methods?"

Evan rubbed his neck and tried to keep the old truck from swaying into the ruts. "For our needs, the generators provide a quick and easy way to get your home up and running. Since we're racing the clock in trying to locate Daria, the sooner we can power your home, the better off everyone will be."

Kyla reached for the radio, "Cover your ears Mer-An, I'm pumping up the noise!"

Evan shook his head, "I think you meant volume."

"No, I did not!" Kyla laughed to see Mer-An make a sour face and clapped her hands over her ears.

Chapter 16

After jouncing over uneven roads for what seemed like days, the trucks turned onto the dirt avenue that would bring their journey to an end. Daria was glad that it was finally over. She was sore, she was tired, and she was ready to be out of the malodorous truck.

Their driver slowed his approach, giving Daria time to assess the complex in which Travlor had chosen to sequester them. Hacked from the stifling, endless green was a place that looked like an unassailable fortress. Towers that were more like machine gun turrets stood at every corner, manned by heavily armed guards. With their blackened faces and menacing looks, it seemed to Daria that the men were not only ready to fight off outside threats, they were hard-bitten enough to fight the jungle into submission. *As if anyone could ever find this place, or would want to.*

She quavered. Hopes of Ni-Cio locating her vanished as surely as the sun sets in the west. "Looks like you're prepared to face an invasion."

They stopped before an impressive iron gate on which was etched a very fancy coat of arms. Travlor stirred. "I am not unused to topside ways, but even if I were, I have myself as an example. Guard your back; if not, you are never prepared for any contingency."

The gate slowly swung open. As they drove through, Daria could see how thick the concrete block walls were. Expecting to see prison-like surroundings, she was astonished by the pure opulence spreading out before her eyes. "Oh my God! What is this place? Some drug lord's refuge?"

Travlor chuckled. "My, my; you are full of surprises. That's exactly what this place was before I acquired it."

Daria took in the gaudy splendor of the estate and couldn't help but think about the effort expended to bring such a place into being. Reflecting pools were adorned with nymphs, naked and gleaming, looking as though they would spring from their pedestals in wicked abandon.

The grounds, abundant with flowers, bushes and plants of every kind imaginable, crowded the eye with a profusion of colors and confusion. To Daria, there seemed no rhyme or reason. She muttered, "The landscaper must've used Alice's walk through Wonderland as his guide." She eyed Travlor, "Does this cacophonous landscape reflect the drugged-out dreams of the owner?"

Travlor ignored her question although he tended to agree with her observation.

The house, certainly a misnomer, came into view. Daria had been shocked by the grounds, but the building, a testament to crazed splendor, failed in its attempt at grandiosity. So huge that it extended out of sight, the architecture was a mishmash of Spanish Colonial, Mediterranean Revival and Beaux Arts.

Arched corridors, columns, cornices and balconies, replete with random wrought iron, fought for attention. Rather than validating an exquisite eye for detail and design, the estate flaunted a voracious appetite. The place was soulless. It occurred to Daria that Travlor had probably picked it for that very reason. If he had, she didn't want to dwell on that idea.

The driver pulled up to the front entrance where two men waited. Dressed in camos, their faces dripped with sweat. Their dark green T-shirts were stained nearly black, so that it looked to Daria as if they had just stepped out of a shower.

Travlor helped her out of the truck. Humidity slapped her in the face like a wet towel and it was hard to take a breath. As they closed the distance to the attendants, the men attempted to stand even straighter. They looked highly uncomfortable and Daria suspected that their anxiety was more from having to face Travlor than it was from the tropical heat and humidity.

"Are the rooms prepared?"

The taller of the two men stepped forward. "All is in readiness. Would you care for some refreshment or would you like to be shown to your quarters?"

Travlor led Daria up the wide staircase and into the foyer. "I am certain the lady would like to be taken to her rooms." He turned a questioning gaze to her and she nodded her consent. He directed one of the men and signaled for Daria to follow. "Make yourself comfortable, my dear. We will be here for quite some time. You will find clothing and all the toiletries you require. Should you need anything, then you must come to me. I have instructed my men not to engage you in any conversation."

"If I'm to be here, what about a doctor for my pregnancy?"

Travlor crooked an eyebrow. "You are a healer as am I. Together we will keep the child safe and in perfect health. You need not fear for her."

Somehow Daria didn't feel comforted by that statement, but she decided to let it pass. "Seems you've thought of everything."

"I have certainly tried. Now follow my man. Tidy up, then join me for supper."

Hot, sweaty, exhausted, and helpless, Daria glumly followed the attendant to her quarters.

Chapter 17

GAWKING AT THE prior owner's ideas of interior design, Daria kept banging into tables and chairs as she ogled a collection of art that ran the gamut from high-blown and overpriced to profane and overpriced. There were so many sitting areas, she lost count of the overstuffed leather and the tropical fabrics that clashed with the objects d'arte spread willy-nilly over, on, and around each room.

The window walls, thrown wide, invited the outside in and opened onto an enormous tiled veranda that looked out over a vista to a vast garden area. Daria stopped and gaped. She actually rubbed her eyes and blinked hard.

The backside of the estate rivaled an Olympic venue. Commanding the center section, an Olympic-sized pool, complete with three and ten meter boards, was surrounded by waterfalls, fire pits, loungers, tables, and chairs. Shady umbrellas sprang up like weeds to provide escape from the searing rays of the sun.

Off to one side, men's and women's changing rooms contained showers, hot and dry saunas, lockers and god knew what else. On the opposite side, a cabana that looked like something from a Texas-sized hotel sheltered a fireplace big enough to cook a moose, a dining table that could have doubled as a runway for a small plane, and a fully loaded kitchen and bar.

Beyond that over the top Busby Berkeleyesque setting, frenzied landscaping wound around and through a regulation beach volleyball court, a croquet lawn court, and tennis courts of every type of surface ever invented. It was an adulterated version of grandeur.

The attendant grew restive as Daria tried to take it all in. She roused herself from the spectacle. "I'm ready to find my rooms, please." She was overwhelmed. She didn't want to see anymore.

The man turned toward a sweeping staircase that spiraled through several stories. Luckily, her rooms were located on the second floor. The man walked down a wide hallway and signaled her door. Holding it open, he closed it gently behind her.

Daria swiped at the sweat trickling down her neck. Before she could take stock of her surroundings, she had to find the bathroom, now.

She spied a side door, hurried over, and as she barged through the door, she gasped. Tiled in travertine from floor to ceiling, a glass-enclosed shower big enough for ten people and friends adjoined a sunken tub that resembled someone's chaotic idea of a garden pond.

A walk-in closet concealed a wardrobe large enough to clothe a small village, and stretching the length of one wall, a fully loaded vanity glowed with gold his and her sinks. She sighed, "I just need a toilet."

Once, she had seen to her urgent needs, Daria walked back to her assigned set of rooms.

The rampant pomposity was absent and whether the designer had taken a break or just run out of ideas, she was relieved to see a large, comfortable sitting area, table, and chairs for in-room dining, and a king-sized, recessed bed with built-in night stands. Throw rugs added touches of color to Mexican tile and a large set of shuttered windows looked out on the front grounds.

Daria had an unobstructed view of the bricked drive and entry gate. The two visible towers were manned and active. Guards held their posts as if their lives depended on it. "Which they probably do," she muttered.

Daria shook her head and closed the shutters. She decided that if she had to be imprisoned somewhere, this was as good as any and probably a lot better than most.

She saw another door, and upon investigating, found a much smaller room that had been readied as an office. A desk and chair stood adjacent to another set of widows and there was a duo of leather chairs, between which rested a dark wood table. "Not sure if I'll need this room." Feeling sticky, she backed out and closed the door. She needed a shower and a change into something less travel weary. Lifting the heavy hair from her neck, she rummaged through the closet. She found some light, loose clothing, and headed toward the bathroom. "Might as well settle in."

Chapter 18

ROGERT AND HIS CREW had moved most of the bodies from the Great Hall of Poseidon. He thought that another couple of hours would bring an end to their hideous undertaking. With a strong clamp on his emotions, he refused to think about the two beloved family members he had just placed inside the burial tunnel.

However, his endurance and fortitude were slipping. His façade was crumbling and he didn't think he could maintain a grip on his decorum much longer. Rather than leave, he determined that all his men needed time away from their grisly work. *"That is enough for now. You have done well, but we must break ... we need to reacquaint ourselves with our beloved ocean ..."*

Cries of assent echoed through his mind and his men quickly gathered round. *"A fifteen minute swim will help calm our spirits. Go wherever your body takes you ..."*

They wound through the broken remains of their home and accessed the portal exit. Each man was lost in his own thoughts, his own grief, and each one of them needed time alone. Without looking at each other, the Atlanteans dove into the water and flew through the portal. Reaching the tunnel mouth, they blasted off in all directions.

Rogert started to race toward his favorite coral reef; however, the shadow of a large figure loomed into view. He knew who it was before he saw him. Every Atlantean considered the huge fish to be the guardian of this particular portal and the behemoth had been loved by all.

"Gallendar, my old friend . . ." Rogert floated, arms crossed over his imposing chest and waited for the gentle leviathan.

Gallendar flicked his massive tail and sailed effortlessly to Rogert's side. His usual clicking and showing of teeth was absent, indicating his own sadness. *"My heart hurts, Rogert, as does yours . . ."*

Though he had walled himself off from the enormity of his loss, that his friend had cared enough to seek him out disintegrated the barriers shielding his heart. A lump rose in his throat, and though he swallowed repeatedly, it refused to budge. His eyes prickled, then stung. With his next breath, the dam erupted and tears poured from his eyes.

The bioskin prevented him from swiping his tears, and try as he might, Rogert was helpless to staunch the river that cascaded down his cheeks and over his chin. The stoic Atlantean cried so that shudders wracked his body and he could no longer hold himself upright.

Gallendar moved next to him. Using his own rigid body, he supported his grief-stricken friend. The great fish didn't waver and barely drew breath. Gallendar knew that the deaths of so many Atlanteans precluded Rogert from choosing another mate. For his friend, more than family had been lost; Rogert's future had been lost as well.

He waited as Rogert unleashed all of the anger and the hurt that he'd kept bottled inside.

At last, Rogert's emotional storm subsided, his tears lessened and as his sobs quieted, he slowly ran his hand over Gallendar's smooth scales. Ripples of light followed his movements and Gallendar shimmered with glowing neon colors. Entranced, Rogert continued to stroke his friend's body and as he did, a silent gift of love and caring flowed into his aching heart. His sorrow lessened and although his hurt remained, it seemed manageable. He no longer felt like he was being be ripped apart.

Rogert finally stopped his motions, righted himself, and gradually backed away. He brought his hands up in prayer pose and bowed his head, "*Thank you old friend. I am sorry to burden you . . .*"

Gallendar displayed his teeth. "*Rogert, you are strong and you will survive, even against your own desires . . . trite though it seems, time does help and I promise, you will find joy again. Do what you must to release your emotions or they will choke the life from you, and I do not refer to the life of your physical form . . .*"

"*I will try, Gallendar . . .*" Rogert couldn't think of anything else to say; however, he was able to show his teeth to his enormous friend.

Gallendar backed away, flicked his massive tail once, and was gone before Rogert could blink. Shrugging his shoulders, the Atlantean took a deep breath and turned back to a place he no longer recognized as home.

Currents of Will

Ni-Cio and his team were still hard at their labors. Using the disinfectant that Aris had given them, each man worked tenaciously to wipe down every surface of Atlantis. Ni-Cio and his squad scrubbed the kitchens and gathering areas, as well as the surviving living quarters. He had sent the rest of his crew to work on decontaminating the remaining tunnels and the garden retreats that were scattered throughout their home.

The crew reached the last of the council hall/hospital when Ni-Cio threw his rags down. He stood and stretched his back. *"How are you doing, Aris? Do you need a break?"*

Aris stopped scrubbing and looked up. *"We are nearly through and I would suggest that we tackle the Great Hall while we still have strength. I believe Rogert and his men have cleared quite an area where we can continue our cleaning..."*

Ni-Cio grabbed his rags and bent to his work. He sent a quick thought to his other men. *"How do you fare?"*

Replies were forthcoming and progress was being made faster than Ni-Cio had originally planned. *"Good, as soon as you have finished, meet us in the Great Hall; we will start where Rogert's team left off..."*

The men worked quickly to get the connecting tunnel disinfected and stepped into the Great Hall of Poseidon where they were joined by the others.

It was a gruesome sight, but Rogert's group had moved most of the bodies to the burial site. Ni-Cio motioned to his friends. *"If you could begin taking the bodies out, the rest of us will start disinfecting. Aris, how are our supplies?"*

"Running low, but I believe it will be enough to finish the area you have designated. It is without doubt that we will have to return..."

Ni-Cio had already decided that the initial pass would take more time. So, before returning to their assignments, he suggested that his men take a break. *"Whether you would like a swim or would rather just wander, please give yourselves some time. Meet back here in fifteen or twenty minutes..."*

Nods flowed around the room and the teams left through the tunnel to the council hall. Ni-Cio knew that most of his men would opt for a swim. He eyed Aris and raised his brows questioningly.

Aris shook his head. *"I am well enough. I intend to push on; the sooner we get this done, the sooner we can start rebuilding. I am anxious to be back in our home..."*

"Very well, let us continue..." Ni-Cio knelt onto the floor and continued his scrubbing. He watched his friend carefully for signs of fatigue, emotion or anything else that would give him an idea as to his state of mind. Still, he could discern nothing. Aris scrubbed as though he was on autopilot. Ni-Cio decided to follow suit, and leaving Aris to his own thoughts, lowered his head and scrubbed, wishing he could just as easily scrub away the acute pain of loss.

Halfway through their work, Rogert entered, followed by his group. Ni-Cio was glad to see them and stood to take Rogert's outstretched arm. *"You have done well, my friend. I think another couple of passes and the bodies will be where they will remain; without doubt, the cleaning process will continue long after we have sealed off the tunnel. I do not intend to take any chances..."*

"Agreed..." Rogert signaled his men to finish what they had started.

Ni-Cio wondered at the deep blue lines that colored his friend's face. It was evident that Rogert had suffered a terrible outpouring of grief. However, because the colors were receding, Ni-Cio could see that Rogert had found a measure of comfort. For that, he was blessedly thankful. He knew how hard Rogert had strived to suppress his grief. He rinsed his rags, knelt back down, and scrubbed harder.

At last, the monstrous display of bodies was gone. Removed from all of the existing halls, tunnels and the Great Hall, the remains had been placed in the designated burial tunnel. It made everyone feel a little easier to know that their families, lovers, friends, and even the mercenaries, had been given a place of rest.

The last action was to blow the tunnel so that the bodies would be forever sealed in their makeshift tomb. It was the only way to make certain that the rest of Atlantis was safe from contamination.

Ni-Cio straightened up, rubbed the small of his back, and surveyed the room. *"We are done. Rogert and Peltor, stay with me. Aris, take the rest of the men, get to the biospheres and ready them for departure. We will blow the tunnel and when we join you, we will return to Evan's compound to find rest and food. You have done well..."*

The men threw down their various tools and rags and trailed out of the huge room. Peltor went to the set of explosives that Evan had provided. The topsider had helped him set the detonator, but had warned caution. "No matter what you think, act like this is nitro glycerin. There are not enough safeguards for this kind of work."

Peltor gingerly picked up the box that contained the charges and Ni-Cio and Rogert fell into step beside him.

The tunnel was not far, so it wasn't long before they stood at the entrance. Ni-Cio watched Peltor and Rogert carefully plant the bundled explosives. Evan had drawn a detailed diagram to indicate how the charges were to be set. The men followed his instructions to the letter.

When they were done, Peltor and Rogert backed away and carefully eyed their efforts. Peltor looked at Ni-Cio and nodded, *"We are ready..."*

Rogert added, *"It would be well to be at the biospheres before the charges fire. I do not trust our handiwork that much..."*

Ni-Cio agreed, *"Peltor, set the detonators to give us enough time to get the 'spheres..."*

Peltor adjusted the timing, then leapt up. The three men darted for the exit. They raced into the portal cave where the others were standing by, crafts at the ready. As Ni-Cio, Rogert, and Peltor ducked inside their craft, a muffled WHOOOMP echoed through the tunnels.

"Out, now!" Ni-Cio's thoughts bellowed through his men's minds.

Hatches materialized and the biospheres sped through the pitch-black tunnel. Everyone was ready to be back in the open sea.

Chapter 19

TRAVLOR STOOD BEFORE the group. Eyeing them carefully, he knew that they were entirely under his control. "You are my elite. I have trained you as I have trained no others."

He paced before the line of men, back and forth, back and forth. Unhurried, he considered his next statement and reinforced it with a compulsion. "You are to guard the woman's quarters as well as mine without regard to personal safety."

Not one muscle moved as the soldiers intently trained their eyes on the horizon. Travlor continued, "You will react immediately to any command I issue without hesitation. Is that clear?"

The men shouted as one. "Yes sir!"

Travlor sent another compulsion. More insidious, it took a toll on his flagging energy, but he was willing to risk the drain. He didn't want them to be susceptible to any other thought-forms, not from the topsider and certainly not from Ni-Cio, should he ever find them. He needed the men willing and ready to fight to the death.

His demand raced through each of the soldier's minds and Travlor could see the change. Their eyes narrowed and their faces became even more hardened. The men he had hired as his killing machines were now powered by a thought-form that was impregnable. No one else could break through.

He stepped back and felt his legs start to give out. Grabbing the nearest chair, he steadied himself. Stiffening his back, he straightened with effort and resumed, "Never let either one of us out of your sight and when it is time to change watch, be ready to brief your counterpart. Any questions?" Not one twitch among the men. Travlor smiled to himself, then roared, "Dismissed!"

Seated at the dining table, Travlor waited for Daria to join him. Although he had allowed her time to freshen up, he knew she needed sustenance, especially now. The chef he had flown in had usurped the kitchen from the prior cook and now used him as sous chef. Travlor had been explicit in his orders regarding what they were to prepare and when they were to serve. He wasn't about to let the topsider's health slide because of lack of nourishment.

"Are you near?" Hungrily eyeing the food-laden table, Travlor could feel his own stomach grumbling in protest.

"Yes, I'm coming. Where else would I be? Your goons are tracing my every step. . ."

"Ah, Daria how you mistake my motives! I have but ordered my men to attend to you for your own health; you have no idea the risks the surrounding jungle holds. There are wild things roaming that you do not want to meet. My men are here to keep you safe. . ."

Daria entered the room with her assigned contingent. Ten men surrounded her, dwarfing her small form with their sheer size and bulk. Travlor had chosen his men carefully, with an eye to size and fitness and inclination to fight.

To a man, no one was shorter than six feet and the muscles that flexed and rippled in their bodies were there not because of gym time, but because of hard use. The mercenaries were experts in different types of martial arts including Jiu Jitsu, the marine's deadly LINE techniques, and the Israeli's highly lethal Krav Maga.

Travlor was delighted to see that Daria was barely visible in the midst of her bodyguards. She was crucial to his plans and he wasn't about to give her any chance to flee. And should the unthinkable happen, and Ni-Cio find the woman, Travlor was fairly confident that the Atlantean could be taken out before he got to her. *"Soon you will get used to them and you will view them as no more than shadows ..."* Travlor stood and offered her a chair.

Daria stared at him with open distain, but took the chair without hesitation. He knew she was famished. He pulled the warming domes from the silver trays and presented their fare. "Help yourself. My chef has outdone himself and I know that you will find most of his offerings quite delectable."

She didn't wait to be asked a second time. Daria piled food on her plate and ate as though she hadn't tasted a morsel in weeks. She barely noticed the wafting aromas and scintillating flavors as she concentrated on satisfying her hunger.

They consumed their meal in silence until most of their needs had been met, then Travlor sat back, wiped his mouth and scrutinized his guest. "You are a most quiet companion. Since we are to share so much time together, I would suggest that you try to initiate some conversation or we will quickly become quite bored with each other. And I have a feeling that you have as many questions for me as I have for you."

Daria put her fork down. "What could you possibly have to share with me? Any question I've asked, you've either refused to answer, or you've acted like you didn't hear."

Travlor was surprised to find that he was discomfited by her steady blue gaze. "So, what would you like to talk about? Humor me and give me a clue." He tried to suppress the sneer that twisted his lips. It was not how he wanted to start.

He grimaced and tried again, willing himself to smile. "I would like to know about your past. How it is that you came to Santorini? Don't you have people topside that are looking for you?"

Her gaze never wavered from Travlor's dark, gray eyes, and Daria took her time. She finished the last of her juice, dabbed her mouth and then pushed her chair back. "You could care less about who's looking for me. I think you're merely trying to pry into my life for reasons only clear to yourself."

Travlor wiped his mouth and pushed his chair away from the table. Crossing his legs, he sat back. "Alright, what I really want to know is why Evan didn't kill you. That was his duty; that is what I had outlined for him to achieve. Nevertheless, I know he never told you about Santorini and I am mildly curious as to how you ended up there. However, if you do not care to share, then so be it. I have other duties that beg my attention." Travlor threw his napkin to the table and stood to leave. When he saw Daria's shoulders slump, he quietly took his chair and waited.

Daria shook her head and shrugged, "I don't know about Evan killing me. Obviously, he didn't. I think by asking me to marry him, he was trying to keep me close so that when you got together, I would already be under control." She thought a bit. "Something just didn't feel right to me."

Daria traced the edges of the table, feeling the fine lace of the tablecloth. She glanced at Travlor and clasped her hands in her lap. "I cared for your son, but I wasn't in love. He kept badgering me to marry him and I was tired of the merry-go-round of why and why not. I decided to give myself time to think things through." She reached for a glass of water and gulped it, as much to give herself time as to quench her thirst, then began again.

"Santorini came up when an Atlas I was holding slipped out of my hands and fell open to that page. My focus was drawn to that particular island. It was as if my life couldn't go on unless I booked a fight as soon as possible.

"Once everything was in place, the compulsion left and I was just happy to be going somewhere, anywhere away from his clinging grasp." She ran her hands through her hair. "Na-Kai told me that Kai-Dan probably led me to Atlantis. I would like to think that she did. All I know is that I was there when I was supposed to be. And, well, you know the rest."

She sighed and placed her elbows on either side of her plate. "Now, it's my turn." She pulled her chair closer and leaned in. "Why? Why did you have to kill everyone?" Her voice broke and tears came, she cleared her throat and tried again. "Na-Kai would've transcended soon enough. Why couldn't you have just waited to kidnap me until that happened?"

All at once, her control snapped and her grief and fury locked on the target. She launched to her feet and slammed her hands onto the table. Silver, china and glassware jumped, spilling food and liquid everywhere. Her chair flew back and

Currents of Will

clattered to the floor. She threw herself at Travlor. "You killed everyone! You murderer! You vile, stinking excuse—"

Before she could finish, Travlor had her in his iron grip. His eyes bored into her like a drill and his mouth was so close to hers, that for one crazy moment, she thought he was going to kiss her. She struggled violently to get away, but his grasp was impervious. She couldn't wrench free.

"Enough!" His vehement whisper stabbed her like a lance and she held quite still. With his next words, Daria's insides turned to ice. "The reasons are mine alone! Bring it up again, and you will be imprisoned in your room and the only sights you will see will be the ones outside your window!"

With every ounce of willpower he possessed, Travlor stayed the hand that was raised to strike her upturned face. When he thrust her from him, she stumbled into the table, just catching herself before she fell.

In that moment, Daria lost all fear of the monster before her. The only thing she knew was that she wanted to hurt the man that stood in front of her with such impunity. She flew at him, hands outstretched like talons. Two strides before she could strike that mocking face, she was surrounded and subdued by the guards.

The fight leaked out of her as quickly as it had flared. She was appalled by her loss of control and she was instantly filled with a deep sense of shame and remorse. The rage and hurt she had expressed were a mirror for everything she knew about Travlor. She coughed and straightened herself. She gently tried brushing the soldier's arms from hers. Squaring her shoulders, she eyed the men. "Let me go."

No one moved.

"Let her go." Travlor's orders were immediately obeyed.

The men stepped aside and Daria approached the Atlantean. "This will not happen again. I apologize." She studied the man standing before her. She was surprised to find that her fear and her anger were gone. She looked closer and saw a hint of the man behind the mask. Although his eyes flashed hot with temper, Daria glimpsed a pain buried so deep that she knew no one in Atlantis had ever noticed. She hadn't thought she would ever feel anything other than disgust for the Atlantean. Unnerved by the depth of his pain, she examined the first thought that came. *Your hurt is even deeper than mine.* And for the first time since knowing the man, she felt something other than abhorrence, she actually felt sorry for him.

Shaking, she reached for a silver pitcher and splashed some juice into her glass. She knew Travlor would never willingly acknowledge a hurt running that deep. Draining the beverage, she changed the subject. "What kind of juice is this? I've never tasted anything quite like it."

Travlor turned away, but as he was leaving, decided to join the game. Their mutual dislike was something they would eventually have to deal with. Right now, his main interest still centered on her health and that of the child's.

He snorted and crossed to the overturned chair, picked it up, and placed it next to Daria, then casually sat down. "It's something I devised to help enhance your energy. It's a combination of pomegranate, blueberries and kumquat. I find it quite tasty myself."

He poured himself a glass and drank. When he was done, he gently placed the crystal goblet back on the table and rested his hands in his lap. "You should feel nothing but glowing health while you are here. Rest, let the child grow, and try to find a way to experience some happiness. That is just as important to you both as anything else." He tiredly rubbed his eyes.

Daria scooted her chair back. "You have a point." Standing, she hesitated, then begrudgingly offered her hand. "Will you show me around so that I can acquaint myself with the property?"

Shocked, Travlor never thought to see the topsider offer anything but extreme dislike. That she offered to take his hand made him balk. Gruffly he declined. "I have much to do. One of the men in your detail will show you the grounds. There is a pool if you are inclined to swim. As you grow in size, it will be a boon to have so that you can ease the weight."

He left without another word. Daria was amazed that he had offered anything to her. Maybe at some point, she and Travlor could reach an understanding, a compromise of sorts. She watched his men follow him up the stairs and to his quarters. Travlor's shoulders were hunched and his gait was slower than before. *It's evident his powers are weakening. I'll bide my time, but if I see even the smallest chink in his armor, I'll use it to my advantage.*

Chapter 20

"It's time, Ni-Cio." Evan studied his friend. "I've done all I can to help, but I've got to get back to Boston to take care of business."

Ni-Cio knew Evan had to return to America, but he did not have to like the idea. "You have been instrumental in helping us. You have not only provided us this safe haven, you have made it possible for us to return to our home. Without you, I do not know where we would be."

The two friends meandered through the waiting vineyards. The decrepit fields had been scraped clean of all the dead vines and stood fallow, ready for new plantings. Evan was happy to see that, because in the back of his mind, he had determined that the vineyard should be revived. It was a challenge to see what kind of wine could be produced, and if it was palatable, it would provide a ready source of income for his friends. He bent to feel the soil and brought a handful of the red dirt up to his nose. He inhaled relishing the rich, earthy smell and glanced up at Ni-Cio.

"My other concern has to do with Daria's friends and co-workers. We can't keep the ruse of an extended honeymoon going any longer. 'Daria' is going to need to be seen."

Evan stood up and clapped his hands, scattering the dirt, then wiped his palms on his jeans. He continued his walk with the Atlantean as Ni-Cio shook his head. "I am not anxious to see you leave, Evan. However, I understand the urgency. Are you thinking to mask Kyla so that she will look like Daria?"

Evan smiled. "Yes, she'll have to make some appearances as Daria. I'll be at her side every step of the way so that I can coach her regarding Daria's friends. And she'll have to give notice at the antique store."

The men halted, then turned around and headed back to the cabins. Ni-Cio reached a decision and slapped Evan on his back. "I know you must miss your home. I have been consumed with our needs and have been remiss in considering yours. How soon will you depart?"

Evan lowered his gaze and regarded the ground. "I've ordered my jet to pick us up tomorrow."

Ni-Cio didn't let his inward discomfort show. "That is sooner than I anticipated." He stopped and regarded his friend. "What is that topside saying? Something about getting the show on the road?"

Evan chuckled, "That's the one."

"I wish you much success so that you may return that much sooner." His gaze was solemn, "Take care of my sister. I will miss you both."

The men hugged, then resumed their walk into the compound. "Don't worry about Kyla; I'd give my life to keep her safe. She's my life's breath, but if I know her, she's going to love this adventure."

Chapter 21

A WEEK HAD SLIPPED by and Daria was becoming accustomed to the estate. She had begun to sleep better but last night, her sleep had been restless and filled with countless scenarios in which she searched for, but never found, Ni-Cio. After breakfasting alone, her mind still felt lost in dreams that clung to her like a spider's web. She longed for a swim and knew that the cool water would help revive her spirits and clear her head. She pushed from the table, and followed by her guards, made her way up the stairs and to her rooms.

Among the clothes that Travlor had provided, she found a swim suit. Donning the garment, she was gratified to see that it fit rather well. "He certainly has good taste," she mumbled. Hurriedly grabbing a brightly colored beach towel, she slid into woven flip flops and made for the pool.

The day was dripping with humidity and with each passing minute, Daria felt herself wilting like an old flower. Taking in the cool blue of the swimming pool, she thought, *Even tepid water will feel better than this.* She used her towel to swipe her sweat-dampened face.

Walking to the nearest lounger, Daria tossed the towel onto the seat, shoved off the flip flops and approached the water's edge. She curled her toes around the travertine-tiled side and dove smoothly into the deep end. The water was deliciously cool and she almost felt giddy as it glided across her skin. Her nerves began to unwind and her mind relaxed.

Swimming a few laps, she tested her muscles and was gratified to feel them loosen and stretch. Finally, slightly winded by the effort, Daria rolled over and lazily floated on her back. Gazing at the crystal-clear, blue sky, her mind wound through recent events. As she drifted in the comfort of the cool, sweet water, she found herself back in an untouched Atlantis, preparing to take her first swim at depth. Her heart warmed and she smiled at the memory.

She had been so frightened; even though she considered herself an excellent swimmer, all of her water knowledge had been pool-based. She had never even snorkeled. She remembered standing in the exit chamber, nerves pinging and feeling jumpy and hypervigilant. However, Ni-Cio had wrapped his arms around her, and nuzzling her ear, whispered that he wouldn't let anything happen. The bioskin surrounded her, swaddling her in comfort and warmth, and her fear diminished.

Ni-Cio slipped into the pool as easily as a seal, then turned and held his hand up to guide her in. When she was firmly in his grasp, he flashed a radiant smile and before she could object, they had gone under.

At first she held her breath, afraid that the bioskin wouldn't work properly. When she exhaled and tentatively took her first sip of air, she was amazed to find that the 'skin functioned effortlessly. The air she received was pure and sweet and her breathing came as easily as if she had been standing topside. The 'skins had been engineered so perfectly that even the smallest expenditure of energy was recycled and reused in almost perfect, perpetual motion. Ni-Cio had explained that if they ever figured out a way to eat, they could live in the 'skins indefinitely.

As she listlessly kicked her feet and floated, she remembered being astounded that she could see so clearly at such remarkable depths. The bioskin not only felt like a replica of her own skin, the material sharpened her eyesight so that even in the darkest water, there was no visual impairment. She imagined that the 'skins functioned in a similar manner as night-vision goggles. As they ascended the depths and more light was reflected, the night vision effect lessened. The bioskins were a technological miracle. And as she flew through the surrounding blue with Ni-Cio's arm around her, she succumbed to the barrage of new sensations and experiences. Ni-Cio carried her through the deep as though she was as light as a feather, and as they swam toward shallower waters, the rainbow colors and immense beauty of their undersea world opened before her.

Coral reefs teemed with life so that she was dazzled by all the motion. Fish darted about like flashing neon signs and the coral grew in an astonishing array of shapes and colors. Plants swayed in a continual dance with the currents, and grumpy crustaceans slid back into holes that had become homes. Daria had been enchanted.

When they had finished discovering all the many homes of the reef dwellers, they descended into deeper, wider seas and Ni-Cio introduced her to some of his larger friends. Whales, dolphins, even sharks slid gracefully through the water to welcome her to their world. Daria learned their names and some of their history, and to her delight found that quite a few of Ni-Cio's friends were really funny. She had laughed at the jibes they had traded with the Atlantean.

Tired but incredibly happy, Ni-Cio had finally taken her back home. Stepping out of the pool, he had gently wrapped a warming robe around her and given her a deep, intimate kiss.

Daria drifted toward the shallow end of the pool and her eyes misted at the memory. Not wanting to stop the thoughts that flowed through her, Daria continued her reverie. Closing her eyes, she watched as, arm in arm, she and Ni-Cio had walked back to his rooms, disrobed and made slow, passionate love.

That entire day had become swathed in a dreamlike quality and Daria had known then that she would always hold that particular time close to her heart. For that had been the night they had conceived their daughter.

She paddled easily, enjoying the flow of water over her body, imagining it was Ni-Cio's touch caressing her skin. Calculating from the night of conception, she was excited to find that she was further along than she had thought. If she was correct, she was two months along.

She smiled, feeling alive and wonderful. There was no doubt in her mind that Ni-Cio would find her. She corrected that thought and slid her hands over the hard bump that pushed against her skin. Ni-Cio would find *them*.

Relaxing against the side of the pool, she laid her head back against the tile and slowly kicked her feet. A thought slipped into the Ethernet, *"I miss you so ... I am well and our baby is growing. You are a daddy..."*

She languished for a while longer until her fingers felt numb and started to resemble prunes. It was time to get dressed. She waded to the stairs, swiped water from her body and walked to the lounger. Reclining into soft cushions, she rubbed her hair with the sun-warmed towel and settled back to dry.

It was then that another pain hit. Worse than the others, she ground her teeth and tried not to scream. She jolted up. She had to get back to the house. She rose unsteadily, but was hit again with another cramp. Her legs gave way and she screamed as she dropped to her knees. Her guards crowded around her while one of the soldiers broke from the pack to find their boss.

However, her shriek fired through the Atlantean first, *"Travlor! I need you!"* Travlor fled his office.

Almost blinded by pain, Daria writhed on the ground, arms wrapped around her abdomen while the men looked on helplessly. On the verge of blacking out, she heard Travlor's harsh voice. "What happened? Why is she on the ground?" The guards parted and Travlor thrust himself at Daria.

Through her tears, she felt him gently pry one of her flexed hands from around her belly. Mixed into the pain and her dimming awareness, she felt oddly comforted by his touch. She sucked in a breath and willed her body to relax. It was no use. Another contraction hit and she convulsed again. Fear for her baby was suddenly worse than the pain and Daria started to cry.

Travlor tried to comfort her, but it was not something that he did easily. Feeling clumsy, he tried to massage her back in disjointed circles, but as he did, Daria moaned and shook her head. He felt rather than heard her plea to stop his motions.

Travlor bent low, and keeping his voice steady, issued gruff assurances, "Shhh, there now, you'll be all right. Try to breathe." Daria didn't respond.

Sitting back, he anxiously scanned her body. He could find nothing wrong so could detect no reason for the seizures. The fear that gripped him was unlike anything he had experienced in quite some time; he was finding it hard to take a breath and he had trouble focusing his thoughts. Deep in his gut he knew he didn't have the ability to help either the mother or the child if something truly happened. Once again, slapped in the face by the inescapable march of time and a terrible sense of déjà vu, Travlor raged. *By the gods! I will not allow this to happen again!*

Sweat trickled down his back and he looked at the guards as though they could offer aid. Nothing but blank stares met his questioning gaze. He wanted to kill all of them. The only reason he stayed his hand was because he needed help getting her back to the house. "Pick her up and get her to her quarters, now!"

He started to release his hold, but Daria lifted her head and grabbed his hand. Her plea slipped through clamped jaws. "No, please, don't let go; the pain is easing."

Travlor wasn't at all certain about her request, but he held tightly to her hand as the soldiers lifted her and carried her to the house.

Daria felt much better once she was back in her bed. The pains were gone and she found that she suffered no ill effects.

Travlor dragged a chair to her bedside and sat. Worry for Daria and her baby had carved deeper furrows into the lines of his face. However, his relief was evident, "I can find nothing wrong."

Daria stretched her back. "I can't find anything either, but I noticed yesterday that she seems to be growing at a fairly rapid pace. Never having been pregnant before, I don't know if that's normal or not."

Travlor considered that for a moment and frowned, "Having been around Evan's mother for much of her pregnancy, I can tell you that it is unequivocally not normal. Possibly her growth is the source of your pain."

"If I calculated correctly, I'm about two months along, but I don't think the baby should be this big." Daria looked at Travlor then asked, "Have you scanned for a growth pattern?"

"No, I've been so concerned about your pain, I have quite overlooked that step." Travlor did another quick scan, then he opened his eyes and smiled. "She is well. She smiled at me."

Daria didn't know what to say. She never thought to see anything but a scowl cross those lips ... ever. She tried to harden her heart; nevertheless, she hoarded the glimpse of humanity that had slipped through Travlor's walls.

Lost in his thoughts, Travlor was quiet for a while. When he roused himself, he took a deep breath and blew it out with relief. "I believe you are right. She does seem larger than a baby at two months should be."

He stood up, went to the window and stared out across the expanse. He reached a decision and turned to Daria, "We need to contact a doctor. Although you are an accomplished healer and I have the ability to help, neither of us is used to anything like this."

Daria started to get up.

"Stay in bed. I will have one of my men go to the local hospital and return with someone who can help us."

Daria stood anyway. "I'm fine." She gazed at her jailer. "Thank you, Travlor, if nothing else, a visit from an obstetrician will help relieve both our minds."

Daria looked at her stomach and smiled, "Well, the only contractions I feel now are the ones associated with hunger. After all the excitement, maybe we should see what the kitchens have in store for us."

Travlor nodded and Daria went to the bathroom and changed. Holding the door to let her pass, Daria preceded the Atlantean into the hall and down to the kitchens. At that moment, whether Travlor was hungry or not, the only thing she cared about was that she was famished.

Chapter 22

THE SHOCK OF ANOTHER cramp hit Ni-Cio with such ferocity that he collapsed to the dirt. He almost passed out. Mer-An came around the corner just in time to see him fall and raised the alarm. *"Ni-Cio is hurt! Come!"*

People came running from every direction, fright slashed across their features in flashes of reds, purples and sickly yellows.

Ni-Cio felt the pain subside and scrubbed his face, then realized that his hands were covered in dirt and mud. He glanced at Mer-An, "I am all right. I am better now."

He struggled to sit up, but Mer-An pushed him back as Aris and Rogert burst through the anxious gathering. Without asking, Aris grabbed his friend by the shoulders and Rogert got down by Ni-Cio's legs. Together they picked their leader off the ground and carried him to the nearest cabin.

Inside, they placed him on one of the lower bunks. The men could tell that their leader was starting to feel better because Ni-Cio sat up and started protesting. "Do not fuss. I am fine. I do not know what came over me, but I am better." When his friends wouldn't leave him alone, he shouted a cranky order. "Stop! Now!" Taken aback, Rogert and Aris stepped away and Ni-Cio stood up. "I am not some sick child. Quit worrying over me."

Rogert's face was colored with stripes of deep purple. His fear was evident. "Ni-Cio, I have never seen this happen. Do you think you might have inhaled some of the poisonous gas? Could you be suffering a side effect?"

Shrugging, Ni-Cio bent over to retie a shoelace. "Other than those sharp abdominal pains …" He hurriedly glanced at his friends, "I feel fine. However, that is not a bad thought; I will question Evan about the gas."

Aris ploughed in. "Ni-Cio, you are never sick. I am very worried that Rogert might be right. Do not waste any time contacting Evan. It is better to know."

"Yes, yes; now if you would leave, I will do just that." Ni-Cio smiled. Aris looked as if—what was that topside saying? The cat that swallowed the canary. Ni-Cio chided, "What is it? I know that look, Aris; you have something to tell us."

A red the color of fire coral slid over Aris's face and his mouth split into one of the widest grins Ni-Cio had ever seen. "We're pregnant!"

Rogert and Ni-Cio crowded Aris, alternately hugging him, congratulating him, and slapping him on the back. Their excitement mirrored Aris's as striations of bright yellow, green and red colored their faces.

"When do you want to make the announcement?"

Aris thought a moment. "I think tonight at the evening meal."

Rogert snorted. "Then I need to make a run to town for more beer!"

The men laughed with joy and Ni-Cio beamed. "Aris that is the best news we have had in quite a while. The gift of a child is the greatest blessing anyone could receive. We must make a grand party tonight!"

"That is a great idea." Aris looked at Rogert, "Let us tell the others so that they may begin the preparations!"

The men hurried out the door; however, Ni-Cio tarried. He didn't want his friends to know the extent of his alarm. In his entire life, he had never felt anything like the pains he experienced. He thought Rogert's theory about the gas had merit, so in order to put that possibility to rest, he contacted the topsider. *"Evan, the gas ... what effects might it have on someone? I have experienced extreme stomach pains. Could the gas Travlor's men released cause something like that?"*

Evan's reply came back swiftly and with such certainty that it allayed Ni-Cio's worries. *"No, Ni-Cio ... no effects as you describe. Can you think of any other reasons you are having these pains?"*

Ni-Cio couldn't imagine what was happening. Evan's next suggestion was wiser than Ni-Cio cared to admit. *"You should find a doctor in town. Maybe he could help ..."*

"I believe I will. I am disturbed by the reoccurrences. Are you and Kyla well?"

"We are more than well; another time I will tell you all that has happened, but promise me, find a doctor ..."

Ni-Cio nodded, Evan was right. *"Take care of my sister ..."*

"Trust me, she's in good hands ..."

Ni-Cio laughed; he missed his topside friend. *"That is what I am afraid of ..."*

He decided to find Rogert. He could ride into town with him and while Rogert purchased the beer, he would try to find a doctor. "Although, I am not certain what topside doctors can do."

He sorely missed Daria; she would have had him well immediately. With that thought, Ni-Cio felt like his heart would break. "Is it possible for a heart to weep?" He pulled a chair closer and sat. He dropped his head into his hands and bent forward, elbows on knees. He suddenly felt old and tired and bereft of finding her. "Without you my love, I am only half a person. Where are you? And why have we found no trace of Travlor?"

He ran his hands through his hair and felt the loose grains of dirt scrape his scalp. *"Where are you, love? Please be well, I cannot live without you …"*

He let himself feel the loss of her for a few minutes more, then he abruptly sat up. "What is this moroseness? It helps nothing. Ni-Cio, get hold of yourself! Things have a way of falling into place. Always, one foot in front of the other."

Those thoughts helped lift his flagging spirits. He stood and swiftly departed to find Rogert. A party was exactly what they needed.

Chapter 23

Evan had taken Kyla out for dinner to his favorite restaurant high above Boston. The city lights sparkled like precious jewels and a light patter of rain gave everything a soft, misted glow.

Kyla had readily accepted topside food and was working her way through a huge salad. Evan couldn't eat for the love that filled his heart. The brilliance of the lights had been forgotten as he once again drank in the Atlantean's beauty. He was proud to have her on his arm. "This place suits you."

Kyla looked up and smiled. "Every place suits you." She knew he had more to say, so she stopped eating and waited for him to continue.

"I'm glad I've made the decision to sell. It would be too much of a hassle to have someone manage the business. I would have to continually oversee everything and I wouldn't be able to concentrate on you."

Kyla waved her fork playfully. "I like it when you concentrate on me. I think that is what you should always do."

Her statement brought its own dose of reality and Evan unbuttoned his suit jacket, leaning forward. "I've given it some thought, and it may take a while, but once I've sold the business, we'll return to Santorini. I want to revive the compound and regrow the old vineyard into a viable business. I've been thinking it would be a great place to raise our children and still give you easy access to your home."

"Oh, I had never thought of that." Kyla put her fork down. "I just assumed we would live in Atlantis." She was quiet, for a moment. Then she sighed and took Evan's hand. "I cannot imagine you would feel right about living in a place that holds so many painful memories. It was selfish of me."

Her downcast expression went straight to Evan's heart. He gently rubbed each knuckle on her slender hand. Then, he turned her hand over and placed a tender kiss in the middle of her palm. "Love, I don't know why I didn't think to ask what you wanted. Do you not want to live topside?"

Kyla was silent for so long that Evan released her hand and reluctantly picked up his fork. He speared his food but had lost his appetite. In truth, he didn't really care where they lived as long as it was together, though he didn't think it would be easy to live underwater full time. *It would be worth a shot if that's what she wants.*

Kyla tilted her head, placed her elbows on either side of her plate, and rested her chin on her fists. Her eyes glistened in the candlelight and Evan could see the love that radiated from her heart.

She held out her hand and Evan reached across the table, placing his hand in hers. Kyla smiled. "Evan, I would live anywhere with you. I think your idea is magnificent! Why, it would give us the best of both our worlds."

Evan swiped his mouth, dropped his napkin next to his plate, and stood. He held Kyla's chair and helped her up. He didn't care if the whole world watched. Taking her in his arms, he kissed her so passionately that older couples in the restaurant wished they were younger and younger couples felt as though they were witnessing some excellent training.

When Kyla and Evan finally released each other, the entire restaurant broke into applause and whistles. Evan laughed and called for the waiter. "Would you happen to have enough bottles of Cristal to serve everyone here?"

The waiter gawked but quickly reacquired his dignity and stood at attention. "Why certainly, sir."

Evan smiled and nodded at the other patrons. "Then please, if you would, a bottle for every table!"

Everyone in the restaurant rose in a standing ovation and amid boisterous cheers and more applause, the waiter disappeared, signaling for the rest of the staff to follow.

Returning with the first bottle, he made a gracious show of producing and pouring for Evan and Kyla. He quickly settled the Champagne into a chilled bucket of ice and left them to themselves.

Evan raised his glass and looked deeply into Kyla's wide, amber eyes. "To the most beautiful woman I have ever seen, to our long life together, and to our new home. May we be blessed with children and grandchildren, with love and laughter, and the time to enjoy … oh, and great wine!"

Kyla laughed and they clinked glasses. To Evan, her eyes sparkled more than the Champagne.

Chapter 24

THE MAN CAME IN heavily escorted by Travlor's armed guards. In one hand, he carried a rather large, black leather bag. He looked extremely anxious and kept swiping his face with a rumpled, dingy white, handkerchief that he clutched in his other hand. His sparse dark hair fell in damp strands over his high forehead and his wide mouth seemed to be moving in some kind of prayer. He was dwarfed by everyone present.

Travlor raked him with his eyes. He didn't trust anyone but Daria as a healer; however, he had no other ideas. The man didn't look too accomplished. "Who are you?"

Nervously clearing his throat, the man opened his mouth, but the words wouldn't come. He tried again. "I—I am Doctor Diaz. I am from the local hospital."

"Do you know anything about pregnancy?" Travlor held his hands clasped behind his back. To the man standing surrounded by soldiers, he probably seemed like his executioner. Travlor didn't care; he just needed to be sure that this man could help Daria.

The Columbian's deep, brown eyes lit with hope. "That is my specialty. I deal in troubled pregnancies and I will be glad to help you." He glanced warily at each of the guards.

Travlor stood in thought for just a moment, then nodded. He sent a compulsion to the doctor. *"You are to examine her and that is all ... if the woman tries to enlist your help to leave the premises or asks where we are or asks you to get in touch with another person, you will not acknowledge ..."* The man's eyes blanked and Travlor signaled the soldiers to take him upstairs to Daria's room. As the men rushed off with the doctor, Travlor rubbed his face. The stiff growth of whiskers scraped his skin and it wasn't until then that he realized he hadn't gone through his daily ablutions. He detested feeling grimy. While the doctor was looking at Daria, he decided to go to his quarters and clean up.

Daria was standing by the window when she heard the knock. She turned in time to see the door open. The man they had brought to the house hesitated and she waved him in. He edged into the room and cautiously closed the door. Trying not to look as desperate as she felt, she quickly walked over to shake his hand. "Hello, I'm Daria." She could tell he was less than happy to be here.

"Hello, I am Doctor Diaz." He shook her hand limply, then shifted his gaze to the floor.

She hurried closer and whispered urgently, "I am being held against my will. Where are we? Please, can you help me?" Daria held her breath and waited for the doctor's response. When he didn't say anything, she glanced up and could see that his eyes had glazed over. "So, he's given you a compulsion. I should've known." She sighed dispiritedly and gave up any thoughts of having him contact Ni-Cio. She switched her attention back to the reason that had brought him here: her baby's health. "Thank you for coming. Are you familiar with pregnancy?"

The doctor offered a small grin and nodded. "I trained in the United States."

Surprised, Daria asked, "Where did you go to school?"

The small man looked shy, yet at the same time, proud. "Harvard."

Daria couldn't help herself, she laughed. "Well, if I'd known that, I wouldn't have been so scared about your visit."

The man nodded as if he understood. "We had no hospital where I grew up; it was my dream to go to the States and study medicine so that I could come back and help my people."

"Well, hopefully now you can help me." Daria motioned to the bed. "Will that be all right?"

"Si." He stripped the sheet from the bed and handed it to her. "Please, try to make yourself comfortable. If you could wrap this around you, I will proceed with my examination."

Daria went to the bathroom and did as instructed. When she reentered the room, she walked to the bed and lay down. The doctor spread another sheet over her, then went to his medical bag and snapped it open. He took some instruments out, placing them on a clean white towel that he had spread out on the bed. He then pulled on some latex gloves and gingerly approached Daria. He explained the procedure. Daria closed her eyes and nodded her understanding.

The doctor began his examination. To Daria, it seemed to take forever. She tried to think of other things, but all her prayers and hopes centered on what he would or wouldn't find regarding the health of her baby. At last, she heard the snap of latex as he removed his gloves. He located a trash can and deposited them into it. "You may get dressed now."

Daria pulled the sheet tighter and hurried to the bathroom. When she came out, Dr. Diaz was seated with his legs crossed and a deep frown furrowing his brow. He waited for her to sit next to him. She tried to read his expression but she only noticed that his dark eyes were filled with compassion.

"You are healthy and I believe the baby is healthy." He hesitated, causing Daria's alarm to ratchet up.

"But ..." she wanted to yank his reply out of his mouth. She tried to steady herself for the bad news.

"But, I have never seen such a rapid growth rate. The child is twice what she should be." He shook his head. "I have seen nothing like this and I have birthed many babies."

Daria released her breath, "Is she overweight?"

"No, she is perfect ... just larger than what would be expected this early into your pregnancy."

Daria was confused. "Well, what does this mean for us? Will she become too big to carry?"

The man scratched his chin. "It is possible. Again, I have no knowledge of this particular condition." He considered Daria's problem for a moment. "Let me contact some of my colleagues and see if they know of this." He sympathized with the young woman's trepidation and took one of her hands. "I will get back to you as soon as possible." He gently patted her wrist. "I wouldn't worry about your stomach pains. As bad as they are, it seems to me to be caused by the rapid spurt of growth that neither your womb nor your child is accustomed to."

Daria was almost overcome with relief. She grabbed the doctor's hands and squeezed. "If the pains are due to the growth of my daughter, then it's a small price to pay for a healthy baby." She smiled so wide her face hurt. "Thank you so much! You don't know how much better I feel. I was so worried."

The man blinked twice before rising from his chair. He helped Daria up. "I am still worried about the accelerated rate. If it continues, there will come a time that your body will not be able to contain the baby. And for the sake of your life and that of the child's, we must be prepared for a Caesarean."

"Oh my God, I didn't even consider that." Shaken again, Daria showed the doctor to the door.

"I will let your guardian know that I should continue to look in on you."

Daria, lost in thought, hardly noticed when he left. When she heard the door click closed, she stood up and walked to the window, pushing the shutters aside. The news was not even close to what she'd been expecting. It was imperative now that she find a way to break Travlor's hold over her thoughts. She had to let Ni-Cio know. She was so frightened. "I can't go through this without you. I need your strength."

The back of her throat prickled and tears threatened. She gulped air and went to the sink for water. As she was filling a glass, she heard another knock. She didn't feel like talking to anybody, but whether she wanted it or not, the door swung open to admit Travlor. The sternness with which he addressed her erased any thought of the man ever softening his attitude.

"So, now that we must endure regular visits from this man, you are going to have to pick one of the kitchen staff to be with you when you are examined." He stepped out of the room holding the door handle. "I will not have you talking to anyone other than me; is that clear?"

He slammed the door behind him and Daria forgot about the water. She went to the bed before her knees gave way, then lay down and buried her face in one of the pillows. Her tears spilled out and her shoulders shook, but of one thing she was more determined than ever. She sat up and hiccoughed. Wiping her eyes, she glared at the door. "If it's the last thing I do, I'll break through your barriers! I will get through to Ni-Cio and he *will* come for us!"

Chapter 25

DOCTOR IN TOW, Travlor rushed down the stairs and stopped in the middle of the great room. "Everyone in here, on the double!"

Soldiers raced to comply, boots clomping hurriedly against tile. Within seconds twenty men were assembled and awaiting their orders.

"You three!" He pointed to each man. Stepping forward, they came to a halt and saluted. "Take the doctor back to the hospital. Give him leave to find the medical instruments and things he will need to set up an operating room in this house. Do not let him stint on anything. I want the newest equipment and I want any recommendations he might have for the birth of this child. Questions?"

Nothing but silence, the men stared into space, and no one moved, they hardly dared breath.

"All right, you three, get to it! The rest of you, dismissed!" Travlor waved his hand and the men jumped to comply. The three volunteers ushered the diminutive doctor out of the house and into the waiting vehicle. The rest of the soldiers returned to their assigned posts.

Travlor was alone. He crossed to one of the many seating areas and dropped to a chair, then lowered his head to his hands. "This complicates matters." He let his mind roam for a while, then had an idea. "My fame is not spreading fast enough." Spurred by that thought, he raised his head and glared in the direction of Daria's rooms. "I will initiate another healing before the topsider becomes too weak. This child frightens me."

He knew what he had to do. "Ten men, on the double!" They quickly filed in, received their orders, and departed.

Travlor stood. With great effort, he straightened himself and grimly scanned his body. His legs were weak and his breath didn't come as easily as it once did. He shook his head and walked to the stairs. Grabbing the handrail, he took several deep breaths and began the climb to his office. "It won't be long before I need another healing session."

Chapter 26

Covered in thick makeup, Ni-Cio sat in the passenger seat watching Rogert wrestle the truck to town and he hid his smile. "I think the truck is winning."

One side of Rogert's mouth quirked up and he glanced quickly at his friend. "This vehicle and I have become friends; the obstinacy you observe is like a handshake. The old man knows I will overpower him, he just wants to make known his objections."

Ni-Cio watched the contest of wills between man and machine with no doubts as to who would win the battle. Rattling over the ruts, they finally reached their destination. Rogert located a spot and jammed the truck into park. "We will meet back here. I will not be long—the place for the beer is just over there."

He pointed to a shop and Ni-Cio nodded. "I will locate a doctor's office. Evan has told me what I need to do."

They took off in opposite directions and Ni-Cio, with a few wrong turns, located an office with a sign proclaiming that the doctor was in and that walk-in patients were welcome.

He pushed through the door and entered an office that, while not spacious and grand, certainly was clean and welcoming. Seated behind the front desk, an attractive young woman greeted him, "Good morning, how can I help you?"

Ni-Cio was floored that her English was so good; he had been prepared for Greek. "Good morning. I am in need of assistance. Is the doctor available?"

The woman glanced at the schedule and nodded. "He's just about through with a patient. If you can fill out some information, I'll get you in to see him shortly."

She handed him some papers that looked very confusing. Ni-Cio's brows knitted together. "I will do the best I can."

He took a seat and scratched his head as he looked over the forms. He could read English, but the questions were unknown to him. He had no idea what any of it meant. He glanced at the receptionist. She was busy typing, so Ni-Cio decided on a mild deception.

He bent over the paperwork and scribbled here and there until the young lady opened the door. "Please, follow me."

Ni-Cio smiled and stood. Holding the clipboard next to his chest, he hesitated, "I have not finished these papers. May I take them with me?"

The woman smiled. "Certainly. Just drop them off at the desk on your way out."

She took Ni-Cio through a small hallway and opened the door into another room. Ni-Cio noticed a couple of chairs. However, unfamiliar with an elevated table that stood in the center of the room, he pointed and asked, "What is that?"

The lady glanced at the examination table and looked back at Ni-Cio. She shook her head and shut the door without answering. Quirking his brow, Ni-Cio took the chair and settled to wait. It wasn't long before a tall, gangly man came in and offered his hand. "I'm Dr. Ayers."

Ni-Cio was again surprised. "You are American." The man's glasses gleamed in the light, framing kind, sparkling eyes.

The doctor grinned. "My wife and I came to Santorini on our honeymoon and we just never left. I started my practice and voila! The rest, as they say, is history." He took out a pen and started to take notes. "Now, tell me your name and why you're here today?"

"I am Ni-C, er, ah! Evan Gaddes. I am having stomach pains and they are increasing in intensity."

"Well, let's have a look." The man put his tablet down and patted the metal table.

Ni-Cio quailed. "Uh, no."

"I have to examine you. And you'll need to get up on the table." The doctor looked confused.

Ni-Cio shook his head. "I cannot take off my shirt."

"Fine, leave it on. I just need to palpate your stomach." The doctor sounded exasperated.

Ni-Cio slid up onto the table.

"Can you lie back?"

The Atlantean's eyes widened, but he did as he was asked. "Now what?"

The man studied his patient. "Have you not seen a doctor before?"

"I have never needed to."

Nodding his head, the doctor explained what he was going to do. When Ni-Cio consented, he bent to his examination.

He poked and prodded, took Ni-Cio's temperature, heart rate, and blood pressure.

Puzzled, he finished his cursory observation and stood back, tugging his ear. "Are the pains constant? Or do they come and go?"

"They come and go." Ni-Cio got off the table and straightened his clothes.

"Have you noticed how far apart the pains are?"

Ni-Cio frowned in thought and shook his head. "I have only experienced them maybe two or three times."

"Well, I'm stumped; you're a perfect specimen. All your vitals are excellent. I don't feel a mass in your stomach, so unless you are willing to submit to further tests, I have no way of knowing what's wrong with you."

"What other tests?"

"X-ray, MRI that sort of thing."

Ni-Cio vehemently shook his head. "Out of the question." He slid off the table, ready to leave.

The doctor placed his hand on Ni-Cio's arm. "Mr. Gaddes, are you married?"

"What business is it of yours?" Ni-Cio scowled.

The man's brows lifted. "Well, if you have a wife and she is pregnant, I would almost suggest that you are experiencing sympathy pains. But, as I say, unless you want more testing, that would be an extremely wild guess."

Ni-Cio couldn't speak. His brain had seized—he felt like he had entered a dream and everything was moving in slow motion.

The doctor thanked him for coming in, but Ni-Cio barely noticed his departure. As the door closed, Ni-Cio dropped into a chair, eyes unfocused. He ransacked his mind for an indication that the man could be right. He ran through the times he had felt the pain.

Slowly, a light dawned. At last, the full realization hit and Ni-Cio slapped both knees. He jumped up, threw his head back and let out an enormous Atlantean yell. "I am going to be a father!"

He started laughing so hard, he didn't know if he could stop. The relief was staggering and his heart swelled with joy. Daria carried their child and she was alive and well! His spirits soared. "I am going to be a father!" He shouted again.

He banged the door open and rushed back to the front office. Startling the woman at the desk, he tossed a stack of money to her and yelled with delight, "I am going to be a father!" He heard her echoing laugh as he tore out the front door. *"Rogert! Where are you? This party is going to be better than we thought!"*

Possibilities and thoughts raced through his mind until he latched onto one magnificent certainty. *"Daria, my love, I swear ... it is only a matter of time before I break through!"*

As he ran back to the parking area, Ni-Cio knew, as he knew Rogert would always get the better of the old truck, that it would not be long before he found the woman of his heart.

Chapter 27

Dr. Diaz had come and gone and evening shadows were encroaching into the last moments of daylight. Daria's stomach rumbled with a vengeance. "Wow, that's something new." Chuckling at the urgent demands her precious daughter imposed upon her body, she rubbed her growing belly. "Patience, little one."

She vacated her room, and tailed by her groupies, hurried to the dining area. Travlor was already seated. Not waiting for him to rise, she slid into her seat and started eating. She didn't feel like talking.

"I did not think you would join me."

Between ravenous bites, Daria managed a reply. "I didn't want to, but my daughter's needs seem to be the driving force these days."

Travlor huffed, "I am in no mood to suffer one of yours."

"I really don't care." Daria didn't look up and continued to eat as fast as she could work the food from the plate to her mouth.

Travlor swept his napkin into his lap and picked up his fork. He stabbed a piece of blood-red beef and raised the bite halfway to his mouth. He paused, "I have decided on another healing. The word is not spreading as quickly as I need it to. So, we must be prepared to make more of a splash." He shoved the meat into his mouth and chewed, looking at Daria from under his eyebrows.

She refused to meet his stare and she didn't feel like rising to the bait. As quickly as possible, she loaded her fork and crammed more food into her mouth. She chewed so fast, she thought she might choke. However, it was no longer the hunger that drove her. She needed to be away from this reprehensible man, but from the way he poked at his meal, it was obvious he was in no hurry to leave.

"Are you listening? My men are scouting another site for a healing. If you can cease eating for a moment, I need to know if you're up to it."

Daria threw her fork down and pushed away from the table. She stood up, trying to tower over Travlor, but all she accomplished was crowding his space. Pushed to her breaking point, she bent closer to him and looked him in the eyes. "I've just had news that I don't quite know how to take. I'm not sure what's happening to me or to my child. I don't care about your schemes or your plans or you!" She picked his plate up and dumped the food in his lap. "I'm sick of this! I'm sick of your control and I'm sick and tired of trying to understand you!"

She ran out the back doors, and after crossing the large yard, found herself at the croquet set. Without thinking, she picked up a mallet and whacked one of the balls as hard as she could. It blasted past the lawn and sailed over the terrace.

The wooden ball hit the glass with such force that cracks spread over the windows like thousands of creeping vines. Daria cringed and held her breath. Pieces of glass started to drop away. The tinkle of falling glass, shattering on tile, took on a somewhat musical quality. Daria dropped the mallet.

She hadn't meant for that to happen. She really hadn't thought the ball would go anywhere, but now she felt supreme satisfaction at having caused *something* to happen, at having damaged something that belonged to him. She had an overpowering desire to stick out her tongue and waggle her fingers in her ears, but even she knew that discretion was sometimes the better part of valor. She turned and fled. Travlor wouldn't be able to catch her. Her groupies, however, stayed close.

Chapter 28

PRIOR TO TRAVLOR'S and Daria's arrival, the local hospital had received a strange demand; any and all signs referencing location or name had to be covered. The only explanation given was that the honored guest required anonymity. So, the baffled staff complied.

Two weeks later every plaque, every sign, and every name tag had been hidden or draped. The staff had done such a thorough job that Daria had no idea where she was. The hospitalist escorted them to the over-crowded cancer ward. In shocked silence, she surveyed the gruesome scene.

Children of all ages lay in varying stages of the rotting disease, tenaciously clinging to life while edging closer to death. Daria's soul ached to see so many bald heads, sunken, purple-reamed eyes, and exhausted, emaciated bodies. The poisonous introduction of chemotherapy had ravaged their tender systems.

As Daria waited for Travlor's lead, she remembered back to the day that had initiated this moment.

After her crazy mallet swing, she had thought Travlor would seek retribution. Instead, he had respected her space. Eventually, he had wound his way through the gardens seeking her out. He had even brought more food. When he located her in one of the gazebos, she readily accepted the meal as she was still famished.

She realized that the food was as much of an apology as she would ever get. Somewhat pacified, she had followed Travlor back to the house and listened while he discussed his plans for the local hospital. She quickly agreed. She had always loved children, but her heart held a special place for those in pain. She not only wanted to go to the hospital, she needed to go. She would heal all of them if Travlor allowed it. However, if all she could do was help one child, she was willing … no matter if it furthered Travlor's cause or not.

Travlor had already requested that his "healing" be done in complete privacy. No parents, no doctors, no witnesses. His insistence that he wasn't seeking publicity rang so false that Daria couldn't believe others didn't see through his act. Nevertheless, the hospital had quickly and efficiently opened the way for his dog-and-pony show.

The hospitalist shook Travlor's hand before leaving the room. "If you can do as you say, then we will be eternally in your debt. You do understand why I am doubtful?"

Travlor nodded and signaled the man to leave. Once the doctor was out of the room, Daria heard Travlor's thought.

"Administer a sedative. I do not want the children witnessing anything..."

Daria immediately uttered the healing tones for the administration of a gentle sedative to wrap each child in sleep. Almost as soon as she did this, the children's eyes grew heavy and closed. All of her charges faded into an easy, dreamless repose.

Travlor shifted and jerked his chin toward the sleeping children. *"All of them. Heal them all ..."*

Daria was so excited she couldn't find the words to express the feelings that engulfed her heart. She stepped to the first bed and began the rites that would bring the slight child back to glowing health. It didn't take long before she was able to move to the next and then to the next. Each little body responded so well that their color returned instantly. Shy smiles spread across pink cheeks as though even in sleep, the children sensed that their sickness had disappeared.

When she stepped to the bed of the last child, she didn't slow her healing tones, however, she stopped her healing motions. The boy was closer to death than the others. His breathing was nearly nonexistent. She glanced at Travlor. "I don't feel I should interfere. He's too close to death."

Travlor brooked no argument. "Continue; everyone must be healed."

Daria didn't want to go on, but rather than risk Travlor's wrath, she began the proper ministrations that would increase the power of the healing.

The child stirred and she could see that he was trying to open his eyes. She sent more sedative through his tiny body. He relaxed so much that his breathing stopped altogether. Her panic flew to Travlor. *"He's dying. I don't know what to do ..."*

Travlor came to her side and took her hands. He infused her with his strength and followed her motions. Daria continued the healing. Time passed and still more time. Sweat trickled down her back and she could feel the heat radiating in waves from Travlor's body. They never ceased their motions, but Daria did increase the tonality of her ethereal song. Finally, the child's chest began to rise and fall and his breathing evened out.

After more time had elapsed, Daria noticed the color creeping back into his sunken cheeks. She meticulously scanned his meager body. There was not a single trace of cancer. Her hands dropped to her sides and she sagged against Travlor. It took her a moment, but she realized that her body was holding his drooping form upright. His voice came out in a cracked whisper. "Call the men to take us to the car."

Daria forced herself to stir. Barely able to speak herself, she managed enough noise so that one of the soldiers looked in on them. Daria nodded and the guard summoned the others.

The squad crowded into the room and lifted both of them, then rushed back to the car. Held securely against a rock-hard chest, Daria caught the doctor's eyes on their way out. She smiled weakly. The man raised his arms in praise and gratitude and all she could think was, *Here we go again.*

As soon as her head hit the car seat, she let go of everything and plummeted into nothingness.

Chapter 29

YET A SECOND ATLANTEAN PARTY was in full swing. Reveling in the warm, summer night and the beer that Rogert kept in ready supply, the Atlanteans had been so focused on getting the compound into shape and scouring the walls, ceilings and floors of their adopted home that everyone was ready to let go.

It was a much-needed release, but the festivities were made even more boisterous with the news that Aris and Mer-An had shared two weeks ago. That a new life was to be born in their midst lifted every heart, bringing them even more reason to celebrate. The way his people smiled, sang, danced, and laughed was almost like their life before Travlor happened.

Ni-Cio sat removed from the noisy fray. Content to let the attention center around Aris and Mer-An, he had decided not to tell anyone about Daria's pregnancy. Without a more thorough set of exams, the doctor couldn't tell him definitively that the source of his pains was a phantom link to Daria. But he knew with every fiber of his being that the man had hit upon the exact reason for the sudden cramps. He released a thought. *"I am with you, my love. I know that you carry our child and I am thrilled ... look to yourself and your health ..."*

He mulled over the problem for a bit. He knew that Travlor still walled the gap between his and Daria's thoughts. But he still hoped that something would slip through. So, he persisted. *"I will find you so that we may be together when our child comes into this world. I love you to the depths of my soul ... be well ..."*

Daria stirred. When she raised her head, she saw that they were still in the car and that Travlor slept like the dead. His mouth was slack and his breathing was labored. He had helped her rescue that boy from death but at what cost to himself? The man was a mystery. She closed her eyes and let her mind drift; she didn't have the strength to ponder the workings of a deranged mind right now.

Somewhere in the depths of her longing and her memories, she felt rather than heard a whisper. It was a whisper so infinitely soft that had she not been in her current state, she would have missed it.

"... to the depths of my soul ..."

She sat bolt upright. Her thoughts rocketed from her. *"Ni-Cio, can you hear me? Ni-Cio!"*

Furtively she looked to make sure Travlor still slept. Suddenly a thought blasted through her mind.

"Daria, where are you?"

She knew they shouldn't waste the precious time but she couldn't help herself. *"Ni-Cio, I love you! I'm carrying our child!"*

Topside, on Santorini, Ni-Cio leapt into the air. Contact! He didn't know what had happened but he realized that their time was probably limited. He had to get them both under control. *"Daria! Listen! Tell me where you are!"*

Waiting apprehensively for her reply, he was afraid to move, afraid one errant breath would make him miss her reply. He stood so still that he heard his own heartbeat. As his wait lengthened, he thought that they had lost contact when finally, her answer gentled into his mind.

"I'm not sure ... somewhere in South America, I think ... are you well? How is everyone else?"

"Fine, love ... we are fine. You have no idea where in South America you could possibly be?"

"No ..."

It was the last thought he received. He didn't wonder how or why they had been able to breach the silence because he was too overjoyed. All he could think about was that now, at least, they had a direction. Maybe it was an entire country, but Daria had narrowed it down from the whole world. His thoughts screamed through the atmosphere to find Evan. *"South America, Evan! They are somewhere in South America!"*

Chapter 30

TRAVLOR OPENED HIS eyes. Turning his head to face Daria, she saw the cruel smile with which she had become so accustomed. "So, you have broken through to your precious Ni-Cio."

Fear froze the blood in her veins but her heart pounded like a jackhammer. A stupidly succinct observation occurred to her when she saw the quick jump of her shirt as her heart thudded against her chest. *I've done it now.*

The man raised himself slowly. Nodding his head in time to something only he could hear, she watched him lean toward her. Even inside the car in a seated position, he towered over her. "That is the last time. Do not expect me to ever, EVER help you again. I will never again use my strength to aid you. I refuse to let you slip through my barriers because of my weakness! I will strangle you with my bare hands before I let that happen again!"

The wildness in his eyes frightened her more than his words. He looked completely mad. She shrank from him and scooted as far back into the corner as she possibly could. But he barged into the space as though they were connected at the hip.

His eyes bulged and he looked crazed. He crushed her with his weight as he angled into her. "Never! Do you hear me?"

Daria could barely nod. Her body quivered like Jello. She tried to shield the baby from her rampant fear, but all she could do was wait and watch. Impaled by his stare, she felt like a bug pinned to a board. The man meant every word. It took all of her will power not to avert her eyes.

After what seemed like a lifetime, he eased back. Since he didn't completely move away, she resigned herself to even closer scrutiny. She closed her eyes; whether she wanted to or not, she had to cut the sight of Travlor out of her fevered brain. She couldn't imagine how the fear that coursed through her body would affect her baby. She tried, without much success, to still her mind.

The car finally pulled up in front of the estate. The men lifted both of them out of the car and carried them upstairs. Daria was placed on her bed and the men left, closing the door softly.

She was afraid to stir. She was so frightened she didn't dare venture outside of her rooms. She roused herself and picked up the house phone and requested food to be brought to her. Her hands shook and she almost hung up; instead, she ordered another tray to be taken to Travlor. She didn't feel like helping him now—her baser nature wanted him to suffer. However, as the only remaining sovereign healer of Atlantis, and because of the lessons Na-Kai had bequeathed her, she was bound to that calling, no matter what she thought about helping the vile man.

Shrugging out of her clothes, she made her way into the shower. The hot water created an abundance of steam. Daria took long, slow, even breaths and sent every calming thought she could think of to her child. Finally, she felt the baby move.

It was all she needed. She was so thankful to feel her daughter's kick, she sank to the tiles. Wrapping her arms around her legs, she dropped her head onto her knees and let the hot water wash away her fears.

No matter what happened now, she had heard from Ni-Cio. The only goal she focused on was the goal of keeping herself and her daughter alive and well. She would do as Travlor asked, no matter what. And as much as she hated to, she promised herself that she would never again try to contact Ni-Cio. He would find her.

IN LOCAL NEWS

Health

MAN PERFORMS MIRACLE HEALING!!!

By Luis Salazar, Reporter, Mondi Times
lsalazar@monditimes.com
LuisSal on Facebook

Palmore, Magdalena, Columbia

Today in a children's cancer clinic in the rural town of Palmore, a modern-day miracle occurred. A white male referring to himself only as Travlor, along with his female assistant, were granted access to several cancer-riddled children at the approval of the hospital administrator and parents. The request was particularly unusual because he insisted on complete privacy. Though there were some doubts, most of the children were out of options.

While hopeful parents, doctors, and staff waited outside the room, Travlor and his assistant attended the children in private. After nearly an hour, the assistant called for help. Both she and Travlor were carried from the room, apparently exhausted, while parents and doctors rushed into the room to find every single child completely cured of their cancers.

Dr. Escobedo, with tears in his eyes, spoke in open amazement, "I have never seen anything like it. These children, who were in the last stages of the disease are completely cancer free! Every child, healed!" The hospital staff are dumbfounded as to how the healings worked.

The identity of the man remains a mystery as he and his entourage left immediately following the healings.

Chapter 31

EVAN JUMPED OUT of bed. Morning light streamed into the room and he heard the sounds of Kyla making breakfast. However, all he could think about were Ni-Cio's thoughts that had just fired through his mind. He ran a hand over his rumpled hair. *"How did you find this out?"*

"Somehow Travlor lost his hold and Daria and I were able to touch each other for a few moments ..."

"So, all you know is that they are somewhere in South America?"

"Yes. She doesn't know anything other than that ... will that be enough to help us find them?"

Evan threw some clothes on as he considered Ni-Cio's question. *"I'm not sure, but it's a start. It's more than we had ..."*

"What would you have me do?"

Evan wasn't sure. He knew that Travlor was set on world domination, but he wasn't sure how the man was going to accomplish it. *"About the only idea I can come up with is to search the news. Look for any unusual activity, maybe a buildup of an army? Or unusual healings?"*

"All right. I will inform the others. We will continue to clean Atlantis and reform the compound. If we hear anything, we will be in touch..."

"I'll research from my end. It's going to take a while to sell off my assets but we'll move immediately if we hear anything. I'll let you know..."

Evan went to the kitchen and settled himself at the bar. He took a moment to admire Kyla as she prepared their food. She turned around in dubious expectation. "Ni-Cio and Daria have made contact. Somehow they were able to break through Travlor's block."

Kyla set the pan down and came to the bar. She grabbed both his hands in hers and squeezed. Excitement colored her face in tones of scarlet. "That is wonderful! Do we know where she is being kept?"

Evan shook his head and wrinkled his forehead. "The only thing she was able to share is that she thinks they're in South America. Exactly where is the question. Either she doesn't know or she didn't have time to tell Ni-Cio. Communication was shut off. I can only guess how *that* happened."

"Well, if anyone can find out, it will be you. What do we do to help ourselves?" Kyla placed his hands back on the counter.

"Not much. Do you speak Spanish?" Kyla's nod made Evan smile. "Of course you do. Well if we could locate some South American news channels on TV, you might possibly hear something interesting."

"Like what, love?" She turned back to her preparations.

"I'm not sure. I'm hoping we'll know it when we hear it. But it could be possible that he is building an army. That might be something to take notice of. We also know that he kidnapped Daria for a reason. Why? She's a powerful healer, but how would he use that? His tendencies certainly don't lean toward kindness, but if we hear of any miraculous healings, it would be another avenue to explore."

"I will start listening today." When she heard Evan's lengthy sigh, she placed a hand on her hip and pointed the spatula at him. "I do not want to hear that discouragement. We have just learned some very important information—we are one step closer than we were yesterday!"

Despite himself, Evan smiled. She was right. "Woman, get that food ready, I'm starving!"

Kyla playfully batted at him, then turned back to the stove. "Ah, I miss our kitchens!"

Chapter 32

Ni-Cio flew into the crowd of dancers and they scattered like paper scraps in a strong wind. Aris grasped his friend's shoulders. "What is wrong with you? Have you lost your thoughts?"

Ni-Cio grabbed Aris's shoulders. "I have heard from Daria!"

Their excitement spread like confetti. Everyone crowded around to hear the news and people grabbed Ni-Cio in rowdy hugs.

"We will get our healer back!"

"Daria is to be returned!"

"We knew you could do it, Ni-Cio!"

Before the happy throng got too out of hand, Ni-Cio held up his arms for quiet.

It took a while, but he finally got their full attention. "The wall of communication between Daria and myself was breached, briefly. She believes they are somewhere in South America; however, she does not know her precise location."

Questions whipped through the crowd.

"How can we help?"

"What must we do to get our healer back?"

"We are ready now, Ni-Cio."

Ni-Cio held his arms up for silence and waited for the rapid-fire questions to cease. "There is not much we can do other than listen for unusual news stories. Until we know the exact whereabouts of Travlor and his soldiers, we must stay vigilant with our news watch and hope that Evan and Kyla hear something that will give us a clue as to her location.

"My sister and Evan will stay in America to complete the sale of his businesses, but when they come back to Santorini, we must be ready to move. For that reason, we have to intensify our cleaning efforts. And we must continue to survive topside until our home is once more habitable."

The Atlanteans crowded closer, encouraging Ni-Cio, and promising to redouble their efforts. Ni-Cio couldn't bring himself to suggest that they might be heading into another war, so he kept his thoughts to himself. But he had already decided to put Rogert back in charge of training. The *Cabala of Ares* was not a discipline he could let lapse. The arcane, secret fighting art had been handed down from Ares, the god of war. The technique, translated loosely as *Last Strike*, turned anything into a lethal weapon. *Last Strike* required total concentration, impeccable timing, agility, and unerring precision. He had a strong feeling that that particular discipline would have to be employed again.

Chapter 33

TRAVLOR WAS EXTREMELY weak. The healing had sapped his strength and whatever generosity he had shown her had been snuffed out like a shooting star. He had retreated back into his old, closed off, angry, mad-at-the-world, self. Still, she didn't want him slipping further into his hate-encrusted shell. The negativity released into his system would only cause his health to deteriorate at a faster rate. Daria racked her brain to think of a way to cajole him away from such an unhealthy state. As she stared out her window, she could see the press of bodies beyond the front gates.

She backed away from the upsetting view and rubbed her arms, feeling the chill from the refrigerated air. She went to the closet and grabbed a sweater. She was disgusted by Travlor's unconscionable display of "miracles" that preyed on the intense desire of people to believe in another savior.

Certainly, Travlor's plans for spreading religious fervor had exploded like a supernova. Once word of the children's miraculous healings was leaked, hordes of people, makeshift supplies on their backs, packed the roads in a never-ending train of religious pilgrims. Outside the gates, the masses stood silently, through every kind of weather, hoping to catch a single glimpse of Travlor. Many of them carried photos, yellowed and cracked with age, hoping that the new Messiah would heal their loved ones. Their faith made them patient. Their hope kept them going.

Rosaries and other religious souvenirs were sold up and down the road to the estate, clogging traffic so that no one could get a vehicle through. To reach the complex, people had to travel on foot over many hot, humid miles. Still the multitudes came.

However, since the children had left the hospital amid a frenzy of news coverage, Travlor had not left his rooms. Any and all sustenance was brought to him on trays and left outside his door until he was ready to eat.

Daria carried the trays herself in order to make sure that he was eating enough; he had to be well, because her fate, and the fate of her child, were tied to his. When she returned to collect the hardly touched contents, she heard him on the phone hour after hour, barking orders. Different men, ramrod straight, and clothed in every uniform imaginable, entered the premises at every hour of the day and night. She tried to figure out what he was up to, but she had no idea. Whatever it was, she knew it didn't bode well.

She really hadn't felt like leaving her rooms either, but she didn't want Travlor starving. Since she had broken through his wall of silence and had heard from Ni-Cio, she desperately needed the tranquility of her own room to help contain her excitement. She needed her solitude to continue helping her baby feel loved, calm, and well.

After the healing, she had recovered so rapidly that she was amazed at the lack of downtime. However, she was learning to recognize when, during a healing, she approached the edge of her energy drain. With the small boy who had been so close to death, it had taken every bit of her strength, and if Travlor hadn't supplied the additional help, she wouldn't have been able to save the child.

For his unbidden intervention, she was incredibly thankful. It would have been tragic to have saved the others and lost the one. The boy's parents would never have gotten over it.

Travlor had not come to her for the healing sessions that he needed so badly. Worried, she decided to approach him.

Following the woman bearing his tray, guards following her, they wound their way to Travlor's rooms. Wading through the soldiers that crowded the hall, she knocked at his door. Travlor's voice barely reached her. "Enter."

She opened the door and stepped aside, admitting the woman with his food. Travlor acknowledged her presence, but didn't say anything.

He was seated at his desk and the tray was placed before him. The woman quickly removed the covers and exited the room. Travlor pushed the tray away then raised an eyebrow and waited for Daria to speak first.

"You need to eat that food." She nodded toward the tray, but he just stared at her. She frowned and crossed to the desk. She propped both hands on his desk and stared at him. "You're acting like a spoiled child. I'm here for your healing."

Surprise flitted across his face. "I did not think you would be willing to offer your services."

"I have no wish to see you deteriorate, no matter what you think. I know you are weak. Let's get you to the bed so I can help."

A big sigh scoured the air between them. Daria didn't respond. She rounded the desk and held her arm for Travlor. There was just a fraction of hesitation before he placed his hand in hers. Rising, he leaned heavily against her. She put an arm around his waist and gasped. He was so frail.

"I know. I have shocked myself."

She helped him into the bedroom and waited as he made himself comfortable. When he signaled that he was ready, he closed his eyes and she began.

The eerie sounds of her healing tones filled the room and her hands began to work of their own accord. She could feel Travlor's body accepting and relaxing into the healing touch.

She worked slowly and thoroughly, without thought for time, for herself, or for her child. She threw every amount of energy she possessed into the healing. And she was gratified to hear Travlor's labored breathing ease. She worked until she felt the drain pulling her down. At last, she lowered her arms. She was pleased to see that Travlor slept.

She walked to the desk and sat in his chair. Pulling the tray of food toward her, she devoured the contents, leaving nothing for the Atlantean. It would be a while before he awakened, and the sleep would help him as much as anything. She wondered again how old the man was. It was incredible that no one seemed to know that fact. It had not been in Na-Kai's memories. She had just told Daria that he was ancient; since that was a relative term, it was anyone's guess.

She was grateful to be able to help him. It was small payment for the life of the tiny boy. She ate with gusto, but when she finished, she picked up the phone and ordered more food. She wanted something for Travlor when he woke. She would shovel the food down his throat if he resisted.

She placed the empty dishes back on the tray and took it to one of the soldiers in the hallway. Closing the door, she took her seat back at the desk. Out of curiosity, she picked up one of the papers that littered the desktop.

Shuffling through some of the piles, she saw requisition requests, bills, receipts and order forms. She had no idea what any of it was for. It seemed to be mostly military in content, but she wasn't used to any of the terms. She shook her head. "What are you doing?"

She heard Travlor's breathing change and knew that he would soon be awake. She dragged a chair to his bedside. As she seated herself, his eyes opened. Relieved to see that his vision was clear, she scanned his body and found that he was thoroughly rested and refreshed. "How are you feeling?"

He took a deep, cleansing breath and sat up. "I feel reenergized. You truly are a marvel."

"Good, now let's get you to the desk for some food."

He rose without aid and traversed the room, entering the outside office, he seated himself. "I feel younger already. You came at the right time."

She had done all she could for him so she took her leave, but not before she scheduled another healing. Even though she didn't want this man to regain full health, it seemed that she had no choice in the matter. She closed the door gently.

The soldiers parted to let her pass. She went down to the great room and glanced out the guarded door. More people thronged the gates. It made her nervous to see such crowds. People in the throes of passion could so easily turn into a mob; she wondered if they needed more guards.

Travlor was pleased with his recovery. Daria's skills surpassed any other healer in his vast reservoir of memories. He wondered at her bloodlines, that they should be so strong at this time. He knew she was descended from Kai-Dan, but he had never known genes to jump so many generations. "Ah well, it is not for me to ponder the mysteries of science."

He ate quickly because there was so much work to accomplish. He had issued new orders to his generals. They were to start building their divisions. He had men at his disposal and command, but for what he planned, he needed an army. The first step, now that word of his healing was spreading throughout South America, was to enlist the religious minded into a new sect. "I must think of a catchy name. One that will draw people in … how does 'Army of the New Messiah' sound?" He rocked back and lifted his hands to the back of his head and grinned at the sight of so many people at the gates. "I will work on it."

He bent forward and reached for the phone. "The minions at the gate are growing. It is time to build our church."

He hung up, grabbed a sandwich, and started gobbling his food. Everything was going nicely, better even, than he had planned.

Chapter 34

Standing in front of the closet, Kyla couldn't reach a decision. She had never had so many clothing choices. In her studies of topside habits, she found that women changed their clothes often, sometimes more than once a day. However, she still wasn't sure which outfit would be the most appropriate for what engagement.

Evan slipped in behind her and hugged her waist. She nestled the back of her head against him. His chest moved gently with the rise and fall of each breath and she loved the feel; it soothed her. She hadn't known it was possible to feel this deeply about anyone, so at times, she needed the tactile feel of him to ground her in reality. She turned around, and gazing into his eyes, caressed the back of his neck. She stood on her toes and kissed him in such a way that she had no doubt it would hold him through the day.

Breathless with the feel and taste of him on her lips, she finally released him. "I can make no sense of this. Do you have any suggestions?"

Evan, out of breath himself, pulled out a filmy dress. "How about this?" He held it up to her eyes. "You're so beautiful. You do the dress justice, not the other way around."

Kyla giggled and took the hangar. She held it up in front of her and studied her image. "It is beautiful. You have exquisite taste and I love everything we purchased." She turned back to him. "Blue it is."

She hung the dress on a hook and Evan took her in his arms again. "I won't be able to be with you much today. I've scheduled meetings regarding the sales of my stocks and other investments. Will you be all right on your own?"

Kyla shook her head and smiled. "Do not worry about me, love. I am looking forward to finding things on my own."

Evan squeezed her waist. "Good, the car is ready whenever you are. Just call this number and tell the driver to bring it around. He'll be at the front entrance before you can get down there."

She knew he was concerned for her and she smoothed his brow. "I will be fine. I have seen you do this all the time. Now go—you do not want to be late for these important meetings. Would you still like to meet for lunch?"

"I'll call you and let you know if I can get free. Don't lose this phone."

She took the cell and went to the front room. In a great display, she showed Evan where she was placing it in her purse.

He rolled his eyes. "OK, you're good." He kissed her one last time and they walked arm in arm to the private elevator. Evan pushed the button and the doors slid open noiselessly. He stepped inside and waved as they closed.

Kyla missed him already but she was looking forward to her adventures in Boston. She was ready to experience the city on her own and she wanted to find some garments that could possibly surprise Evan.

She went back to the closet and ran her hands over the dress. It was so soft and the gorgeous sky blue would reflect the balmy Boston day; she loved it. She hurried to finish dressing.

Chapter 35

SEATED AT AN OUTDOOR café, Kyla basked in golden sunlight that sparkled off the waves in Boston harbor. The morning had created new surprises and infinite delights as she soaked up topside life, culture, and shopping. She felt incredibly alive. Watching people pass by, she carefully scrutinized their mannerisms and dress. These bustling topsiders fascinated her. She loved their high energy and mad dashes to unknown and important destinations.

Evan had called to say that he was running late, so she hadn't ordered. She wanted to wait, but she was getting quite famished. Her stomach was making all sorts of angry noises and she was becoming embarrassed. When another loud rumble actually made the patrons at the next table look up, Kyla decided not to delay any longer. She signaled a waiter and placed her order. When the young man left with her menu, she looked at the phone again. No message. Well, he would come when he could. She sat back and continued to admire the view.

Evan had suggested this café. Situated on a pier, it offered sweeping vistas of the bustling bay. She felt nearly at home in the surroundings; it almost reminded her of Santorini, only much busier. She enjoyed the different ships and boats coming and going and people casting their lines from the boardwalk.

Her musing was sharply interrupted when she heard someone shout Daria's name. She was afraid to look around. Still masked by Evan's thoughts, she resembled Daria, but she had no idea what she was supposed to do or say. She thought she had been prepped and prepared for every contingency, but neither she nor Evan had counted on a chance meeting.

The woman shouted again. "Daria! Over here!"

Kyla stiffened her spine and looked around. A woman, waving and smiling like they were the best of friends, stood on the other side of the far railing. Kyla gulped and clinched her hands into tight fists. Her palms tingled and she felt the heat rise in her face. She froze. She hadn't the slightest idea what to do.

"Daria, don't you recognize me? It's Megan!"

The plump, stylish, red-haired woman walked to the entrance and hurried to her table. She threw her arms around Kyla's neck and squeezed. Then she kissed both her cheeks, hauled the bags she had been carrying up and over Kyla's head, and settled herself in the opposite chair. It looked like she planned to stay forever. Kyla closed her eyes and tried to stop her nerves from unraveling.

The woman talked so fast, it was hard for Kyla to keep up; however, it saved her from having to join the conversation. The woman was overly excited to see "Daria" and rambled on about certain events at someplace the two of them may have worked.

Kyla did her best to look interested and tried to parry the woman's questions. However, when Megan drew closer with a funny look on her face, Kyla nearly jumped out of her chair.

The day was no longer fun and she secretly writhed beneath the woman's scrutiny.

"What's wrong with you? You don't act like your old self. Married life already over?"

Kyla shook her head. The question was one that she could answer with absolute honesty and she felt like she was back on even ground. "Married life is amazing! I couldn't have found a better man if I looked the entire world."

Megan grinned. "I'm so glad to hear it. I knew you weren't happy with the fact that Evan kept bugging you, so when I heard that you were going to Greece, I figured you were just trying to get rid of him."

Kyla was gaining more confidence and rhapsodized, "Greece turned out to be magical! He came after me and everything clonked."

The woman's brows furrowed and she looked puzzled. "Clonked?"

She had said the wrong thing! She fisted her hands again and wildly searched her mind for topside expressions.

Suddenly, Megan brightened. "You mean clicked?"

Kyla threw her head back and laughed. "Exactly!"

Megan laughed, too, and reached out to touch her shoulder. "Maybe you're still jet lagged. It takes a while to get over a trip like you had. That reminds me. Pictures—I need to see pictures!"

Kyla thought she was going to be sick. Panic rose along with the temperature of her body and she could taste the bile in her throat. She started to rise and leave with any excuse that would come to mind, but when she heard Evan's shout, she plopped back into her chair with a huge sigh of relief.

"Daria! I'm here!" He darted from the cab and flew to the table. Kyla hadn't even been able to send him a thought-form she had been so nonplussed. He bent to kiss her then stood and pulled out a chair. He sat, shook a napkin into his lap and gazed suspiciously at the unexpected guest. "Megan?"

"Evan."

"What are you doing here?"

"Daria and I were just chatting. It's been ages since we've seen each other and I just wanted to catch up."

Evan stood and if Kyla hadn't known him better, she would have thought that he was being rude. He glared at Megan and barely managed to keep the snarl out of his voice. "Don't you have someplace else you need to be?"

The woman's affable manner departed. She frowned with a show of contempt, and without ceremony, stood and grabbed her bags. Nodding curtly to "Daria," she said something that sounded to Kyla like, "Harumph," then she stalked out of the café, using her bags as battering rams to angrily brush aside anyone who got in her way.

Evan watched her like a hawk sighting prey. "Just in time."

Kyla, bewildered as to Evan's reaction, took his hand. "Who is she? I was so frightened. She asked to see pictures of our wedding and honeymoon."

Evan waved his other hand as though he was swatting a fly. "Don't worry about her. She and Daria used to be friends. She's a terrible gossip and she spread some pretty filthy lies about her. When Daria confronted her, they mutually decided it would be best to end the friendship. To my knowledge, they haven't spoken since."

Kyla felt a blush rise over her cheeks but she knew the makeup hid the Atlantean effect. She was surprised when

Evan grinned. "I can see that you're embarrassed; you might think about applying more base."

Adopting a haughty attitude, Kyla pulled herself up and with all the dignity she could muster, looked down her nose and then up. "I was thinking that, once again, you have come to my rescue." She batted her eyes like the heroines in her books. "You are my hero."

Evan had taken a drink of water and almost snorted it out of his nose. He wiped the liquid from his mouth and laughed. "Certainly a different day." He reached to touch her cheek. "I've cancelled the rest of my meetings. What would you think of a trip to a museum of impressionist paintings? It's supposed to be an outstanding show."

No longer hungry, Kyla searched through the pile of shopping bags. Beaming coquettishly, she brought out a bag that was quite small and tied with a bright pink bow. She waved it playfully in the air and teased, "I think you might rather see a fashion show."

Reaching into his pocket, Evan threw some money down and took Kyla's hand. "Well, what are we waiting for?" He called for the chauffer.

The cries of hungry gulls floated over the water as they surrounded the returning fishing boats. Ship horns honked merrily, and as Kyla followed Evan from the small café, Boston took on the patina of an impressionist painting in the amber haze of soft summer light.

Chapter 36

ANOTHER TWO MONTHS had come and gone and Daria was showing so much that nothing fit. Grumpily, she tried to stretch the shirt out and away from her belly. "I don't even think a queen-sized sheet would wrap all the way around me." She scrunched her face and tried once more to pull the shirt down over her stomach.

She grimaced, "Whether Travlor likes it or not, someone is going to have to get me something I can wear!" She stomped out of her room to locate the insufferable man. She felt like she was carrying a baby elephant.

She passed the "hospital" room that Travlor had ordered and couldn't help wondering how he made things happen so quickly. She knew he could compel people but she also knew that he had quit using that particular ability in an effort to retain his strength. "He must have an endless supply of money."

"Almost."

Spooked by the curt reply, she swung around to find Travlor standing behind her. "I didn't hear you. Where were you?"

"Working. No need to worry." He eyed her clothing and raised both brows at the sight of her protruding belly. "I believe you could use a larger size."

"Tell me about it." She tugged the top that threatened to become a midriff. "Can't someone go to a store and get me a tent?"

Travlor chuckled. "Come my dear, you need breakfast. Perhaps it will improve your attitude, and to answer your question, I have dispatched someone to acquire the things you need." Leading the way down the hall, his voice barged through the corridor. "Even though you are my prisoner, there is no reason for you to look like one."

Grumbling, she followed Travlor down the stairs and into the dining room. "Well, you can just tell them size elephant."

Travlor held the chair for her. "Shall we feed Dumbo?"

Daria chuckled despite her mood. Sometimes Travlor managed to say the right thing at the right moment—not often, but when he did, it helped. She scooted in and picked up the glass of special juice and gulped it down. She took a moment to savor the garnet-colored liquid and was glad that Travlor had retained such a chef. He truly was remarkable. "So, what's on your agenda today?"

Travlor replaced his coffee cup. "Would you be interested in seeing my new church?"

Chapter 37

TEMPTED TO RUB her eyes to make sure she was seeing right, Daria knew her jaw had dropped open, but there was nothing she could do about it. She had never seen anything like it in her life. Not far from the estate, a sight that was as astounding as it was outrageous appeared.

In a cleared section of land, a grand testament to Travlor and to religion soared high into the air. The building's polished marble walls glistened in the early morning light and stained glass windows threw rainbows of color across a well-manicured lawn. Resembling something out of old Rome, columns rose in mighty splendor underneath a wide portico. Enormous wooden doors, imported from God-knew-where, stood open, ready to receive the masses. At the very apex of the red, tiled roof—lest people not realize to whom they worshipped—a statue of a berobed Travlor, hands raised in benediction, towered over the entrance.

Daria didn't know what to say. What could she say? Her thoughts raced and her eyes glazed over. *He's doing it! The man has created a religion!*

Travlor raised his hand, looking eerily like the statue. "Care to see the inside?"

All Daria could do was nod. She was too dumbfounded to speak.

He led her up the stairs and into the vestibule. Displayed on one end wall was the "story" of Travlor's life. She watched, in unabashed awe, as the film scrolled through scenes of Travlor feeding the hungry, binding the wounds of war victims, walking through villages handing out money. A sound erupted from Daria between a snort and a laugh. "My God, you make Saint Teresa look like the devil."

Travlor put a hand on her back and ushered her into the main room. On a raised dais high above an arena stood, for lack of a better word, a throne. The chair glowed in gold and dripped with carvings and intertwining curlicues and mock angels ready to sound various sizes of trumpets. Daria felt faint. She wobbled over to one of the pews.

"Well, what do you think?"

"How did you make this happen so fast?"

"Did you ever stop to think how many people are willing to move mountains for their new savior? This was nothing!"

"But, why? Why do you need all this?"

Travlor walked over to her and ran his hand slowly over the polished wood. "Have you not taken stock of where we are? These countries need a leader. The people need someone they can look up to. If I were to try to lead without such an ostentatious display of power and wealth, my religion would only appeal to the masses of poor that already run amuck.

"No, I must appeal to the wealthy as well. Not only do I need their money to continue to fund my campaign, I need their compliance."

"Compliance? For what?"

"Your naiveté continues to astound me." He lowered himself next to Daria. "The coup I have put into place. The present government will be deposed and I will be elevated, not only as the new Messiah, but also the new dictator of this magnanimous country."

The man's assurance was unassailable; he spoke as though everything had already been accomplished and he was just waiting for the coronation to take place.

Daria couldn't reply. She couldn't even think of anything to say. *What do you say to a megalomaniac ... Don't do it?* She shook her head but Travlor mistook her meaning.

"Yes, it amazes even me. This edifice cost me quite a bit, but I intend to make that back very quickly. Have you noticed how many people this will hold?" He pointed to the balcony. "Notice the television cameras? Oh yes, my word will encircle the globe now."

Daria felt defeated. What could anyone do? He had amassed an army—generals were at his beck and call. And now, through massive telecommunication efforts, he was going to brainwash everyone with his superficial, religious drivel. Who could possibly stop this man? She pushed her tired body off the hard bench and stood, rubbing her aching back. "Can we go now?" The 'ow' echoed dully through the church.

Evan was in bed and Kyla had gone to the kitchen for a snack. He brushed his hair back, reflecting on the vision she had presented when she had walked out of the bathroom wearing ...

Currents of Will

well, not much. He was living a dream, a waking dream that stretched before him with nothing but the love he had sought and craved all his life.

He sat up and retrieved his laptop from the side table and flipped it open. He needed a distraction or he would accost the poor woman before she returned from the kitchen.

Scrolling through the news, his eye caught the snippet of a headline. He stopped, opened the blurb and scanned the brief account. A bloodless government takeover had transpired in Columbia, South America. He rapidly searched for more of the story, but all he could glean was that the entire executive, legislative, and judicial branches had unanimously resigned in order to form an autocratic theocracy. The vast country of Columbia was now being led by someone they recognized as the New Messiah.

It had to be his father! Evan slammed the cover down and rolled out of the bed. Grabbing his robe, his thoughts flew through the stratosphere. *"Columbia, Ni-Cio! They are in Columbia, South America!"*

Yelling for Kyla, he almost ran into her when he rounded the corner to the kitchen. She looked frightened.

"I know where they are!"

She raised a hand to her heart. "Where?"

"Columbia, South America. He just took over the entire government without so much as a single rifle shot. I don't know exactly where he is, but it's a start!"

"Have you told Ni-Cio?"

"He wants us to come back to Santorini. I don't know what he has planned, but we've got to be in the air as soon as we can."

"I will pack."

Evan paused to think. "Not tonight. Let me have the jet fueled and waiting for us after lunch. I have to be here tomorrow morning to sign off on the sale of my company. After that, we're off. I can't believe we've found the bastard!"

REGIONAL NEWS

Nation

FOLLOWERS THRONG TO MEET NEW MESSIAH!

By Juan Perone, Editor, Bogotá Gaceta
juanperone@BogotáGaceta.com

Bogotá, Magdalena, Columbia

Nestled in the thick jungles outside La Ciudad Perdida (the Lost City), massive throngs of Columbians trek to the heretofore unknown complex of the man hailed as the New Messiah.

The man has garnered the acclaim and attention of multitudes because of his spontaneous healing of the terminally ill children at the Since Cancer Clinic.

Walking, hiking and hitch-hiking, through all kinds of weather, believers gather to wait patiently outside the heavily guarded gates for just a glimpse of this illusive man.

Mr. Carlos Espinoza of Barranquilla had this comment, "One has to ask, who is this man?" Holding tightly to a worn picture of his wife of fifteen years, he continued, "Without this woman, I have no life. The new Messiah will heal her."

While their belief is touching in today's cynical world, one still has to ask, who is this man and where did he come from? Was the healing a one-time event or can he do it again? Is he truly the new Messiah?

These questions and more demand answers, in the meantime, people wait and hope that this man heralds the dawn of a new age.

Chapter 38

RUNNING FULL SPEED into the compound, Ni-Cio summoned everyone. *"Travlor has been found! Come to the courtyard as soon as you can!"*

People scrambled from every direction. Excited faces appraised him as he waited for the others. It had been a long day scrubbing Atlantis, but the preparations were nearing an end. With all of the men helping, the work had moved along rapidly. If need be, they could now move back to their home without fear of sickness or contamination.

Ni-Cio signaled Aris and Rogert. They disengaged themselves from the crowd and quickly joined him. He lowered his voice so that only they could hear. "Travlor is in Columbia, South America. We need to come up with a plan and we do not have time to waste. I need you to help me think of ways to get to that country and how we can rescue Daria." The men nodded curtly.

Ni-Cio moved to address the others. Looking over the tightknit group of survivors, he felt an immense sense of pride. Against all odds, his family had flourished. New life was coming into the world, the compound looked more robust, and everyone was finding ways to laugh again.

He dreaded what was to come. He had no idea what Travlor was up to, but he couldn't afford to lose any more of his people. As willing and ready as he was to sacrifice his own life to get Daria back, he wasn't ready to sacrifice any more Atlantean lives. "The search for Travlor has ended in Columbia, South America."

Clapping and cheers resounded throughout the courtyard. Ni-Cio held his arms up. "I do not know where in Columbia he is, but that is what I am determined to find out. Our home is nearly ready to inhabit. However, the topside equipment is not strong enough to sustain air and water for all of us.

"That means that some of us must stay in the compound. As council leader, I would offer a vote. Who would be willing to stay topside?"

He counted the show of hands. "Thank you." He looked back out over the assembled friends and continued, "Who needs to be home again?"

He could tell that people were reluctant to respond. "It is all right. I do not need to know now. Please, go to your families and talk it over. I will take the count again tonight. Just know that you will be well protected with either decision you make."

The assembled throng sought their families. Leaving in tight groups, Ni-Cio watched his people drift away. Aris and Rogert stayed behind. Aris spoke first. "When do you expect to leave?"

Shrugging, Ni-Cio motioned for his friends to follow him. He led them to the kitchen, and grabbing a pad and pen, took a seat at one of the tables. Flanked by Rogert and Aris, he tried to sketch a plan of rescue, but he had to admit he hadn't a clue what he was doing. He looked at the two men helplessly. "I have no plan. I have no idea how to proceed."

Rogert placed a hand on Ni-Cio's shoulder. "Do not worry yourself. Let us begin with the first step. Let us wait for Evan as he contemplates his father's plans in depth and at length. We will seek his guidance, but in the meantime, we will research South America and this Columbia."

Aris declared, "We will find her Ni-Cio, but Rogert is right. We must remain calm, plan accordingly, and act only when we are ready. Otherwise, if we somehow alert Travlor to the knowledge we have, we may lose her again."

Grabbing the hands of both his friends, Ni-Cio tried to infuse himself with their calm. "I would not be able to do this without your guidance and your friendship."

He loosened his grip and was so quiet that Aris asked, "Ni-Cio, what else bothers you?"

Ni-Cio glanced at both men and then rubbed his eyes. "Rogert has previously addressed an issue that looms over us like a black cloud. We have worked so hard just to survive that I have refused to let myself think about it."

He placed his hands, palms up, on the table. "The machines Evan brought into Atlantis are only a temporary measure. They give us the ability to visit our home, but they are noisy and certainly cannot sustain us long-term. I am at a loss; I have no idea how we make the transition back to our normal way of life."

Neither Rogert nor Aris said anything and the looks on their faces told Ni-Cio how alarmed they were. Their bronze glow dulled and thin strips of black swirled over their faces and up into their hair.

A deep rumble came from Rogert. "Ni-Cio, have you thought that we may never recover our home? The energy source handed down from Poseidon works only when enough people continue to reach the age of transcendence. That gift has been taken from us. It is as I explained to Evan—unless a miracle occurs, we will never be able to inhabit our home again."

Aris's voice was heavy with sadness. "Let us not dwell on this now. We have no way of knowing the future. We still have much work ahead of us. For now, let us finish the tasks at hand. It will help keep our minds occupied."

The men filed out of the kitchen and into the bright morning sun. Aris faced his friends. "I know it seems hopeless, but it was not long ago that we felt hopeless about finding Daria." Aris nodded at Rogert. "Our friend tells us to put one foot in front of the other. While we wait for Evan's return, we keep working and we keep our spirits up. When Evan arrives, everything will fall into place."

A ghost of a smile flitted over Ni-Cio's lips. Eyeing Rogert, he asked, "How about that garden?"

Rogert shook his head. "I will leave you two to the gardens and I will gather my men. We will continue our efforts in Atlantis."

Ni-Cio nodded and Rogert took off toward the cabins.

"Come Ni-Cio, you and I need to get our hands dirty." Aris pushed his sorrowful friend in the direction of the gardens.

Chapter 39

EVAN WRAPPED UP the sale of his company faster than he had thought possible. His company, his most important asset, was what he had needed to turn quickly. The other investments could wait.

The big step forward had been somewhat bittersweet, and he alternated between nostalgia and excitement as he cleaned out his office. His secretary would see to the furnishings and he had given her detailed instructions on what he wanted done with the Van Gogh. He went to the painting to admire it, as his, one last time. Gazing at it in awe, it was hard to believe how old the painting was; the colors were exquisite, so vibrant. With gentle reverence, Evan touched the thick splashes of oil, marveling at the texture of the brushstrokes.

He had hoped that one day he would have the time to take up painting. "Well, it's not the time now." He stood back and took in the whole. The museum would be very grateful for this donation. He was pleased that he had found an excellent home for this particular piece.

He sighed and lifted his box of mementos, then readied himself to face the poor woman outside his door. She had been with him from the beginning and never seemed ruffled by his brusque manner, which if he were to be honest, most times bordered on rude. Feeling guilty now, he was sorry that he had never taken the time to fully appreciate all she had done to keep his affairs in order.

He thought maybe the check he was going to give her would go a long way toward glossing over any past offences. He closed his office door and strolled over to the aging, grandmotherly figure.

The woman held herself as if she stood at attention. "Mary, I don't know what to say or how to thank you." He stumbled over words that he should have said long ago.

Kyla had opened his heart and he was a much better man because of her. He was grateful for the change, but he still felt awkward voicing his feelings to anyone else. He reached in his suit pocket and retrieved the envelope. He handed it to his steadfast assistant. "I think this will suffice. The new owner is a good man. I think you'll like working for him, but if not ... well, let's just say you won't have to worry about retirement."

Awkwardly, he walked around her desk and gave her a hug. Her response was hesitant. Evan stepped away, nodding. "Take care of yourself."

Making his way through the rest of the offices, he said his goodbyes to the other employees, assuring them that they had been well taken care of and that they would retain their jobs. As he entered the elevator and the doors started to close, he heard Mary's delighted scream. A wide grin spread over his face.

Downstairs, Kyla waited for him in the limousine. He slid in beside her and the driver closed the door. Evan felt Kyla's thought as they reached for each other.

"I feel your sadness. I am sorry..."

He hugged her even tighter. As the car slipped seamlessly into traffic, Evan looked into her gleaming topaz eyes. "It was the stepping stone for everything else. I'm fine. I have you and you're all I ever need." He released her and they sat back. "The jet is ready. While we're in the air, I'll do some research and see what else I can find. If I know Ni-Cio, he's standing at a biosphere ready to leave for South America right now."

"Do you have an idea what you will do when you find your father?"

"That's the problem. We've got to come up with some kind of workable plan. If he's got a big enough following to depose the present government, then there's no way we can fight openly against that. Our approach will need to be stealthier. That's about the only thing I'm sure of."

"Well, between you and Ni-Cio, I have no doubt you will come up with a plan that will not only be workable, but will succeed marvelously."

Trying to share her faith, Evan closed his eyes and leaned back in his seat. They would be at the airport soon enough. His mind had churned last night, keeping him awake. If he could catch forty winks before takeoff, it would help. He drifted down into sleep.

NEWS FROM SOUTH AMERICA

SudAmerica

FLASH!...Bloodless Coup

By Frederico Pena, Brasília, Brazil
jbalsa@sudamerica.com
@jbalsa on Twitter

Reporting from the Capitolio Nacional de Colombia, Bogotá, D.C.

    Today, in what is to become known as The Bloodless Coup of Bogota, the nation's president, the Senate and the House of Congress unanimously resigned the nation's democratic rule amid wild cheering and tumultuous celebration. For weeks, thousands upon thousands of Columbians have poured into the city of Bogota demanding change. As word of mouth has spread about the New Messiah, a tidal wave of unprecedented religious conversion has shaken the very foundation of the Columbian body politic established so long ago.

    Following the overwhelming will of the people, the New Messiah appeared on the steps of the Capitolio Nacional at precisely 10:30 a.m. EST and graciously accepted the role thrust upon him by staggering popular demand. Working closely with Travlor, a seamless transition of power has been accomplished as the men holding office prior to their resignation now return to serve the New Messiah.

    Rarely seen in public, Travlor, speaking perfect Spanish, honored the occasion with these words: "The great honor you have bestowed upon me today is cause for great humility. I accept your trust and this burden with equal measures of awe and trepidation. I promise to lead you on the righteous path and in accordance to the divine will."

    Falling to their knees in worshipful hunger, people's faces, flowing with tears, reflected the joy in their hearts. Images flashed across the airwaves as throngs of religious followers descended upon his church outside of La Ciudad Perdida to receive the news on holy ground.

    Surrounded by a sea of bodyguards, Travlor departed amid an overwhelming mood of hope and joy basking in the faith of his followers. On this miraculous day, one man, heading a benign, autocratic theocracy will hold the reins of power in his very capable hands.

Chapter 40

CARS ARRIVED IN DROVES and people scurried about the headquarters. Travlor was locked in his office, phone attached to his ear, emails flying. Men exited his quarters with terrified looks. His orders were being executed quickly and to the letter, and the only people allowed into his inner sanctum were his generals, the lady bearing food, and Daria. Even she was only allowed entrance at certain times.

Daria reluctantly attended his health while trying to keep her spirits up for the sake of her baby and for her own state of health. She was bigger than ever and grew more uncomfortable with each passing day. The stomach pains had increased in intensity, but at least she had learned how to mask the worst of the cramping.

Sitting idly by the pool, her swirling feet creating little eddies in the water, Daria thought about Travlor's first service. It had to be seen to be believed. The congregation had overflowed out onto the lawn and down the road, and the road had been blocked for hours before the pomp began and had remained so until well after the Travlor show had ended.

The initial kickoff of his mega-church was such a spectacle that it made a three-ring circus look tame. But his oratory was possibly the most heinous bit of sacrilegious brainwashing Daria had ever heard. The virtual spin of religious ideals spewed out of his mouth like lava from a volcano. She watched people listen, spellbound by honeyed words that covered his lies and his spiritual corruption. He made a mockery of all that was good and right about religion. But what sickened her most were the decent people in attendance. Most of them tried to live their lives by tenets that included love, joy, compassion, and peace. But they had absorbed his lies as easily as a mosquito sucks blood.

She hadn't wanted to be there, but he'd given her no choice. He had secreted her behind the curtain that was the backdrop to his "throne," and she had suffered through every pause, every indrawn breath, and every audience gasp as he disgorged his pious doctrine.

It literally made her sick to her stomach and she had thrown up in the nearest trash receptacle. She was not surprised that even her body rejected the air of unctuousness that poured off Travlor like week-old sweat.

Afterward, his flock had mobbed him just to touch the hem of his robe, catch a glimpse of him, or simply revel in being in the vicinity of the New Messiah. When he finally extricated himself from the noisy throng of supplicants, he had joined Daria in the car. All the way back to the estate, he had gloated about how gullible people were and how readily his plans continued to roll forward. Daria had exited the car without a word; she couldn't escape his vile presence fast enough.

She sneered at the offensive memory and then eased into the pool. She walked slowly around the shallow end, hands trailing behind. The easing of the baby weight was a godsend and she was glad that at least her prison had a pool.

Travlor had opened satellite offices in other key cities to handle the number of pleas that flooded in daily. The local post offices were inundated and screaming for more help, and emails clogged the Internet by the thousands. Everyone hired to handle correspondence worked at full speed and still needed more help. It was pandemonium—fervid, religious chaos.

Churches were jam-packed with a melding of the old faithful congregations and the newly-minted fanatics. Priests, ministers and pastors were spreading Travlor's doctrine faster than he could send out sermons.

While she swam a few lethargic laps, cars continued to enter the gate like flocks of birds and men in military uniforms swiftly entered the foyer for their meetings with Travlor.

The new theocratic rule had spurred further religious hysteria and, like dominoes, other countries fell before Travlor's religious onslaught.

Thousands of followers soon burgeoned to millions and his goal of global domination leapt toward fruition in bounds. Nothing stopped his forward momentum throughout the rest of South America. Governments, dictators, presidents, premiers, worshippers all, fell to their knees without as much as a sniffle of discontent.

Daria tried to pick up bits and pieces of Spanish to better understand the conversations she was able to overhear, but Travlor had forbidden any newspapers, radio, or TV to come near her.

The available books in the library were all in English and all fiction. She slapped lazily at the water. She was frustrated to be so helpless. If there was any way short of murder to stop the man, she would do it, as long as it didn't endanger the safety of her baby.

One thought kept niggling at the back of her mind and when she stopped swimming and let herself delve further, she was astonished. *Travlor is able to compel people with his thoughts. What if it's an ability I have, too?*

She chewed on that idea for a while then decided to try an experiment. She sent out a request to one of the kitchen staff for more juice with a bucket of ice and a pear.

The only way she could exit the water now was to use the stairs, so she waddled out of the pool and dried off. The sun was warm on her skin and she settled on a lounger to wait and see what would come of her first attempt to control someone.

The sun crept higher in the sky and she waited. Clouds drifted by and still she waited. Feeling sleepy, she berated herself for even trying something so foolish. However, as she started to close her eyes, one of the kitchen staff hurried toward her across the wide expanse of lawn. The woman wasn't carrying a tray, so Daria had no idea why she was coming.

When the woman stepped into the pool area, she approached with an air of deference, eyes cast down, hands clasped. She didn't speak; she only waited patiently for Daria's orders.

Although the woman spoke English, Travlor had her under a strong compulsion. She never said a word to Daria or even conveyed that she understood any of her requests. Daria imagined that even if an extreme emergency regarding her pregnancy occurred within the woman's presence, she still wouldn't break her gag order. Daria sighed. "If you could please bring some of that juice I like with a bucket of ice and a pear, I would appreciate it."

The woman nodded and rushed off to do her bidding. Daria lay back and closed her eyes against the glare of sunlight. *Probably just coincidence, but I'll keep experimenting.*

She relaxed again and as the first wisps of a dream started to color her mind, the gates creaked open and three cars entered the grounds in rapid succession. Tires scraped against the brick drive as they halted at the front entrance. Doors flew open and men ran up the stairs, yelling and gesticulating wildly.

Daria lurched up and grabbed her towel. She waddled to the house with as much haste as her size would allow. Upon entering the great room, she found people running in all directions. Phones rang all over the house and the stairs were crowded with men elbowing their way up the stairs to see Travlor.

Daria couldn't make sense of anything. With the smattering of Spanish she had acquired, everyone's speech was far too rapid-fire for her to follow. She thought she heard 'Brazil' but she couldn't be sure, so she headed toward her rooms.

People swarmed past her like bees on their way to a new hive. Of one thing she was certain: Travlor had orchestrated another horror on the trusting South American population.

She reached her rooms and closed and locked the door. She was so tired that she felt like falling asleep on her feet. Swaying with dizziness, she eased her way to the bed. Gently lowering herself to the mattress, she adjusted the pile of pillows for the most comfort and lay back with a groan. She stroked her stomach and sang a children's song that had surfaced in her memory. The baby kicked and she smiled to feel the strength of her child. *"Ni-Cio would love to feel you..."*

A soft knock at the door interrupted her reverie. "Come in."

The attendant that had come to the pool carefully walked in with a tray of her recent requests. She set the contents on the desk and turned as if to inquire if there would be anything else. She did not open her mouth to speak.

"Thank you, that's all."

The woman crossed the room and started to close the door behind her.

"Wait."

She looked back, timidly.

"Do you have a name? Anything I can call you?"

The woman looked so fearful that Daria got up from the bed and went to hug her, feeling guilty that she had inspired that response in another being. The poor woman backed away as though Daria had threatened to expose her to Ebola. Before Daria could reach her, the door slammed tight and the staccato sounds of footsteps reiterated again just how isolated she was. Travlor was winning.

News from South America

SudAmerica

With Host Martina Godiva

E TU BRAZIL?

LAST SOUTH AMERICAN COUNTRY SUCCUMBS TO MESSIANIC CONTROL!!!

...And Around the World

World News

London Globe
Est. 1848

STOP THE PRESS !!!

RISING TIDE OF MESSIANIC ARMY...

RAPID ASCENSION OF NEW MESSIAH...

WORLD SUPER POWERS GRAVELY CONCERNED !!!

Chapter 41

IT WAS DARK AND STARS dotted the Grecian sky when Evan and Kyla walked off the plane. During the flight, he had browsed the Internet for news of happenings in South America. He had shown Kyla photos of masses of people, arms outstretched in worship, eyes wide with awe.

He read her some of the stories about the healings that his father had concocted. He then ran across an interesting article, picked up by the Associated Press, that wasn't quite so effusive in its praise. This piece posed some hard questions regarding Travlor's methods and the rampaging spread of Travlormania. Nevertheless, it was a small story and had probably been lost in light of all the articles flooding the web about the man who could work miracles.

Together, Evan and Kyla tossed some ideas around as to how they could find his father. But the inherent problem, once they located Travlor's hideout, was how they were going to slip past his guards so that they could locate Daria. By the time they touched down, neither of them had come up with anything concrete.

Evan took Kyla's arm and led her to the car rental counter. He paid quickly and by the time they made it to the vehicle, their bags had been loaded. "Do you want to stop in town and get something to eat?"

Kyla shook her head. "No, we need to get to the compound. I am sure they will have something ready for us."

Evan started the car and accessed the main road. The night was breathtaking. The air was warm and island breezes stirred the trees into a gentle dance. Kyla opened her window and turned off the air conditioning, then took three deep breaths. "Love, you must do the same. We have been in the jet for nine hours. We are both exhausted and in need of food. Enjoy this while you can."

Evan knew she was right, but he felt Ni-Cio's urgency and hadn't wanted to think about anything else. He did as she suggested and rolled his window down. He inhaled the perfumed air. "Oh my God. I had forgotten how wonderful the mix of salt, wind, and olive trees could be. I not only *want* you in my life, you are my life's blood."

A trace of color ascended Kyla's neck. Underneath her makeup, the faintest striping of rose swirled over her cheeks and curled up under her hair. When she turned to him, her topaz eyes, luminous in the light of the car dials, gave her an otherworldly quality. Evan almost gasped. He blinked hard to reenter reality and turned his gaze back to the road.

He felt the trace of her touch as she stroked his hand. "You are my life's blood as well."

Night sounds climbed through the air, bringing a rhythmic cadence with which to serenade the lovers. Evan's mind started to unwind. He relaxed into the joy of Kyla's company and even managed to appreciate the drive to the compound.

Chapter 42

THE TABLE HAD BEEN set for two. Ni-Cio, Aris, Rogert and Peltor waited for Evan and Kyla to arrive. It was late and Ni-Cio had sent everyone else to bed. His men needed all the rest they could get for what was to come.

Everyone had eaten and Ni-Cio and his friends were settled around a smaller table, pad and pencil out. Ideas had been bandied about. Some that seemed workable at the outset had been reluctantly rejected. Logic determined too many complications or too many working parts. Obstacles arose so as to make most of their plans impossible to complete. They needed something simple. But what?

Ni-Cio threw the pencil down. "We know he is guarded. We also know he is able to requisition men easily, for the flow of his money seems as endless as his followers."

Rogert rubbed the bridge of his nose. "I would think that now he would not even need to use much of his own money. If he is the government, he can produce the funds from the national treasury. And we have seen that people are joining his army by the millions. It would be considered a high honor to be a disciple in his religious army."

Ni-Cio smiled at his companion. The man was becoming more loquacious by the minute. That in itself was a small miracle. "You are right of course. Travlor will probably confiscate the monies into his own supply; as a dictator can do whatever he desires. His wealth will continue to grow as will his army. Do any of you know if Columbia has an air force or a semblance of a navy?"

They shook their heads and waited for Ni-Cio to continue. "Well, Evan has probably done his homework and will be loaded with statistics on the available manpower in Columbia. But with each country that falls under Travlor's control, it will not matter who has what. He will gain control of every last person, vehicle, ship, or airplane. After that, it will be anyone's guess as to how long the entirety of Central America, as well as Mexico, will stand against his advance."

Grabbing the pen and pad, Aris started drawing. Ni-Cio tilted forward to follow his diagram and scratched his chin thoughtfully. "That could work."

Aris drew feverishly until he tapped the table with his pen and held up the pad for everyone to see. Silence greeted his presentation.

However, the silence carried its own weight and the moment stretched. Quick glances flew around the table as the men looked at each other for confirmation of their own thoughts. Before anyone could comment, a car horn sounded. Evan and Kyla had arrived. Chairs scraped and the men hustled to the courtyard.

Taking turns, Evan and Kyla were passed around. Hugs and smiles and warm gestures of welcome were exchanged.

Ni-Cio released Evan and slapped him on the shoulder. "Not a moment too soon. We are glad you are here."

"We came as soon as we could."

"Let Aris and Peltor take your bags to your cabin. We have food prepared. We will tend to your needs first and then we will discuss what we have found."

"Sounds good. Lead the way."

Rogert took off and held the kitchen door open. Gladly taking seats at the table, both Kyla and Evan loaded their plates. Ni-Cio grabbed some wine and glasses and uncorked the bottle. Pouring generous portions, he handed a glass to the weary travelers. No one declined the offer.

By the time Aris and Peltor rejoined the group, the food had all but disappeared. Ni-Cio patiently waited for them to finish eating. "Do you need to take showers or freshen up?" He was proud that he was adopting some of the Terran slang that Kyla was able to employ with such ease.

Evan spoke for them both. "We're here to talk strategy. We can rest later."

Ni-Cio splashed more wine into their glasses. "You need to see Aris's plan."

"If you are through eating, move over here and I will show you what I was thinking." Chest thrust out, Aris sauntered to the other table. He seated himself and held out the pad.

Dragging extra chairs over, Evan and the others took their places. Aris handed the pad to Evan and waited while he studied the drawing. His eyebrows finally lifted and he looked up with astonishment. "This could work." He glanced back at the sketch. "My God Aris, this actually could work!"

He passed the notebook to each person and everyone, again, carefully studied the plan. Peltor was the last one and when he was finished, he threw the drawing on the table, stood, and clapped Aris on the back. "I do not know how you thought of this. It is so simple, it is brilliant! I do not know why one of us did not think of it."

Aris beamed under the effusive praise. Evan looked equal parts perplexed and delighted after he finished commending Aris. He stood back, looking at him. "I sometimes wondered if you were smart enough to come out of the rain, now you come up with this! You've destroyed all my preconceived notions about you."

Good-natured laughter rippled through the group. Ni-Cio walked toward the screen door. "Aris always was one for getting in and out of trouble. And his plan tonight just proves that. Let us all get a good night's sleep. We still have much to do before we leave, but tomorrow will be soon enough to start."

After they made their goodbyes, the men trailed out of the kitchen, leaving Evan and Kyla alone. Evan didn't hesitate before sweeping Kyla into his arms and kissing her with all the longing in his heart and soul. When she lifted her gaze to meet his, he read everything he needed to know in her expression. He led her back to their cabin; their night had just begun.

Chapter 43

Travlor had come to her room. He sat in the nearest chair and looked steadily at Daria. "I am unable to rest in my quarters now. I will start coming to you for my healing sessions. I need a little peace."

Unwilling to rise when he entered, Daria still languished on her bed. She didn't want to go through a session with him today. She wanted to be left alone. She slowly sat up, swung her legs off the bed and faced Travlor. "I'm too tired for a session today. Can we do it tomorrow?"

Travlor eyed her suspiciously. "You do not seem overtired to me. I have given you a quick scan; everything is proceeding well."

Daria stood up. Even with Travlor seated, she didn't feel that she intimidated him in the least. "Fine, then. Let's get it over with."

She stepped aside to let him take the bed. He looked at her before lying down. "You need a change of attitude. You don't want your child to inherit a bad disposition."

She glowered at Travlor and had to concentrate to keep her lip from lifting in a sneer. Daria pushed Travlor back and began to scan his body. She could see that because of her efforts, the decay had eased. As a matter of fact, some of his organs looked better than before she had started. She wasn't surprised to see those results, but she had hoped that her ministrations wouldn't be quite so successful.

Beginning the healing tones, Daria dragged her hands over his body. Her mind wandered as she worked, until she almost forgot Travlor was there. When the last notes sounded, she did another scan. She stopped and rubbed her lower back. She was puzzled. Nothing looked as it had. His body was different, changed somehow. He didn't seem so robust and the organs didn't look quite so filled out. She did another scan just to be sure. Again, the same results. Daria glanced at Travlor as he sat up. She waited to see if he noticed anything. As the man rested, a tick started under her right eye. She didn't dare touch it.

Travlor finally stretched and took a deep breath. "I am always invigorated by your touch. I feel younger every day." He got up from the bed and strolled toward the door. "By the way, you might be interested to know that Central America is starting to come under my control. I calculate that it won't be much longer before Mexico falls into line. Ahhh, the power of a few miracles. Which brings me to the fact that it is time for another one."

Daria blanched. "I thought the hospital would be quite enough."

"Oh no, we must continue to stoke the fire. We cannot afford to let faith waiver. It must be fed and strengthened. People are weak and have short memories. I am being a good shepherd and tending my flock. I do not intend to lose even one of them." He opened the door and looked back, an evil gleam in his eye.

"There are many wolves out there. We must be ever vigilant." He slipped out the door and gently closed it behind him.

Daria sat down on the bed. She was used to his bragging so she hadn't been as attentive as she had been in the past. Instead, her mind was fixated on the scan that she had done after the healing. *What happened? The difference was microscopic and obviously Travlor didn't feel any different. But what was it that shifted? Was it something I did incorrectly?*

She reviewed the healing, moment by moment, searching her mind for any mistakes she might have made. However, she couldn't find a single flaw in her technique. She felt fidgety and her eye still twitched. "Thank God he didn't notice anything."

Rubbing her hands over her arms, she went to the window. Men were everywhere, running here and there with orders both urgent and unexceptional. But it was clear that, to a man, everyone was elated to be in the shadow of the mighty Messiah.

No matter his will, their faithful hearts leapt to do his bidding. She ran her hands over her belly and felt the lack of clothing where her shirt had started to pull away from her pants, again. She felt dismal. "Time for another wardrobe expansion."

Later that night, as Daria drifted on the edge of sleep, her earlier thoughts about the healing brought her upright. *That's it! That's what I can do!*

She threw the covers aside and plodded out of bed as quickly as her belly would allow. She paced the length of her room, turned and came back. As she circled the room, her mind raced. *I didn't want to do this healing. I wasn't tired, I just didn't feel like it! That has to be it. If my heart and soul aren't in the healing, it must have no effect or even may have small negative effects.*

Apparently the health of the individual isn't reduced so much that it's noticeable, but as a healer, I'm able to see the difference.

She continued her pacing while she wracked her brain for something, anything Na-Kai had said about a reverse healing, but there was nothing. *Maybe the healers were always willing to employ a healing no matter the circumstances. If that's true, then maybe I can effect microscopic changes in Travlor that he won't be able to detect until it's too late.*

She stopped in mid-stride. Hugging her daughter, she whispered to the child as if she was in on the secret. "We might just have a way out of here after all. Sleep well, my dearest one. We're going to be busy challenging this idea."

The baby kicked once as though in agreement, then she settled. Daria yawned. Energy depleted, she sank gratefully onto the soft mattress, whispered her good nights to Ni-Cio and their child, and then fell into a wonderfully dreamless sleep.

...AROUND THE WORLD...BREAKING NEWS....AROUND T

EMERGENCY SUMMIT!!!

LEADERS OF WORLD'S SUPERPOWERS CONVENE IN GENEVA

"What can be done to stem the onslaught of Armies of the New Messiah?"

Chapter 44

Morning came too soon. Evan and Kyla were still wrapped in each other's arms. However, the banging of the door signaled that it was time for them to get up and get moving. Evan groaned and yawned. "What an incredible night. Another one that I won't soon forget."

Kyla wrapped her arms tighter around his groggy form. "I hope I did not keep you up too long. Did you get enough sleep?"

Evan kissed her gently then released her. He stood up and stretched long and hard. "Nothing a little strong Greek coffee won't help."

He offered his hand. But Kyla shook her head, grinned wickedly and fell back onto the pillow. "I do not have to plan; therefore, I will get more sleep. Have a nice day, dear."

She ducked under the covers before Evan could grab her. Her muffled laughter slipped into his heart, filling him with energy. "Don't worry, I'll make sure the next time you have a chore that needs tending that you are up until the wee hours of the morning. And then, *I* will laze about dreaming the day away."

She pulled the blanket away from her face. "As long as you dream about me, I would not care how long you slept."

He touched her cheek and bent to kiss her. "I'll shower and be out of here before you slide back into dreamland, but just in case, I promise to shut this creaky old door as quietly as possible."

She took his hand and looked him in the eye. "No matter what plans you and Ni-Cio decide, try to take time to run or workout or something. That will help get your blood going."

A rakish thought entered Evan's mind which his smile reflected. Kyla playfully slapped his hand. "Go, before I pull you back into bed and make you forget about helping anybody but me."

Chapter 45

SIXTEEN MEN GATHERED around the courtyard waiting for Ni-Cio and his lieutenants.

They knew that Aris had come up with a plan that seemed workable. They had been chosen as part of a special squad. Their training in *Last Strike* drills had been revived and they were ready to leave at a moment's notice. Though not anxious to jump into another battle, they were prepared to go anywhere in the world and fight to the death to get their healer back.

They wanted and needed to get their lives and their families' lives back to normal as soon as possible. The rest of their friends and families would stay in the compound, working the gardens, tending the vineyards, and caring for their children.

It had been voted upon and decided that people would take turns visiting their home so that everyone could see and appreciate the progress that had been made. By doing so, it would also allow everyone the opportunity and the time to visit the burial wall and pay their respects. As the Atlanteans had been topside far too long, families would also have the chance to become reacquainted with underwater living.

Since the equipment was not strong enough to sustain everyone who wanted to move back to Atlantis, in most people's minds, there wasn't much reason to stay longer than overnight. However, the short reintroduction to their world would be enough. It would not only help reinvigorate those left behind awaiting the outcome of the latest rescue attempt, it would keep their minds occupied, too.

Ni-Cio and his four companions left the kitchen and made their way to the courtyard and into the middle of the group. "All right, we think we have perfected Aris's plan."

His men stepped closer, listening intently. "Evan has strengthened his masking abilities. As we have seen, he is able to mask the compound, no matter the distance and he is able to mask people up to a greater distance than the previous two-hundred feet." Ni-Cio glanced at Aris and nodded.

Aris proudly walked to the center, taking Ni-Cio's place as their leader stepped away. He pulled out his drawing and held it high so that everyone could see. "After I considered the fact that Evan's powers were changing and developing into something even stronger, I thought about the fact that Travlor is surrounded by men he doesn't know and more than likely hasn't taken the time to get to know.

"That made me think that if Evan masked us, we could slip into the culture of Columbia where we could familiarize ourselves with their routines and find out where Travlor is staying. When that has been established, we simply sign up as part of his army. Once we are at Travlor's hideout, we can drop the charade and locate Daria."

He looked around to see if the men had accepted his idea; some of them looked puzzled, so Aris tried to explain. "Think about it this way: if Evan is able to make the compound disappear, then he should be able to make us disappear."

He stopped to wait for comment and commendations. No one said anything, so he plowed on. "I know this sounds childishly simple, but my thought was that if we can get into Travlor's stronghold undetected, then we find Daria and get out before anyone suspects a thing."

Nothing happened once he was done and no one said a word. Aris was quite deflated. He didn't know what else to say, so he gave the floor back to Ni-Cio and went to stand next to Rogert.

The men were deep in thought, but Ni-Cio knew they were searching for any way that the plan could fail. He waited for their responses.

After a lengthy pause, one of the men walked over to Aris and placed a hand on shoulder. "I must tell you—I thought we would end up fighting to the death and I was prepared to do just that in order to get our healer back, but Aris, your idea is so simple that it is quite marvelous." He glanced at his comrades. "I see no reason not to adopt this plan. What say you all?"

Already attached to each other through thought, the men reacted as one. They surrounded Aris and lifted him up into the air and onto their shoulders. They paraded him around the courtyard, their joyous shouts resounded through the compound and flashed through the vineyard. Thoughts raced outward, announcing to all that Aris had come up with a way to get their healer back with minimal effort and an excellent chance of no loss of life.

Ni-Cio and Evan followed the celebrating group. "How soon do you plan on leaving, Ni-Cio?"

Knowing he needed to keep his people buoyed with thoughts of their return home, he tried to think as Marik would have. He had to put the group's best interest ahead of his own mad desire to push Evan into a biosphere and race to South America. He gritted his teeth before he answered, Marik's admonishment echoing in his head. *"Lead them well..."*

"In another month, we will be ready. Our team will be buoyed by the knowledge that the larders are stocked, plants are flourishing, and our home is refurbished enough to welcome families for a visit." He looked sideways at Evan. "I wish Marik had chosen someone else as council leader. I would have us leave this moment."

Evan stopped Ni-Cio. "We still have time on our side. Now that we know where they are and we have some idea of how to break into his stronghold, it's more than okay to make sure that your friends and families are settled and well taken care of. Don't worry. Daria knows you'll come for her and I'm sure she'll be ready with a way to help us when we get there."

The sad, mourning color of indigo twisted up from Ni-Cio's neck. "I miss her so much. I feel as if half my body is missing. I am lost without her."

Evan placed his arm around Ni-Cio's shoulders and gently prodded him toward the kitchens. "My friend, I am familiar with your pain. I've felt that way most of my life. I promise; we will get her back safe and sound."

Shaking himself out of the whirlpool of self-pity, Ni-Cio picked up the pace. "Let us see if we can find some more of that Greek beer. Aris deserves a great toast!"

They hurried toward the sounds of excitement that rang out of the kitchens and into the island air.

Chapter 46

Travlor wasn't feeling as chipper as he normally did after a healing session. He couldn't discern the reason, but the closest he could come to describing the feeling was twitchy. He didn't understand it. Thinking that he probably needed more rest, he promised himself that he would make an earlier night of it. "Alas, duty calls and the requirements of the rise of a world dictator preclude much rest."

Stopping before the door to his rooms that were now his headquarters, he rolled his neck. The muscles were tight, no longer as relaxed as they had been after other sessions. He made a mental note to ask Daria about it. He would be interested to hear her thoughts. And possibly, he just needed another round of healing sooner than expected. He sighed. "Just another detail to reconsider."

He opened the door, already barking orders to his majordomo and the attending general. They departed to do his bidding. Travlor took his seat behind the massive desk and rifled through all the papers. Three men entered and came to immediate attention. Travlor didn't look up, just crooked a finger. "Come."

They approached the desk coming to another ridged stance. They barely dared to breathe as they waited for their Messiah to acknowledge them. Travlor let them wait.

A phone rang in another room and bits of a hurried conversation reached their ears. Travlor looked up. "You have news?"

One of the three generals stepped forward with a smart salute. "Yes sir."

Travlor waited but the man said nothing. "Well, let's have it."

"We have learned that the resisting countries have gathered their armies. They are combining their navies and their air forces into one military might. Their plan is to invade Columbia and bring war to us."

Travlor sat back. The news was nothing he hadn't expected. He knew that as his reach grew, governments would start to fear him and would react in the only way they could: by declaring all-out war on him and his followers.

He steepled his fingers and rested his chin on the top, then eyed his men carefully and compelled them to state the unvarnished truth. "Are your men ready?"

The general quickly stepped back in line and all three of the men replied in the affirmative.

"Do you have your defense plans finalized?"

They gave brisk nods.

"It is as I told you. We do not want to look like aggressors. These countries must fall through faith in me and a firm desire to follow my teachings. I don't want to alarm the rest of the world, especially the United States. We don't want to incur the wrath of Uncle Sam—not when they've got so many nukes at their ready disposal."

Another man opened his mouth then decided better of that idea. Travlor inched forward. "Speak."

The general glanced nervously at his partners then swallowed hard and stepped forward. "Sir, I know we don't want to look aggressive. But don't you think it's prudent to mobilize our forces and take the fight to the other countries. To … take them by surprise before they can determine their course of action and move their armies?"

Eyeing the man carefully, Travlor quirked his mouth. It was a salient point but he didn't want the world to know what a true megalomaniac he was. "I appreciate your candor. The simple answer is no. I can't risk the time needed to move our forces from country to country. We will continue to grow our troops and we will continue to gather the flock into the fold."

Travlor thought to leave them with a spiritual bit of wisdom. He stood and raised his arms to the men. He tried to look compassionate, but even he didn't buy it. "I do not intend to lose one life if we don't have to. I want people of all faiths to watch us and learn from us. Then it will be their choice to join with our crusade, or not."

He rounded the corner of his desk and opened the door to usher the men out. "Just fortify our defenses in every base under our command. Have everyone on high alert and let us see where this takes us."

The men stepped into the hall.

"Do not worry. It is my will that shall be done and together we will bring a new world peace to this quarrelsome planet."

He didn't wait for their response before he closed the door and laughed. "Quarrelsome indeed, a little mind control never hurt anyone."

He crossed back to his desk, seated himself, and went back to work. A sly thought made him smile. *There is no rest for the wicked.*

...FLASH...FLASH...FLASH...FLASH...FLASH...FLASH

FLASH!!!......WAR BREAKS OUT!!!

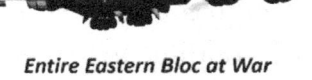

Entire Eastern Bloc at War
Countries Clash!
Governments Join New Messiah

NEWS FROM SOUTH AMERICA

CENTRAL AMERICA
NOW PART OF
TRAYLOR'S
ARMIES!!!

Chapter 47

DARIA WAS GETTING USED to the spurts of growth that she and her baby experienced. The stomach pains no longer troubled her, but the weight was something else. She thought she might have to get a sling for her distended belly. She waded into the pool and sighed as the water closed around her. Pulling the paddle board from the poolside, she placed it under her head and let her feet float up. Her stomach broke the surface of the water like a beached whale. She shook her head in wonder. She didn't even want to think about how she was ever going to deliver such a child. She gazed at the blue sky, filled with billowy white clouds, and tried to imagine different shapes as they drifted by. It was a game she looked forward to sharing with her daughter. She couldn't wait to see what wondrous things her young mind would imagine.

Kicking her feet, she floated to the side and stood. As hard as the extra weight was to bare on dry land, the water made her feel almost weightless. She glanced up at Travlor's windows. The previous owner had installed bullet-proof glass, and as paranoid as that man had been, Travlor made him seem like a novice. Travlor had rigged the jungles surrounding the complex with cameras and trip sensors connected to an intricate alarm system, and it wouldn't surprise her to find that the soldiers had mined the entire area extending all the way back to the city where they had debarked.

She pushed the board away and tried a few backstrokes. She felt awkward and sluggish, without a hint of the grace she had known in her pre-pregnancy days. "That's all right," she crooned to her daughter. "I'll be back to my old self soon enough." She sang a nonsense tune that reminded her of something from her childhood. The baby moved and Daria grinned happily.

It was the first time since she had been taken from Atlantis that she was actually flooded with joy. She and her child were both healthy and her daughter continued to grow even if it was at an outrageous rate. When Ni-Cio came for them, they would be ready.

Between now and then, her efforts to sabotage Travlor's health would go unnoticed, at least for a while. *If he starts to wonder what is happening, I'll just resume the healing touch with a more positive attitude. If I can just keep him yo-yoing until Ni-Cio is here, it could help him in some small way.*

She thought about names for their baby, but she didn't want to decide. That was a special moment that she wanted to be able to share with Ni-Cio. The baby kicked again and a single word appeared in her mind, *"yes..."* Astonished, Daria floundered around, almost losing her footing. *What? It can't be!* She looked down at her stomach.

Another kick, even harder, and another thought, *"yes..."*

Daria focused all her energy inward. Scanning her womb, she almost screamed. Her beautiful daughter was looking back at her. The child acknowledged her with a smile. Then another word whispered into Daria's mind. *"love ..."* The word was followed by a profound feeling of warmth that surrounded her heart like a caress.

Daria grabbed her stomach and danced around the shallow end. Hugging herself, she sent a tender thought. *"I love you!"* She watched in wonder as her daughter closed her eyes and floated back into her dreams. "Oh my God!"

Her mind reeled. It felt like her heart would burst from the infusion of her daughter's love and joy. Grinning like the Cheshire Cat, Daria retraced her steps out of the pool and grabbed her towel and robe. Her stomach rumbled as she dried her hair.

Laughing uproariously because her body was firmly in control and she could care less, she decided to try another compulsion. She issued the order. *"Lunch on the terrace, please. Travlor will join me ..."* She thought she should change, so she snuggled into her robe and wrapped the towel around her wet hair.

However, when she entered the foyer, the woman was waiting for her with a puzzled look on her face. As soon as she saw Daria, she lowered her gaze to the floor. Daria was surprised; the woman's response was certainly quicker than the previous one. "Thank you for meeting me. I am going to invite Travlor to join me for lunch. If you could set up a table on the terrace, I think the fresh air will do us both good."

The woman left without acknowledgement, but Daria wasn't bothered in the least. This was turning out to be one of the most memorable days of her life. Nevertheless, she still had to haul her body up the stairs and to her rooms. She smiled and waddled away as quickly as her bloated body would allow.

Chapter 48

Taking advantage of their al fresco lunch, Daria tried to engage Travlor in small talk. She thought that if she could somehow draw him out, she would find a clue as to why he carried so much pain. However, his heart remained closed tighter than a clam shell. She finally gave up and concentrated on the mouthwatering Columbian cuisine. Between bites, she did wonder at Travlor's preoccupation. He hadn't offered anything in the way of conversation. She studied him carefully and initiated another scan. Nothing was amiss. "Are you feeling all right?"

The man continued to eat and looked as though he wasn't going to talk at all. A few moments passed in which the only sounds punctuating the silence was the clink of silverware against china, the odd bird call, and the incessant buzz of Travlor's cell phone. When he finally lowered his knife and fork, his expression was odd. "I haven't felt as well as I normally do after one of your sessions." He shrugged and cut into another bite of meat. "Maybe you should think about changing our schedules. It would be better to administer the healings at closer intervals. I leave it to you to decide."

Unnerved, Daria glanced back at her plate. She shoved a forkful of food into her mouth and chewed until her jaws ached and the food had almost dissolved. She swallowed hard. She knew that if she didn't remain calm, Travlor would sense her unease.

Her silverware chimed against her plate as she let them rest. Nonchalantly, she placed her hands in her lap. "I just scanned your body and everything looks well. Can you explain what feels different?"

Travlor pushed his plate away with a big sigh and signaled the server to remove it. He pushed his chair out, straightened his legs and leaned back. "I just don't have the energy as before. It's an infinitesimal sensation. However, in prior sessions, I've been so rejuvenated that I have felt the years drop away. Maybe you're losing your touch."

Laughing as lightly as she could, Daria shook her head. "Maybe you're just aging faster than you knew."

Travlor rested his head on the back of the chair. "Ah, the marching of time. It comes to us all. At least I have enjoyed a stretch longer than most."

"Would you care to share how long?"

"Not in the least."

Daria considered Travlor as he rested. "Well, since you have seen so much of the world through your span of time, do you have any wisdom that you could share with me or something I could pass down to my daughter?"

A frown flitted across Travlor's face. Daria thought he would leave rather than answer the question. Instead, he sat up, pulled his chair back around and stared at her. "No one has ever asked me that."

Daria was so moved she almost reached out to touch him, but she stayed her hand. *How sad to have lived as long as he has and never have anyone explore his knowledge and wisdom. His is a very lonely heart.*

She waited for him to speak, but he was lost in thought, eyes closed, elbows on the table and head resting on the tops of his fists. Slight facial twitches were the only indication that he delved into his memories.

Scowling deeply, he absentmindedly picked up an errant tomato and chewed thoughtfully. "If I could share one thing with you, it would be this—love never wins the day. It is one step away from becoming the worst pain you have ever known in your life and it can turn on a dime. Don't trust it, don't look for it, and if you think you have found it ... by God run from it as fast as you possibly can and don't ever look back."

Daria gasped. She had never heard anything so jaded or sad in her life. She couldn't imagine what had happened to Travlor to make him feel that way. She wiped her mouth and slowly got to her feet. Pushing her chair away, she went around the table and faced Travlor. He stood up, head tilted at an angle. Daria stepped into him and before he could move away, she embraced him as close as her expanding belly would allow. She poured out all the love she held in her heart and prayed that he would feel it.

Travlor didn't move. Daria couldn't even detect the rise and fall of his chest to indicate that he still needed breath. She lifted her head and hesitantly lowered her arms. Like the statue on his church, Travlor remained unmoving, unblinking, gaze frozen toward the distant horizon. Daria backed away and smiled. She reached out one last time and stroked his arm, then she left him standing on the terrace, still as death.

Safe in her room, Daria tried to understand why Travlor had felt the lessening of her healing effect at their last session. It disappointed her to think that she might not be able to affect his health in even the most incremental of ways. The man was clearly a very different type of being. *He's more in tune with himself than I guessed. I'll have to discontinue my attempts for now. I'll try again when he's more distracted or maybe I can use the negative energy in every other session so that he doesn't maintain a constant state of health.*

She thought about the hug she gave him. "I can't believe he stood for it." She went to the window and absentmindedly stroked her abdomen. "What happened to hurt him so much that he feels safer wrapped in hate?"

The barren wasteland that stretched through his soul made her heart ache. She had wanted to comfort him in some small way and before she knew what she was doing, she was hugging him as hard as she could. "He has to know that he's not alone."

She addressed her baby. "Pain is an unavoidable part of life; there are no guarantees. But, my darling daughter, the beautiful alchemy is that if you keep loving with all your heart and soul and let it flow through your actions, it always comes back to you, and often in magical ways.

"I will always cherish the love I've received from your father, from friends, from animals and from this incredible earth. And it is this love that will sustain me forever." She lowered her voice to a whisper. "Remember, love is love, no matter the source."

She massaged her back and went to the bed. Propping her pillows, she eased down, brows tightly knit. "Travlor is an enigma, but love is the only key to unlock his heart."

Chapter 49

A WEEK PASSED AND Daria had not seen Travlor at all. Although they had discussed shorter durations between sessions and Travlor should have come to her by now, he remained barricaded behind closed doors. Her attempts to invite him to join her for meals had fallen on deaf ears and his guards had summarily dismissed her with rigid looks and cursory waves of their hand.

She couldn't resist goading one of the soldiers. "Where did you train, Buckingham Palace?" Not waiting for his reaction, she huffed off and that was when she decided to do something different.

Instead of waiting for Travlor, Daria created a full daily routine so that her time felt meaningful. Each morning, rain or shine, she took breakfast on the terrace. As the rain showers dripped to a finish, she went to the pool. There, she swam or read or basked in the sun, and she attempted simple compulsions. Some worked while others failed miserably. Nevertheless, she kept trying.

This particular afternoon, the heat built on top of the humidity and comfort was hard to find; however, Daria was determined to take in the gardens. She strolled through the vast maze of plants that ran haphazardly about the grounds. Bending to admire one of the fire-red hibiscus flowers, she heard a different voice. A young man was explaining to her jailers that he had a message for her only.

Curious, she watched as a painfully thin youth with bright hazel eyes and a kind face waded through her musclebound groupies. He came up to her and smiled. Deep dimples on each side of his face made him look even younger than his sixteen or seventeen years. Obviously he was another fervent volunteer, proud to serve the Messiah. Daria was dumbfounded when he actually addressed her.

"He requests your presence."

"Why?"

He shuffled his feet and oddly, the ground now held his undivided attention. It was obvious that he wasn't going to divulge anything else. She shrugged and tapped the new disciple on his shoulder. "I'll follow you." Her guards, whom she barely noticed anymore, fell in behind. Daria marveled and shook her head. *Travlor was right, the guards have become like shadows playing in the sunlight.* She threw a glance over her shoulder. "But you're still my jailers." She trudged after the youth as quickly as she could and they forged a path back to the house.

Reaching the stairway to Travlor's domain, Daria grabbed the handrail, hesitated, and grimaced. The stairs had become obstacles difficult to surmount. Since the baby had pushed up into her diaphragm, her oxygen intake suffered. She paused every forth step to catch her breath. Halfway up, she stopped and rubbed a stitch in her side. Travlor's men waited patiently while she huffed and puffed. She sent a thought to her daughter. *"Someday, I'll read you the story about the Three Little Pigs and you'll understand why I can play the part of the Big Bad Wolf so well..."* Still winded, she nodded and the group continued the trek up to Travlor's quarters.

The youth opened the door for her and then withdrew. Walking into Travlor's inner sanctum, Daria noticed how tired he looked. His pallor was grayer than it had been in quite some time. She thought that he was ready for a healing until his first words reached her.

"It is time for another miracle."

He hadn't even bothered to look up from his gargantuan pile of papers. She suddenly felt like the cornered canary, mesmerized, watching the cat's tail switch back and forth. In the cartoons, the cat always pounced, then with yellow feathers hanging from his mouth, slinked off to make more mischief.

Guardedly, she sat in the nearest chair staying well away from Travlor's desk. "What will it be this time, and why now?" She waited for the pounce.

"My men have located someone suited to my needs. This person is beyond famous and my healing will attract worldwide attention. It is time to cast my influence throughout Europe and possibly into North America."

His plans were being executed so easily she was still confounded. Initially, she had been skeptical because she had been naïve enough to believe that governments would be difficult, if not impossible, to topple. Since the inception of his mad schemes, governments, dictators, and puppet regimes had fallen away like wisps of clouds in a jet stream. Travlor himself hardly seemed ruffled. The information age had given him all the tools he needed and he was a master manipulator.

⊰ *Currents of Will* ⊱

Travlor's fame, along with his growing numbers of disciples, spread throughout the world like a plague. Tireless in their proselytizing, the true believers now carried his message throughout Mexico, Canada, Australia and Micronesia. His sermons blasted over the airwaves and through cyberspace with the speed of light, and people succumbed to his influence in unfathomable numbers.

Isolated from all but his closest disciples, he handpicked the men who now wrote and preached "his" sermons. His rise was dizzying. Daria inhaled deeply and held her breath for a few heartbeats. Then she released her words slowly, the way air seeps out of a tire. "Who needs the healing?"

Travlor continued writing. "Do not burden yourself with that small detail. However, for your information, we will be traveling by air. Be packed and ready to go in two days' time."

"All right, what kind of clothes will I need?"

"Warm."

"Anything else I should know?"

She never saw his face. Head bent low, he continued to skim the papers before him. "No."

Daria stood. "Am I to know what time we are departing?"

"Early morning. That is all."

Whether she wanted it to or not, the ball was rolling. With no idea who could possibly need her help or who would be so famous as to demand the world's attention, she shuffled back to her room.

Half-heartedly, she retrieved her suitcase, placed it on the bed, and started packing. She tried to think of a world figure sick enough to require a visit from the "Messiah."

As she was folding a red sweater, her head snapped up and she slapped both hands over her mouth. "Oh my God, that's who it is!"

Numbly, she sank down next to her suitcase. Her voice shook. "I'm wrong. It can't be." She hugged herself and rocked gently back and forth. No doubt about it, the cat had pounced.

The more she considered the possibility, the more sense it made. *How has he done it?* Then she caught herself. *Well, that's an idiotic thought.* And she almost laughed. *Maybe I've caught Travlor's crazy. But who else could it be?*

She shook her head, dazed and feeling that the weight of the world had suddenly dropped onto her shoulders. She got up and plodded back to the closet; at least now she knew what to pack.

Chapter 50

THEIR FLIGHT ACROSS the Atlantic had been uneventful and lacking in conversation. Travlor had been in heavy communication with his staff, making sure that all his orders, plans, and pretenses moved mercilessly forward.

On final approach, the jet descended toward Da Vinci airport. The Pontiff's private AW139 helicopter, a gift from the Italian air force, stood fueled and awaiting their arrival. As the jets' wheels kissed the tarmac, Daria watched the scenery flash by. The captain had been given immediate clearance, so upon landing, he quickly taxied next to the helicopter and powered down.

Instantly, people swarmed their plane, transferring luggage and ushering them, along with another phalanx of guards, to the air force chopper.

Cleared for takeoff, they were immediately airborne. A cardinal, sent to attend them, offered them a glass of champagne. Travlor accepted while Daria declined. Settling back in comfort, Travlor raised his glass in a toast. "Your health and that of the pope's."

Daria closed her eyes and rubbed the back of her neck. Travlor set his glass on the small table between them after appreciating a sample taste. "You might as well relax. How many people get to see the part of the Vatican that we'll be visiting?"

"It's not that." She moved closer to Travlor and whispered. "I'm tired of the lie. And I'm less enthusiastic with each healing that *you* perform."

Travlor's lips lifted in a sneer. "Must we go through this every time? You *will* follow my lead, stay as unobtrusive as possible, and heal the man. Do you understand?"

Her heart felt squeezed, like her ribs had shrunk two sizes. She waited to see if the tired muscle would continue pumping or would just shrivel up and quit. When she felt the next thump, she swallowed hard and looked out the window. She detested Travlor's masquerade, but if she didn't go through with it, she endangered the life of her child, and that was unthinkable. "How did you get in touch with the Vatican, anyway?"

"I didn't have to; they begged me to perform a healing on Il Papa. This will cement my hold on the rest of the predominately Catholic countries."

Resigned, she watched Italy, bathed in the splendor of an amber afternoon, unfold like a carpet beneath them. Lush green fields overflowing with sun-ripened vines flew by, and rooftops tiled in burnt sienna hues winked at her as the chopper blades rotated onward.

The flight wasn't long, maybe thirty minutes from departure to their arrival, but as soon as they landed, they were escorted into waiting limousines. A few of Travlor's elite guard stayed close, but made themselves as inconspicuous as possible.

The cars sped to an underground tunnel and soon came to a stop before a private entrance. Without any fanfare, they were taken to a plain set of elevators. Surrounded by both Travlor's and the pope's men, there was not enough room for all of them when the elevator doors opened. Travlor gestured for his men to follow in the next car and the heavy doors closed with a whisper.

Daria was properly subdued when the elevator doors opened and she stepped into the inner sanctum of the man considered by many to be the most powerful religious leader in the world.

She felt like Travlor's cynicism had rubbed off on her with her next thought. *Make that the second most powerful. Travlor's nest is feathered, he's moved in, planted roots, and will not be moved . . . now that's a mixed metaphor.*

The late afternoon sun highlighted the rich colors that dominated the beautiful room. Religious art graced the walls alongside Rembrandts, Monets, and even a Pollack. Frescoes adorned the ceilings and she wondered if Michelangelo had done the work. Furniture was covered in gleaming brocades, dark velvets, and bright silks.

Several cardinals were in attendance. One of the priests separated from the group and crossed the parquet floor to greet them, hand extended. His smile displayed white, even teeth and his eyes sparkled like emeralds in his lined face. His white hair set off his swarthy skin and strong features; he was a striking man. When he spoke, the hint of an Irish brogue was still quite melodious. "Welcome to His Holiness's private quarters. I am Father Patrick. I speak for us all when I thank you for coming."

Travlor took the man's hand and tried to return his smile. It looked to Daria like he had to exert a lot of effort to quirk his mouth out of its habitual frown. "I am glad to be of service."

"If you will come with me, I have refreshment to offer."

Travlor held his hand up. "That is not necessary. We have been well supplied on both legs of our journey."

The cardinal bowed his head, then stepping aside, lifted his arm in a welcoming gesture. "Then please, come with me; I will lead you to His Holiness."

Travlor jerked his chin once and fell in step with Father Patrick. Everyone else, including Daria, kept a careful distance as they followed.

Daria noted that each of the cardinals bowed his head in acknowledgment as they passed. Their expressions reflected awe tinged with doubt, but it was clear that they were cowed by Travlor's personage.

She wanted to kick their awe-filled backsides. Their obeisance was sickening and disheartening. She had hoped the pope's entourage would be a harder audience to convince, but Travlor hadn't even needed to compel them. They were already his, with or without their doubts.

Entering a darkened chamber, Travlor was taken to the bedside of the ailing pope. Daria peered around the men to get a look at the man who had headed the Catholic Church through decades of change and challenge.

She couldn't see much. The light was so dim that she couldn't even make out the pallor of the man swathed in covers up to his chin. She did a quick scan and saw that he was riddled with problems. It wasn't just one disease that plagued the poor man; his overworked system struggled under the weight of a lifetime of neglect.

Travlor didn't deign to look at the others; he knew his command would be obeyed. "Everyone but the girl must leave."

When the cardinal opened his mouth to protest, Travlor turned the full force of his gaze on the man. The scarlet robed priest backed away without another sound. He looked at his retinue, crooked a finger, and closely followed by the others, made a quick, silent exit.

Travlor turned back to the pontiff and Daria sidled up next to him. The sickly man barely had enough strength to draw a breath. She glanced at Travlor and he moved aside, motioning for her to start.

The mystical healing tones cut through the quiet, but were quickly muffled by the heavy fabrics used throughout the room. Nothing ever echoed in this place. Daria's hands moved over the length of the man's decrepit body. The range of issues that assailed his health were many; however, one by one, Daria removed each disease. After a couple of hours, she reached a point where she could do no more. He was so much healthier that it was likely he would live at least another twenty years.

She took Travlor's arm. Surprisingly, she didn't feel drained, which in itself was an incredible boon. She wondered if her ability had grown to a point where any but the most severe healing would tax her system. *Could my daughter and I have combined strengths? Is that even possible?* She would have to consider that idea, especially after the episode in the pool. Now, however, she was just grateful that she didn't have to be carried out on a stretcher.

Travlor prepared himself for his grand entrance and sailed through the door as though he had just wrought a miracle.

In essence, I suppose he has, Daria reflected. Meekly, following like a good minion, Daria kept to her role with unerring precision. She would not risk her baby again.

Travlor stopped before the gathered cardinals and made his pronouncement. "His Holiness rests comfortably. He will sleep deeply tonight. There is no need to administer any of the medications that crowd his nightstand. He will be with you for many years to come."

The men's faces lit up and their thoughts were as evident to Daria as their noses. *"We are in the presence of God!" "He is the true king of heaven!" "The new Messiah has appeared to save us all!" "The one man who walks the face of the earth in holy splendor! Hallowed be his name!"* They crowded around to kiss his hands.

A young man stood holding several dark vials, replicating an ancient ceremony recorded in the scriptures. On the floor next to him was a golden basin filled with water. He knelt reverently, opened each vial, and in turn, poured the contents into the water. The unmistakable essence of myrrh and frankincense rose into the room and teased Daria's senses. She detected another scent that she couldn't quite identify.

As the name of the other oil came to her, the young priest prostrated himself before Travlor in one swift motion.

Cardinal Patrick offered Travlor a chair. "He is prepared to wash your feet in the same manner that Jesus's feet were symbolically washed. It would be our honor to perform this sacred ceremony for you."

Travlor held up both hands. His voice dripped with honey and haughtiness. "While I appreciate your magnificent gesture, I must leave, a Messiah's work is never done."

The men were crestfallen, but quickly recovered. The cardinal led Travlor and company back to the elevators and pushed the button to summon the car. He took Travlor's hand and kissed it with all the fervor of the religious reborn. "Please come back. We are honored to be called your servants. It will not be long before the Church gives you your rightful sainthood."

The doors slid open and Travlor left without another word. Daria shook her head, but wisely kept her mouth shut.

Chapter 51

Landing again at Da Vinci, Travlor offered a suggestion to Daria. "I doubt you have been to Rome. How would you like a nighttime tour and then dinner in an old Italian restaurant with which I am very familiar?"

The man was a dichotomy. She never knew what to expect. Tired but feeling well, she accepted his offer. She didn't feel like climbing aboard the jet quite so soon. "That sounds wonderful. I would like that very much and it will give me a chance to stretch my legs."

The limo rolled over the tarmac to meet them as they ducked under the helicopter's churning blades. Travlor ordered his men to load their bags into the jet and wait for his return.

He helped Daria into their car. When he slid in next to her, she frowned, her suspicions aroused. "Why no detail tonight?"

Travlor snorted. "I had hoped to stay in Rome awhile. However, some matters have interrupted my plans and we are forced to return to Columbia. Before we do, I thought you would like to experience the Roman night." He rolled down his window and breathed deeply. "Ah, there's nothing quite like it. The art, the history, the women."

It was a small glimpse of a past that he never shared. She was hit by a crazy thought. *Maybe he's losing his mind. Oh, wait—that's already happened.*

She still didn't trust his motives. "I don't understand why you've dismissed the bodyguards. Aren't they supposed to be documenting your 'healings' and getting the word out?"

The window stayed down and cooling night breezes swirled through the car. Travlor still faced the window, breathing deeply. "My dear, I dismissed the guards as I tire of their presence. I don't need them to relate our mission. As a matter of fact, other than those of us on the plane, I didn't tell anyone of our Italian undertaking."

He looked back at Daria and when his long hair blew across his face, he raised the window and smoothed his tresses. He looked at her again, gray eyes glittering maliciously. "Don't you realize that those old men in their garish red dresses will spread the word faster than a small town gossip can spread the news about a philandering neighbor? Your healing pumped up a wasted old geezer and His Imminence will soon be replaced by a living saint." The bitter sarcasm lacing Travlor's voice was impressive.

Daria tried to match his tone. "You'd think that some infinitesimal amount of religious or spiritual teachings would've touched you at some point."

Travlor sniffed. "If they ever did, it was so long ago I can't remember." He pushed the window button again and the glass lowered, letting the Roman night swirl back into the car.

.......BREAKING NEWS.......
VATICAN PRESS SERVICE

Il Mondo

circolazione 245,000

By Enriqué Peroni   EPeroni@ilmondo.com

MAN PERFORMS MIRACLE HEALING!!!

Vatican Press Release

CATHOLIC COUNTRIES FOLLOW ITALY'S LEAD!!

Pope Abdicates as Head of Catholicism
Emphatically Issues Mandate
"He *IS* the New Messiah."
Urges Faithful to Renew Vows to Traylor!!!

FLASH...FLASH...FLASH...FLASH...FLASH...FLASH

EUROPE AT WAR!!!
FOLLOWERS of NEW MESSIAH IMPRISONED

.......BREAKING NEWS.......
AROUND THE WORLD

NEW MESSIAH REFUSES MEETING!!!
U.S., ENGLAND, FRANCE
ISSUE STRONG ULTIMATUM
Control Followers or Risk Nuclear Intervention!!!

Chapter 52

BACK FROM THEIR Italian excursion and secured safely within the complex, Travlor sequestered himself again. He hadn't ordered one healing since their return and Daria was jumpy. If he had an inkling that she was sabotaging his health, she would have heard about it. Nevertheless, she felt like she was waiting for the other shoe to drop. She decided that when he called for her again, she would give him nothing less than her best efforts. His guard would be up and all his senses would be functioning on high alert.

The days dragged even though she had resumed her original routine. As she went about her business, men hustled in and out of the house bearing the latest news. Daria was able to glean snippets of their reports, so she knew that countries and governments continued to succumb before the relentless machine that had become Travlor's "Armies of the New Messiah."

Outreach offices bloomed like weeds in the "newly acquired countries" and volunteers streamed to staff them by the busloads. Put into service immediately, they worked feverishly to further Travlor's cause. And so the machine went into maximum overdrive. "El Mesias" was everywhere.

Travlor's healing of the pope had done what even the vast armies of his faithful could not. People fell to their knees at the altar of his supposed divinity. The entire world, with the exception of the superpowers, was stepping into line without a whimper. Travlor was viral and people believed.

Seated on the terrace with a glass of Travlor's special juice nearby, Daria studied the people lining the gate. They were simple people, used to following a religion established long ago. Their hearts and souls cried out for something more in a world that seemed to turn a blind eye to so much suffering.

She sipped the sweet, refreshing liquid. *The healings we've— I've performed are enough. Especially when nothing like it has been seen in our time.*

She used a napkin to blot her brow and swipe the back of her neck. When she set her glass aside, she rearranged the clip holding her hair. She stood, seeking a trace of breeze to cool her, but the air was so still it seemed to be holding its breath. She viewed the mass of faithful followers crowding the gate. She was still puzzled, *I would think, out of all these people, that someone would question how and why this man just appeared out of nowhere. It's almost like they require someone outside themselves to save them from themselves.*

She wanted to shake them awake and scream. "Find it within yourselves! It is in your own heart and soul!"

The numbers of people joining his church defied description. And though she hated her part in the deception, she could do nothing about it. The staggering flood of followers illuminated just how lonely the world had become. Sorrowfully, she shook her head and left the terrace. She couldn't watch anymore.

Three days later, standing before her full length mirror, Daria was in a foul mood. "I'm going to need a wheelchair to get us around." She blew a blond strand of hair out of her eyes. Disgusted after the latest wardrobe replacement, she didn't know how she could get much bigger and stay upright. "Hopefully, there's a seamstress nearby that can keep me covered."

A knock sounded at her door, and without being asked in, Travlor made his entrance. "I need you to attend me."

Daria turned around and looked at the man. She was astonished to see how much he had aged. He shuffled to the bed, shoulders stooped, head low. Grimacing, he eased his pain-wracked body onto her bed. "I am ready."

She went to him and scanned. Shocked at the amount of decay, she had to hide her reaction. *I can't let him know the scope of deterioration.* She lowered her head and went to work, withholding nothing.

The session took longer than any of the previous ones, but she finally sang her way to the completion. She dragged a chair to the bedside and sat, keeping her voice low. "Just rest awhile. It will do you good."

Thinking he had fallen asleep, she went to retrieve a book that she had started. His voice startled her. She went back to the bed and took his hand. "What did you say?"

He swallowed and took a deep breath and tried again. "I feel better. But I know what is going on."

Daria froze and waited for the ax to fall.

"I am aging faster than even I thought possible. It may be that your efforts can't circumvent that process anymore."

Caught off balance, she released his hand and slumped into the chair with ill-concealed relief. "I'm not sure. You've missed so many sessions. I would have to believe that your aging is progressing at a rate that may seem fast to you, but is probably quite normal considering your age."

Travlor's eyes opened and he sat up under his own volition. "You may have something there." Daria was gratified to see that he needed no aid.

The Atlantean was quiet for a moment. "Events are starting to get out of hand. I have no choice but to continue to work as hard as I can."

"Would you care to tell me what is happening that would keep you away?"

A deep sigh rumbled from Travlor as he stood and stretched. "The United States is not falling under my control as easily as I had planned; neither is much of Europe. A while ago, the U. S. and European Union instituted sanctions against South America and Columbia in particular. There is talk that the U. S. is threatening nuclear armament should its people start joining my army.

"Europe, as one unit, has declared that no more news of me or my movement is to be disseminated on their airwaves. Governments are blocking ports of entry from anyone registered within my auspices and borders are closing faster than a junkie can inhale the last line of coke."

He crossed to the window and stared out. "If the U. S starts threatening nukes, China, Russia, and North Korea will not take it lightly." He turned to her, eyebrows raised, "World War III wouldn't be far behind."

Daria was stunned. "I can't believe you just told me all this. Why now?"

Travlor started as if swimming up from a dream. He went to the door and looked back. "I needed to unburden myself to someone and you are the only one I trust. Although that may have something to do with the way I have isolated you."

He grinned diabolically. "Don't think you'll be able to do anything with this tidbit. I will regain control and you will continue to attend my health."

He slammed the door behind him. His tread sounded much lighter and she knew that she had invigorated him. She ran her hands through her hair. She was desperate to think of some way to stop the maniacal man. "There's got to be a way. I just have to keep looking."

...FLASH...FLASH...FLASH...FLASH...FLASH...FLASH...

...ON TWO...DEFCON TWO...DEFCON TWO...DEFCON TU...

BORDERS CLOSED

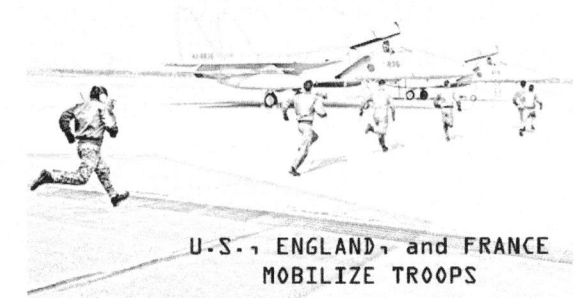

U.S., ENGLAND, and FRANCE MOBILIZE TROOPS

MIDDLE EAST NEWS CENTER

MIDDLE EAST, INDIA BOW TO TRAVLOR!!!

Chapter 53

THE MONTH HAD flown by; however, Ni-Cio was satisfied. The compound was well supplied and stocked with everything his people could possibly need during his absence. He was particularly gratified to see how close they were to becoming self-sustaining should his mission fail. It was not something he considered during his waking hours. But, alone at night he was assailed by nightmares, making sleep futile.

Admiring the work Rogert and his team had effected in Atlantis, Ni-Cio appreciated that vestiges of their old life connected so seamlessly with the new. The Great Hall of Poseidon had risen again, its old grandeur re-established. New tapestries replaced their ruined predecessors and traced their history from the sinking all the way to the last battle waged within their hallowed walls.

Ni-Cio wandered through the renovated kitchens and halls and took great pride in the strength and fortitude of his people. If he and his companions didn't return, his fledgling colony would not only survive, they would once again thrive, whether their choice was to return to Atlantis or to continue living in the compound, topside. That knowledge alone gave him comfort.

He walked to the nearest entry portal and retrieved his biosphere. He had thought to take one last swim, but he was restless. He had done all he could to aid his people; now he needed his mission to get underway. "My heart, we will take that swim together when you are back in my arms."

He stepped into the craft and the hatch materialized. Rocketing out into open ocean, the dark water flowed passed his 'sphere and soothed him. The sea, always willing to share her mysteries and her delights, made him feel less burdened and his spirits rose. *"I am coming love. We have a good idea of your location and once we have entered Barranquilla, we will find our way to you. You are my heart, always . . ."*

Evan waded into the surf as Ni-Cio's biosphere surfaced. He helped his friend disembark, then they walked to shore holding the biosphere high enough that it would no longer be buffeted by the waves. They stowed it under the copse of trees in its assigned space and Evan dusted sand from his hands. "So, we are ready?"

Ni-Cio nodded. "We leave tomorrow. With only twenty men, two 'spheres will hold us, but we will take a third as we will need a spare."

They finalized departure plans as they walked up the trail to the compound. Following behind, Evan did a quick calculation. "With an early start, we should reach Barranquilla by mid-morning."

Ni-Cio glanced over his shoulder. "Good. We will moor in deep water and swim to shore. Once you have us masked, we will circulate through town. With all the notoriety, I am certain we will discover the location of Travlor's hideout; however, with your ability to compel people, the onus may be on you to glean the most information."

"I don't think it will take long."

Ni-Cio stopped and turned around. "It had better not, with the proliferation of nuclear missiles taking aim, the United States and Russia, China, and North Korea are ratcheting up their responses. Borders have closed all over the planet, and Travlor is on the verge of starting World War III."

Evan nodded. "But think about it Ni-Cio—he has to be weakening because of the compulsions he must maintain. It's a superlative drain on his energy."

Ni-Cio looked out across the sea. Lost in thought, he contemplated Evan's statement. He had been so busy with the preparations for his people that he hadn't considered the drain Travlor had placed on his dwindling supply of energy. He watched Evan, "I believe the shift of followers from the Catholic Church had to influence the number of people disengaging from other religions. So, maybe he has not had to compel as many as we originally thought. It is possible that because of Daria's healing, his energy has ceased ebbing and is now flowing as easily as a fish swims with the current." Ni-Cio turned his attention back to the trail and continued the climb.

Evan fell in behind. "That idea occurred to me as well, which in itself is terrifying. If his energy is high, he will be in talks with the Presidents of China, Russia, and the US, as well as the UN, and Prime Ministers of the European block. Unfortunately, if he's too weak to compel the leaders and they don't agree to his terms, the man is mad enough to say damn the consequences and instigate a nuclear war to achieve his goals."

Ni-Cio reached the trail's summit and turned again. The waves cascading onto the beach below mirrored his restlessness. "Evan, your father does not frighten me and though he certainly would not be the first invader in history to throw caution aside, world domination is not a new idea. Our plans are sound; we will stop him."

Evan crossed his arms and shook his head. "Then we'd better get to his hideout ASAP or there'll be nothing left to rescue … anywhere."

Evan spiraled down into his own dread of Travlor. His friends had experienced the lengths to which the man was willing to go to achieve his aims. Even though Ni-Cio wasn't afraid of Travlor, he wasn't sure he realized just how insane his father really was.

Chapter 54

SLAMMING THE RECEIVER down, Travlor pushed away from his desk, stood up, and ran to the door. When he burst into the hall, his men jumped to attention. "Get me that woman and get her now!"

One of the men took off at a dead run. Travlor turned around, slammed the door shut and started pacing, hands clasped behind his back. *I can't afford to kill that betrayer yet!*

It wasn't long before he heard a frantic knock. "Enter!"

Daria stepped into the breaking storm. Travlor whirled around and pointed, his hand shaking. "You! YOU!"

She blinked hard and took a step back. Travlor saw the fear in her eyes and he circled her like a shark. "I have had all of you that I could possibly need in several lifetimes …" He caught himself before he started stuttering like a broken record. Still, the words poured from him like projectile vomit. "I had started to trust you and you betrayed me! Just like all the others. I would kill you if I didn't need you! It is my misfortune to have to wait until that … that spawn spews out of you!"

He stopped for breath and Daria took her chance. "What have I done?"

Travlor grappled with the sides of his head, wanting to tear his hair out by the roots. Rigidly, he clasped his hands behind his back in an effort to keep them from the woman's throat. "It finally occurred to me! I don't know how you figured it out, but you decreased the power of your healings so that instead of increasing my energy and therefore my *LIFE*, I was sliding backwards in incremental degrees! Did you think I wouldn't notice at some point?"

Her arms wound about her stomach and she paled. "I ... I ..." She stopped.

Travlor towered over her. "You have no excuse! You are just like the others! Evan's mother, the bitch, and Na-Kai, that pontificating fool!"

He ordered himself to walk away. He grabbed the back of a nearby chair to steady himself. "No, you're worse ... you're like ..." An eerie calm settled over him and he faced the vile topsider. "You are just like my father."

He sank into the chair and covered his face with his hands. Rubbing his eyes as hard as he could, he tried to stem the tidal wave of rage. "There has not been one person in my life that hasn't deserted me or betrayed me. But *you* are the worst." He raised his head and grimaced. "Your pathetic attempts to slither into my heart bring to mind a viper that steals through the trees and settles to wait. The moment the parent leaves the nest, he strikes the unprotected offspring."

Daria took a step but Travlor held up his hand. "Do not even think of coming any closer." He lowered his head. Unable to stop himself, his pent up feelings poured out of their own accord. "I *never* should have gone back to Atlantis. I didn't have to—they could never have found me. But I did, stupid fool that I was! I stood in front of the Council of Ten and I begged, *begged* them to let me live my life topside! She was to give birth any moment and she was so scared. Her pregnancy had not been easy."

A deep sob escaped, shaking his chest. "She didn't want me to leave her!" He looked up wildly. "I took her in my arms as she lay on the hospital bed and promised her it would be all right. I said that I would only be gone long enough to inform the council that I wanted to live topside. That I wanted to create a life I NEVER HAD!"

Travlor leapt out of the chair as if he was still addressing the council. "It will be all right? Marik I trusted you to lead the others in what was right! It was what I deserved after so many years of doing my godforsaken duty!"

His rage erupted again as he refocused on Daria. He pounded his chest with a fist as he screamed each statement. "My wife died because they imprisoned me! There was nothing I could do to help her! Na-Kai even blocked my thoughts and I could've killed the child before she delivered! I could have saved her!"

His chest heaved and his knees gave way. Travlor fell to the floor. Hot tears streamed down his face and stuck in his throat, inducing such a coughing fit that he couldn't inhale. He gagged and drool pooled between his hands, darkening the carpet like blood. He drew a ragged breath, but he choked so hard, she thought he would suffocate. As he tried to drag a breath into his burning lungs, he felt a gentle touch suffuse his body. It calmed him enough so that he sucked oxygen like a drowning man coming up for his last breath.

The tympani rhythm of his heart that had threatened to break through his chest slowed. He was able to breathe again. Feeling a deep lethargy seep into the marrow of his bones, he yawned. His eyelids fluttered and closed. Surrounded by black, Travlor plummeted to the floor.

Daria cautiously approached. She scanned him and was relieved to see that he slept comfortably. She pulled a chair next to his inert form and shakily lowered herself onto the seat.

She wept. The breadth of Travlor's pain was as vast as space. It seemed never-ending. The lengths to which he would've gone in order to be with the woman he loved made him more human.

Daria wiped her eyes with the backs of her hands and slowly began the healing notes. She stroked the air above Travlor. She focused on his heart and mind and tried, with the force of her entire being, to help heal his broken heart.

She worked so long and so intently, that when she felt the first signs of the energy drain, she refused to stop. Sweat beaded at her hairline and trickled down her brows until it ran into her eyes. Blinking the sting away, she still refused to stop. She worked until she could no longer hold her arms up. Falling to her sides, arms dangling uselessly, she tried to keep her intonations going, but her voice cracked. She no longer had the strength to push the tones out.

Slumping back into the chair, despair enveloped her. *I have failed. Why did I think I could possibly help this man? It is beyond my abilities and he is now beyond my reach.* Her eyelids closed and she joined Travlor in a dreamless sleep.

Chapter 55

Disturbed by a far-off sound, Daria climbed toward consciousness. When she was finally able to focus, she realized that someone was at the office door. She glanced down at Travlor. He still slept. Blearily avoiding his sleeping form, she crossed the room to admit the person that had interrupted her rest. It was one of the generals. She didn't know or care which one.

Seeing Travlor on the floor, the man barged past her and into the room. He bent down, hurriedly searching for Travlor's pulse. "What have you done?" He glared at Daria and back at Travlor.

"He was highly agitated so I administered a sleeping pill. He needs rest. As you know, he has pushed himself too hard, rarely sleeping. It was high time someone helped him to do that." She wasn't sure the man would believe her, but again, she didn't care. She had calmed Travlor the only way she could. And now that she thought about it, the sleep would indeed help him. Whether she had eased any of his pain was doubtful. All she knew was that she didn't want to be there when he woke up.

"I'm going back to my rooms. Have your men get him into bed. Make him comfortable and order a tray to be brought up. He'll probably sleep through the rest of the afternoon and into the night. But he'll need food as soon as he wakes." Not looking as to whether the general affirmed her instructions or not, she left Travlor's headquarters as fast as her swollen feet could carry her.

When she entered her rooms, she was so tired that she had to make herself pick up the phone and request the food that she knew her body required. The phone fell out of her grasp and she just managed to haul herself to the bed before her body pitched forward.

She rolled onto the mattress, almost too tired to close her eyes. Her heart actually ached, but she couldn't stand to feel Travlor's pain anymore. She released him from her thoughts and her lids closed. Daria willingly slid back into the comfort of sleep.

Chapter 56

ROUSING HIMSELF, TRAVLOR was surprised to find that he was in bed. He couldn't remember how he had gotten there. He stretched and as his mind started to clear, the scene with Daria swam back into focus. *What was the aftermath? The infernal woman didn't seem the least bit traumatized. And why can't I remember falling asleep?* He lurched up. *She bloody well better not have tampered with anything.*

He searched his body and could detect nothing amiss. He scratched his head. *Why do I feel less disturbed about her betrayal?* He threw the covers aside and got out of bed. Still in his clothes of the day before, he went to his bathroom and disrobed. He scowled. *And remarkably enough, I feel less inclined to kill her.* That in itself was perplexing.

Catching a glimpse of himself in the mirror, he stopped. Turning his face left and then right, he thought he was seeing things. His skin was a bit flushed. He laughed. "Flushed may be too hopeful a description. But definitely less gray."

He stepped into the shower, turning it on full blast and as hot as it would go. He wondered at the fact that his mind wasn't in turmoil as he went through his morning ritual. He felt almost … relaxed. *What the hell did she do to me? Bah, it was the sleep. I haven't had enough of it lately.*

He felt reenergized and could it be … Optimistic? *Wait a moment, don't get carried away.* He admonished himself. *Maybe I should consider letting her healings continue. The topsider wouldn't dare cross me again. She may even elevate me to more health than I initially thought. I do believe the she devil will work twice as hard as before.*

Slightly annoyed, he turned off the water, stepped out of the shower and grabbed a towel. *I'm tired of thinking about the bloody woman. She disturbs my equilibrium.*

Running through a list of emergency calls that had to be made, his day was planned before he finished dressing. Only then did he spot the tray of food. Suddenly ravenous, he threw his shirt on, not stopping to button it or tuck it in before he hurried to the table. He was starving and he started eating so fast that he hardly chewed. *At least someone has their head on straight.*

When he had completed his meal and finished dressing, he threw open the door and barked. "Get the generals assembled. I want them here within the hour from wherever the hell they are. If it's war they want, then its war they'll get!"

Men rushed down the halls, dragging out cellphones and setting fires under other backsides. Travlor slammed his door, clapped his hands once and crossed to his desk. He picked up the handset on his landline. "Get me the president," he snarled. "Yes! Of the Estados Unidos!"

He hung up and sank back in his chair, hands behind his head. *Those bastards are playing a game with no idea of the rules. If it's brinkmanship they want, I'm their man.*

Chapter 57

AROUND THE WORLD, headlines shrieked:

WAR IMMINENT!

U.S. RESPONDS TO NUCLEAR THREATS

DEFENSE DEPT. SETS READINESS ONE

Travlor threw the paper aside. By God he was ready. He wasn't worried about his safety; he could shield himself to withstand anything those bastards threw at him. But, it was a crapshoot as to how many topsiders he could shield. *Not to worry. I will inherit the earth, even if I'm the last man standing.*

He rocked back in his chair and swiveled to look out the window, then stood and raised his arms. "I will not to be deterred nor will I be thwarted. This battle of wills, I *will* win ... one way or another!"

Daria woke feeling much better. She lay still for a while and analyzed the scene that had unfolded in Travlor's quarters. He had said something about going before the council and begging to be released to live topside. She struggled upright and rested her back against the headboard. *Ni-Cio! I remember what you told me!*

When she was new to Atlantis, Ni-Cio had rescued her from her first meeting with Travlor, but she had been curious about the man. Ni-Cio explained that Travlor had come before the High Council and informed them that the woman and child had both died due to complications in delivery. *He didn't beg them to let him go to her! Why would he do that? Why would he lie?*

She got out of bed and noticed the phone lying on the floor. *I was really tired.* She strained to reach the cord and hoisted the phone back to the desk. She depressed the receiver and dialed.

She ordered breakfast and then went to the bathroom to ready herself. *I have no idea how Travlor will react to the healing. He might feel better, but he could be angrier, although I doubt that's even possible.*

Through with her grooming, she waited for her food as she gazed out the window. *Things are an incredible mess. How the man has brought the world into the net he has cast is beyond me.*

War is coming and Travlor must be stopped. But what can I do now that I can no longer weaken him? I don't even know the truth of his past. Maybe the woman died, maybe she didn't. Evan certainly is alive. What really happened?

She wrapped her arms around her stomach. "Good morning, my sweet. I know how Travlor feels about loving someone so much that you would be willing to give your life. You are safe and loved and wanted, always." A picture of tiny arms wrapped around her neck and a tiny head resting against her cheek made her smile. She sent an answering thought back to her daughter. *"Thank you, my most precious child..."*

The food arrived and she shambled to the door. She was surprised to be greeted by a new face. Without thinking, she blurted, "Who are you?"

A lovely Latina with laughing brown eyes and long wavy hair stood in the doorway. Her soft curves probably enticed the eye of many men. She carried the tray gracefully to Daria's table and set it down with a bright smile. "I am Graziella."

Startled, Daria stammered in abundance before she collected her wits. "You, you're speaking to me?"

Graziella moved the food from the tray. "Of course, why not?"

Daria didn't know what was going on, but she seized the opportunity. "Do you have news of what's going on in the world?"

Fright leapt into Graziella's brown eyes. Picking up the tray, she prepared to leave.

Daria couldn't give up; she pushed the edge of the envelope. "No, please, I have to know. How close are we to war?"

The woman backed up in panic and held the tray to her chest as one would hold a shield. "It is madness!" She whispered fiercely. "The whole world is on the brink! The United States and Europe are terrified of the Savior. Russia refused to open a discourse. China and North Korea are threatening a nuclear strike! Everybody has missiles aimed in every direction! War is coming!"

Her eyes were wide and her full lips were set in a grim line. "I do not understand. Why are these countries so afraid? He is the Messiah, returned as predicted in the Holy Bible. Their fear has escalated into panic because they see that they cannot control him. They do not want to lose the power they have. But when the fighting starts—and it will—we will defend him at all costs." Graziella turned to go.

Daria grabbed her arm. "How is it you are allowed to talk to me?"

Puzzled by Daria's question, Graziella licked her lips and tried to pry her hands away. "I ... no one told me not to." Afraid she had broken a rule that she hadn't known about, she jerked out of Daria's grasp and fled the room. The door swung closed after her retreating form.

Alone with her thoughts, Daria massaged her temples and sat on the chair next to the desk. *It's worse than I imagined!*

She tried to lean forward but it was too uncomfortable. Time was running out. She needed Ni-Cio now. *"My love, if you can hear me, I need you. Travlor is out of control. If his will does not prevail, he is bent is on total destruction! Oh my God, where are you?"*

"Hold Daria! We are coming! Stay strong—it is not long now!"

Shock, fear, joy, and sorrow tore through her until she thought she would run screaming from the room. *Ni-Cio, nearby?*

Her heart thudded in her ears and the baby kicked so hard that she had to press her tiny foot from beneath her ribs. Her breath came in huge gulps until she almost hyperventilated. *I have to calm myself.* She had an uncontrollable desire to run into the jungle until it swallowed her whole.

Deliberately, she slowed her breathing before she responded. She went to the window, her heart on fire. *"I don't know how Travlor's block has been breached but I am here and I will wait. Be careful ... he is sinking into total madness and he doesn't care if he is destroyed as long as he takes everyone and everything with him. He will not stop ..."*

Ni-Cio's reply soothed her torment. *"Do not fear; there is always hope. Keep yourself and our daughter safe. We will find a way ..."*

Four long, anxious months had passed since she had been taken. All the emotions that had been held in check finally surfaced. She put her head in her hands and sobbed with relief. When she was able to find her voice, she whispered to their child. "Your father will be here soon."

Their daughter moved gently inside her womb. Daria put a hand on top of her stomach. "There is *always* hope and if anyone can stop this insanity, the men to do it are coming." Hungry, Daria pulled the chair up to the desk and ate voraciously.

Chapter 58

Having reached their destination much sooner than expected, Ni-Cio and Evan were hidden inside a small gas station bathroom in order to figure out logistics. Masked so that they were invisible to any but each other, the rest of the men waited in back of the station.

As Evan was the only one with a license, he and Ni-Cio were trying to come up with an idea as to how they could acquire a vehicle large enough to carry everyone. Suddenly, Ni-Cio stared off into space, mouth agape. Evan grabbed his shoulders. "Are you all right? You look like you've seen a ghost!"

Ni-Cio focused again and Evan dropped his hands. A smile lit Ni-Cio's face like the sun. "I have just heard from Daria!" His voice was filled with awe as trails of yellow and orange streaks raced up and over his face. His joy was evident. "Somehow, Travlor no longer blocks our thoughts!"

He let loose an Atlantean howl and clapped his hands. "Daria is well, our daughter is well and we are almost to them!" Evan stepped back as Ni-Cio paced the small bathroom like a caged tiger. A dark frown replaced the smile. "Daria says that Travlor has lost his mind."

Ni-Cio stopped his rapid circling and faced Evan. "Evan, your father is out of control. Time is no longer on our side. We must hurry. Let us depart and find their whereabouts."

He started for the door, but Evan stopped him. "Ni-Cio, we have to figure out how to move the men and we need food. We have to eat before we can do anything else."

"By the gods Evan, you are right. I race ahead of myself and forget the needs of my men. But there is not a moment to lose. What do you suggest?"

Evan perched on the stained sink and ran a hand through his hair. "We're going to need a pile of food, which won't be easy to provide. The issue of how we get everyone there has to wait."

Considering their dilemma, Evan rubbed his chin and worked the problem. "Just might do the trick."

"What are you thinking?" Ni-Co was extremely worried about Daria's safety and he was impatient to get started.

Evan stood, "If we could, uh … requisition … a truck, we could load it up with enough food to fuel us for a while."

Nodding, Ni-Cio frowned. "How do we procure this vehicle?"

With a big sigh, Evan went to the door and unlocked it. "As a time saving measure, I steal it."

Walking into the sunlight, Evan masked Ni-Cio. They rounded the station and Ni-Cio sent his orders. *We are all masked now. Spread out and find Travlor's whereabouts and meet back here in …* " He looked questioningly at Evan.

"An hour should do it …"

"One hour... we will know something by then. We leave, but we will stop on the way to refuel. Our plans must be executed quickly. Questions?"

The men were ready for action. With no questions, they took off. Ni-Cio grabbed Evan in a bear hug. *"Good luck, my friend..."*

"I'll be back soon..."

They departed towards their chosen destinations.

Chapter 59

WITH HIS HANDS IN his pockets, Evan tried to look nonchalant as he scoped the parking lot. Clunkers and luxury cars were mixed in together. There were a lot of trucks, but since he knew nothing about stealing a vehicle, his needs were specific. He needed something that was unlocked, preferably with the keys left inside. His education had not included any information on how to hotwire a car.

He strolled through the lot, casually eyeing interiors. One possibility caught his attention—parked in a corner, an older truck with an attached camper shell looked fairly reliable. *Better than the jalopy at the compound.*

Evan walked to the cab and tried the handle. It was unlocked. The door opened, accompanied by a loud cracking sound. Praying no one had noticed, Evan slipped inside and hauled the door closed.

No keys in the ignition. He lowered the visor. No luck. The glove box? Nothing. With his nerves starting to fray, sweat trickled down his back. He did his best to ignore the need to scratch and rummaged under the driver's seat. Exasperated, he thumped the steering wheel and exited the truck. "What the hell am I going to do?"

Then it hit him. Travlor's mercenaries had hidden their keys outside their vehicles in case of emergency. Surreptitiously, he walked around the truck feeling under the fenders of each tire. The third attempt yielded treasure. Evan pulled out a single scratched-up key.

Hopping in, he inserted the key and pumped the gas. "God, don't let this be like the compound truck." He turned the ignition.

The engine sprang to life. Shifting gears, he drove carefully out of the lot, shoulders hunched almost to his ears as he anticipated the cries of alarm that would follow in the wake of his taillights. However, he turned onto the thoroughfare and drove away without incident.

Accelerating through the morning traffic, Evan drove as fast as he dared. It wasn't long before he spotted a good sized restaurant. "That should work." He downshifted and found an unobtrusive spot, turned off the truck, and sprang from the cab. He took the key with him.

The restaurant was fairly empty, the early morning rush having come and gone. There were a few stragglers swapping stories over coffee and a couple of waitresses were clearing and cleaning the tables.

Evan went to the counter. A gray haired, heavy-set woman appeared and handed him a menu. From beneath the counter, she retrieved a cup and saucer. After filling it with hot coffee, she returned.

Evan was grateful for the caffeine even though his adrenaline was pumping enough. He blew across the top of the coffee and still nearly burned himself as the piping hot brew drained down his throat. The waitress brought water and stood, pad in hand. He set the cup down. "English?"

She blew out her cheeks and with a small downturn of her mouth, nodded. "Si, un poco."

Evan pointed at the food then told her how many orders. The woman finished writing and looked up. "Ees, many, eh?"

"Muy pronto, por favor." Evan sipped his coffee.

Eyebrows raised, pencil shoved in her hair, the waitress rushed to the kitchen. When she came back, she held up both hands, extending her fingers. She flashed her hands twice. "Veinte minutos."

Evan repeated her gesture. "Twenty minutes?"

A quick nod and she left to help in the kitchen.

He sipped his coffee and did his best to be patient until the order was finally ready. The waitress came around the kitchen corner with a double stacked, wheeled cart, followed by a boy and then a man, both similarly encumbered. Wheels creaked and metal groaned.

At the register, Evan paid the bill and signaled everyone to follow. The carts bounced over the rough pavement, but they made it to the truck where Evan opened the tailgate and helped load. Once they were finished, Evan took out his wallet and handed each of the workers a substantial tip. With grateful smiles, they dragged their carts away.

Out on the busy streets, Evan found his way back to the designated meeting spot. He knew the men would be more than ready for food. His own stomach had started objecting quite a while ago.

Evan couldn't help worrying as he turned into a back alley. "How the hell are we going to get everybody there?"

He pulled up to the group and stopped. "*Ni-Cio, I have food, but I still don't have any idea how are we going to move the men…*"

Ni-Cio disengaged from his friends and pointed behind the truck. "*Do not worry… we have found transport! There is an abandoned building two blocks over. We will meet you there. We will eat and then I will explain…*" A picture of vacant offices came to mind and Evan nodded. He threw the truck in reverse.

He parked as near to a door as possible when he reached the run-down complex. The men were already there and had managed to get the entrance open.

Evan surveyed the area. It was fairly abandoned; the people he saw were engaged in other activities and hadn't even cared enough to look up. He unmasked the group of men who had crowded around the truck. He and Ni-Cio climbed into the back and handed out the containers. Once everybody's arms were full, they hurried back to the offices.

Inside, spreading out over the floor, the Atlanteans quickly devoured their food. When they were down to the last scraps, Ni-Cio addressed Evan. "There is a tour bus that leaves within the hour. It is taking people to Travlor's church. Travlor's residence is not far from there."

Ni-Cio put his takeout box on the floor and threw his crumpled napkin on top of it. "The church is about a four hour drive from here, somewhere in the mountains. I asked the tour operator if there was room for twenty people, but he said that there were only eleven seats left. It was my thought that the vehicle you have found will provide enough room to carry the rest of us."

Evan wiped his mouth. "Excellent work!"

"There is a slight problem." Ni-Cio held out his palms.

"Yes?" Evan didn't understand.

"We reserved the tickets, but we could not pay for them."

Evan looked at his watch. "Alright, let's load up the men who will be going on the bus." He stood up and dusted his pants.

Ni-Cio quickly chose the riders, who followed Evan out the door. Before he left, Evan looked over his shoulder, "I'll be back soon. Be ready to load up."

It seemed that the path was opening before them.

Chapter 60

STAYING IN THE relative safety of her rooms, Daria did not dare venture out. She couldn't contain the riotous thoughts spinning through her mind and her heart pounded like a runaway freight train. Walking in circles, she paused every now and then to stare out the window, heart in her throat. *When?* She paced until she was forced to lie down. The baby weight made her body ache in places she didn't even know she had.

Her moods were out of control. Swinging from the heights of joy to the depths of fear, her body alternately burned with fever or froze so that her fingers became numb.

With nerves stretched tighter than piano wire, she tried to read, but the book was useless as a distraction. She reread the same sentence over and over and over until, frustrated beyond belief, she had thrown the book across the room.

She was terrified of sending a thought-form. She refused to interfere in the slightest way with Ni-Cio's efforts. With no idea where he was or how much longer it would be, she tried to imagine what they were doing.

At one point, she moaned and dropped her head to her hands. "And I thought Travlor was crazy. I'm driving myself insane!"

The morning dragged and the clock on the nightstand indicated just how slowly time was passing. "Only nine-thirty."

She shivered in a burst of anticipation, the feel of Ni-Cio's arms around her was almost a reality. "Hurry, my love."

Unable to stare at the same four walls a minute longer, she burst out the door, startling her entourage. Without paying any attention to their presence, she headed outside.

On the terrace, she stopped to survey the surroundings. Guards were everywhere. The men in the towers marched back and forth in a constant vigil and were on high alert. Their roving eyes never rested as they scoped the area for anything that might present a threat. The road, once crowded with the religious, was now clogged with military tanks, trucks, and jeeps. Outside the walls, she heard the sound of men running drills. They were as comfortable with the dark interior of the forbidding jungle as the animals that inhabited it.

She couldn't see how Ni-Cio would gain entrance. She lowered herself down the steps, refusing the arm offered by one of her guards.

As she strolled through the gardens, she tried to take in the perfumed air, but all she smelled was her groupies. The humidity was relentless and everyone perspired like they had run a marathon. She tried to increase the distance between them, but the men stayed close.

A riot of colors proliferated in the helter-skelter gardens. She let her fingers trail over some of the flowers. Their different textures tickled her palm and yellow pollen stuck to her hand.

As she swiped her hand down her shirt, a thought wound through her mind.

"We are moving. We will be arriving at the church Travlor built. Do you know how far you are from there?"

Losing her footing, she nearly stumbled. One of the men bumped her as he was trying to catch her, and she almost fell down. He grabbed her shoulders to keep her upright. Covering her anxiety, Daria signaled that she was all right. "Please, can you give me some space?" The unit moved a few feet away and until she was back in the house, that would be all the space they would allow. Satisfied, she lowered her face to a flower, taking her time and inhaling deeply. *"Love, it is not far. The drive is about thirty minutes, but the road is dirt and narrow and bordered on both sides with dense jungle. When you reach the church, there will be a large parking area, most of which will be taken up by military..."*

"I understand. Do not concern yourself. Aris has come up with a very good plan. We leave soon. I will let you know when we have reached the church. You are my heart. Look to yourself and our child..."

"Oh, Ni-Cio, you are my heart too. I can't be without you. Look to yourself... I will be ready..."

Chapter 61

EVAN GOT THE ELEVEN Atlanteans situated on the bus while Ni-Cio loaded the rest of the men into the back of the truck. Aris had the dubious honor of riding up front in the middle. While not easy and certainly not comfortable, their chosen modes of transportation would get them where they needed to go and that was all Ni-Cio cared about.

Wearing their bioskins beneath topsider clothes, the men were as comfortable in the humid climate as they were going to get. Ni-Cio closed the tailgate but left the window up so that his men would get some type of circulation. He went around to the passenger side and jumped in.

Evan started the truck and swung the vehicle around. "The bus is waiting for a few more people. It should not be more than five minutes before they depart."

He drove to a place behind the bus and waited for the rusty exhaust pipe to begin belching black smoke.

When the last of the faithful were ushered on, the driver climbed in after them. In a smelly cloud of fumes, the bus chugged into traffic. Evan stayed right on its tail.

For the men in the back of the truck, the journey was not easy. Two hours into the drive, Evan halted so that they could rotate. They reacquired the bus as the road started its climb into the lower mountain ranges of the Andes.

Another hour trailed by and Evan stopped again. As they were now on the only road leading to Travlor's church, they no longer worried about staying close. However, it wasn't hard to catch up to the bus. They had reached an elevation of twenty-five hundred feet and the bus seemed to be gasping for air. The driver wasn't able to coax anymore speed from the vehicle, which was just as well, as the road was flanked on one side by the mountain, while the other side plummeted in a sea of green into a steeply angled ravine. At times, it looked to Evan like the two wheels of the wide bus hovered over the precipitous drop. He had no problem hugging the mountainside until they had made the summit and the road flattened out.

Another couple of hours passed before the church finally came into view. Evan and Ni-Cio had expected a number of military vehicles but the phalanx surrounding the church was impressive. Evan parked between two Humvees and everyone exited the truck as quickly as possible.

The bus pulled up in front of the church and passengers poured out, cameras and phones snapping non-stop. Gawking like the other tourists, Ni-Cio's crew caught up to the other Atlanteans and they spread through the crowd, following the tour guide into the vestibule.

The gaudy splendor that greeted them elicited a whistle from Evan. "I never expected this. If I didn't know him, this monument would make me think he *was* something saintly."

The number of people in attendance was astounding, the pews were packed. Their guide said that the church could hold two thousand people but to Ni-Cio, it seemed that number had been far surpassed. *"As soon as the group starts its return to the bus, Evan will inform the guide that we have found other means of travel. Once that is done, gather back at the truck and we will initiate our next steps..."*

His men signaled their agreement, and in order to lessen the impression of the size of their group, wandered off in twos and threes. Ni-Cio and Evan stayed behind and found two available seats. They slid into the pew. As if in prayer, Ni-Cio continued going over their plan. *"When we are at the truck, step into the jungle and divest yourselves of your topside clothing. Masked as soldiers, we will find our way to a detail that is being dispatched to the complex..."* Ni-Cio dragged his palms across his thighs. He was nervous and had started to sweat. He sought Evan's reassurance, *"Any last minute thoughts or changes? I do not intend to risk Daria or our daughter in an ill-timed maneuver..."*

Evan brought his hands up to his forehead and sank to the padded prayer bench. Trying to look like another devotee, he furrowed his brow in an attempt to appear pious. *"Our plan is good. We have to be ready for contingencies, but we're prepared. Try to remain calm..."*

"Calm is as far from me as Atlantis is..."

Ni-Cio left Evan to his thoughts and furtively took count of his men. Scattered throughout the church, they emulated the tourists who flocked to admire the immense edifice that Travlor had erected.

The tour was only supposed to take an hour and as it neared its conclusion, Ni-Cio's heart picked up its rhythm. His heart thumped his chest so hard that his shirt jumped in time to the beats. Ni-Cio closed his eyes and thought of home. He imagined how it would be when he and Daria got back. Those thoughts didn't calm him in the least, but they did occupy his mind for a few moments.

He knelt on the bench and placed his hands against his chest in prayer pose. *"Love, we are at the church. I do not believe it will be long before we can climb aboard a vehicle that has been ordered to the house. Watch for us ... we will be masked as military ..."*

"Is there anything I can do to help?"

Stirring, Ni-Cio reseated himself. As if in awe, he stared transfixed, at Travlor's statue. *"No! Please do nothing ... when we are on the grounds, lead me to your room, but stay there and stay safe ..."*

"Don't worry love, I won't do anything stupid ..."

Ni-Cio broke communication and saw that some of the faithful were starting toward the exits. His men were on the move as well.

Standing, Ni-Cio nudged Evan. He rose from the kneeling bench and they stepped out of the pew. They merged with the crowd headed back to the vestibule, then extricated themselves and made for the truck. Their plans were coming together, and Ni-Cio and his men were more than ready.

He and Evan waited as the rest of the men left the tour and gathered at the back of the truck. Evan left to do a sweep of the grounds. People were engrossed in military duties, tours, or prayers. No one paid them the slightest bit of attention. He signaled Ni-Cio.

The Atlanteans casually strolled into the jungle and began to remove their garments. When Evan joined them, Ni-Cio took a moment for questions or comments. No one had anything else to say and they didn't need any more advice. It was time.

Standing in their bioskins, precious crystals lodged in hidden pockets, they waited to be masked. Evan took one more look at the group and smiled. "We will win the day. Look smart and remember—as soldiers, don't respond unless you have to. As your commanding officer, I will step in if you need help."

He considered each of the men before he continued. "You are my friends. I will give my life to protect you. With luck on our side, we will all be back home very soon."

Ni-Cio stepped forward. "We survived the fires of hell when we defended our home." He peered at Evan. "We have all endured much. I do not know what this day will bring, but there are no finer men that I would rather have at my side. Look to your partner, look to yourselves. Now, let us find our way to Travlor's hideout and bring our healer home!"

The men hugged each other and trickled out of the jungle into the mellow afternoon sun. Masked to resemble every military man that rushed around the churchyard, they fell into the squadron as easily as water falls over a dam.

Chapter 62

MIXING WITH THE soldiers that were to become part of a detail headed to the complex had been deceptively easy. Evan had compelled the lieutenant in charge of rounding up the volunteers. Fifty men had been selected and commanded to Travlor's stronghold. Their orders were to guard the perimeter.

Two large, tarped trucks stood idling, ready to leave as soon as the volunteers were loaded. Twenty-five men, including twenty Atlanteans, climbed into the back of the first truck and found their seats.

Resting against the supports, the Atlanteans were determined not to bring attention to themselves, so they stayed quiet. However, Evan kept a vigilant watch for signs that their cover was suspect. He was prepared to use his limited Spanish to intervene if anyone questioned them; however, he sincerely hoped that wouldn't be necessary. He didn't think it would wash if the man in charge couldn't understand one of his officers, so he too, sat very still. However, his gaze never rested. He hadn't told Ni-Cio that if things went south, he was prepared to compel as many of the soldiers as he could in order to give his friends the chance to get to Daria.

The Atlanteans had been anxious about their disguises. The masking was questionable enough that the men were on high alert. Evan had harbored his own doubts, so no matter what happened, he was determined to look as though he had the situation under control. However, he was much more disturbed than he had let on. He knew without a shadow of a doubt that if they were found out, his father wouldn't hesitate to kill all of them.

Evan kept that knowledge to himself. Nevertheless, he was prepared to do everything in his power to keep that from occurring. After his failed attempt at patricide, he wasn't certain he could bring himself to try again; however, if his friends were taken, then all bets were off.

Evan shuffled his feet and repositioned his back against the hard pole. As he did, his shoulder jostled the man seated next to him. He turned to offer his apology, but the soldier eyed him with such suspicion that he shrugged and turned the other way. It wasn't long before he felt a tap on his shoulder. Reluctantly he faced the soldier again.

"American?"

Evan nodded.

"I speak English, I like to try it when I can. Do you mind?"

Evan felt the leery stares of the other soldiers so he barged into the conversation. "I'm from Boston."

They shook hands.

"I do not know where Boston is, but I think you are long from home."

"I brought some friends with me." He gestured at his group. "We're sick of Uncle Sam dictating who we can or can't worship. We came to help in the only way we could. So, here we are."

"I am amazed to be so close to our risen Savior. I never thought to be picked for this detail." A look of rapture swept over his dark features.

Evan tried to mimic the man's attitude and nodded enthusiastically, "We are excited to be here. We didn't think we had a chance of getting any closer either. We were just happy to be in the vicinity of the ... risen Savior."

The man sat back and tipped his cap up. "I would be honored to give my life for him. I pray he can persuade the world powers to disarm. But if he cannot, I have cleansed my soul and I am ready to meet mi Dios." He quickly performed the age old ritual of the sign of the cross and ended by kissing the knuckle of his pointer finger.

Evan was tired of the charade but adamantly sat forward and eyed the other man, "We are prepared to do the same." Letting out a loud sigh, he leaned back against the post and crossed his arms, "Rest. We'll be marching enough once we get there."

Thankfully, the man quit talking and left him in silence. He glanced at Ni-Cio. *"I don't need any more friends..."*

Ni-Cio hid a grin. *"No, I believe the ones you are with have gotten you into quite enough trouble..."*

"Never a dull moment with you ... always stirring up trouble any chance you get..."

Ni-Cio covered his mouth feigning a yawn. *"No doubt something we learned from you and your father..."*

Evan let his head droop down to his chest and sent his thoughts to Kyla. *"We're almost there, my love ... are you well?"*

Her return was immediate. *"I am holding you in my heart ... I am well and everyone at the compound sends their prayers and loving thoughts for your quick return ..."*

"We should not be long ... maybe another day or so. Once we have Daria, we will leave as soon as we can ..."

"Look to yourself, Evan ..."

"I will my love ..."

Interrupted from sleep, Kyla sat up in bed and hugged her knees. She was terrified for Evan's safety and she didn't know how to occupy her time other than with worry. She had gone down to Atlantis hoping that would help calm her, but for some reason it had produced just the opposite effect. She felt worse than ever, and she had returned to the compound, cutting her visit short.

Needing something to help occupy her mind and her time, she had joined Mer-An in the kitchen. However, she found that she had become irritated by the inexperienced workers so she made her excuses and headed outside.

She found her way to the gardens, then grabbed a shovel and went to work. Thankfully, no one felt like talking so Kyla pushed her muscles and found that the hard work helped a little. After retiring to her cabin, she took a hot shower and was gratified to feel tired. She thought that she had done enough to quiet her thoughts; nevertheless, she fell into a fitful sleep. She jerked awake some time later, her fears once again churning her thoughts like salmon swimming upriver.

Restless, she got out of bed and paced the floor. She and Evan had kept their communication to a minimum, so she was thankful to have heard from him. She briskly rubbed her arms, "It won't be long now."

Kyla tried not to dwell on the negative. She refused to touch upon the possibility that Evan might not come home. However, everyone knew that the men were staking their lives on this charade going off without a hitch. Kyla shivered.

Grabbing a woolen sweater and slipping into her tennis shoes, she stepped outside. The night air was chilly and she quickly snuggled into the heavy sweater as she made her way through the vineyard and out to the cliffs. A salty breeze caressed her face and she inhaled deeply. The moon had already started its downward march in its ceaseless game of hide-and-seek with the rising sun.

Kyla fervently hoped that the glowing orb wouldn't wreak havoc on the small band of rescuers. She never discounted the influence of a full moon, so she accepted the fact that things could fall apart. Poseidon willing, their plans wouldn't turn to cinders before the onslaught of Travlor's wrath should they be discovered.

She settled herself onto the grass. It would be long after dawn before she felt sleepy enough to return to the cabin.

Chapter 63

Daria ordered another tray. She couldn't help it. The kitchen probably thought she was nuts, but she had nothing else with which to occupy her time. When the knock sounded, she was at the door faster than she had moved in weeks.

Expecting someone tiredly bearing a food-laden tray, Daria threw the door open and nearly screamed. Travlor stood alone in the corridor. Daria's throat seized and fear sparked through her like an electric current. Her mouth dried up so that she couldn't talk and it took all of her reserve willpower to keep from falling to her knees and groveling for mercy.

Daria beckoned Travlor in. Closing the door carefully, she squared her shoulders and turned to face him. She didn't know what to expect.

He cocked his head to one side and scanned her. Obviously satisfied with what he saw, he crossed to the desk and pulled the chair around. "I have come to thank you for what you did the other day."

Daria's stomach turned over and she almost threw up. She swayed uncertainly and leaned against the door. Steadying herself, she coughed, cleared her throat and managed to string enough words together to form a sentence. "I don't know what to say."

Travlor drifted closer. "I have been haunted by events of the past my entire life. The fact that you could give me reprieve from that awful wound is more than I ever expected. Your abilities are impressive. I think the daughter you carry will be the best of both worlds. It will be entertaining to watch her grow."

Daria uprooted her feet from the tile and went to her bed. She lowered her body to the mattress and willed her beating heart to slow. She shook her head. "I certainly never expected you to acknowledge the healing, much less feel any effects from it. It was something I've never tried before."

"Well, don't let it go to your head. There will not be another time when you will get the chance to override me."

She bit her lip. "Are you feeling well health-wise?"

He nodded. "I think as well as can be expected considering my advanced years."

"Do you want another healing?"

"No, I just came to offer an olive branch. Unless North Korea and China back down, the U. S. and Russia are prepared to release their missiles. I don't know where their madness will take us."

A crazed urge to laugh gurgled up and out of her chest, so Daria pinched herself in an attempt to strangle the sound. When she regained control, she offered, "It might help if you backed down first."

Travlor stood and straightened his clothing. "If I wanted your advice, I would have asked for it."

He strolled to the door and opened it. The woman bearing her tray had waited patiently outside, but it was evident that she wished to be rid of her burden.

"Ah, I see that your appetite grows. Do not follow the ways of so many and overeat. It's not easy to lose the baby weight."

Daria shook her head, perplexed. "Why should you care?"

He shrugged. "You are a beautiful woman; one would hope that you stay that way. Well, I'm sure your healer's metabolism will take care of any excess. Disregard what I just said. Attend your health in any manner you choose."

Stepping aside to let the woman enter, he closed the door behind him.

Daria's stomach was still filled with acid and she wasn't sure she could eat. But when the silver covers were lifted, the enticing aromas ignited her hunger with gusto.

She held the door to let the woman out, then pulled up the chair and dug in. As she ate, she tried to figure out what had happened to Travlor's ability to block her thoughts. *How did we get through?* And then, it came to her. *The healing! Somehow, I broke through the barrier he created and he doesn't know!*

Chapter 64

THE TRUCK HAD BEEN traveling for approximately half an hour and Ni-Cio was becoming more restless by the minute. *"We should have been there by now …"*

He looked skeptically at Evan and his friend raised a hand, palm down, signaling him to slow down. Evan turned to the soldier next to him. "Do you know how much longer it will be?"

The man shook his head. "No, I have never been there."

Evan looked back at Ni-Cio and raised his shoulders. Ni-Cio crossed his arms and glared out the back.

Finally, the gears shifted and the truck began to slow. The men started yawning and stretching and tightening belts that had been loosened during the ride. Some of the men checked their rifles and others looked through their packs to make sure everything was secure.

Evan's masking made it look as though all of the Atlanteans carried rifles and guns and even machine guns. The men emulated the other soldiers and acted as if they, too, checked their belongings.

The truck eventually pulled to a stop. But before they were allowed out, a cadre of soldiers loaded with rifles, grenades, and Kevlar, and holding tight to the leashes of their working dogs, swept mirrors around and under the truck. Assured that nothing had been hidden in the recesses of the vehicle, they opened the tailgate and ordered the arriving squad to pile out.

A man with captain's bars on his shoulders shouted orders in Spanish. The men quickly dispersed and formed a line. Ni-Cio, Evan and their men followed suit, double-time.

Standing at attention, they watched the captain walk up and down their line as he surveyed the new recruits. He motioned to one of the men who stepped forward. Leaning toward the soldier, the Columbian captain waved his hand toward the Atlanteans. "Quienes son?"

The man held his hands up and shrugged. The captain signaled for him to retake his place in line. He approached Evan. "Americano?"

Evan nodded. "Si, mi capitan."

"Habla Espanol?"

Shaking his head, Evan tried to explain, but the Columbian held up his hand. He motioned to someone behind the group and a tall, lean man rushed to the captain's side. "Necesito su interpretation."

The lieutenant nodded and waited for the captain to begin. As his superior spoke, he interpreted for the newcomers. "The captain welcomes you to the sacred site of our beloved Messiah. He wishes you well and knows that you will perform your duties without hesitation. He has asked me to stay by your side in order to relay his commands. Do you understand?"

Ni-Cio and his men stood straighter, eyes forward, and Evan spoke for the group. "Muchas gracias mi capitan, we are honored to be here." He saluted smartly. The captain returned his salute and continued barking orders.

The interpreter did his best. "You are to surround the outer perimeter wall. Shifts will change every three hours. He has asked that I lead you to the back of the complex. Are you prepared to walk?"

Evan nodded and signaled for the others to fall in behind. They gathered in single file. When they were ready, the dusky-skinned interpreter introduced himself. "I am Juan Espinoza. Please follow me."

Juan took off at a rapid pace, pulled out a machete and started hacking his way through the jungle growth. The complex was huge and the grounds engulfed an enormous amount of land. Thirty minutes passed before Juan showed them their post.

Ni-Cio asked, *"Evan, how are we to gain entrance from here?"*

"Don't worry. I'll send a compulsion to the watchtowers. They'll believe that we're still here, so for them, nothing will be different…"

"And what do you propose to do with our interpreter?"

"Bring him with us. We may need him so I'll compel him as well…"

Ni-Cio's relief was evident. Evan patted him on the back. Squinting at the guards in the two rear towers, he sent a very strong compulsion. Although there was no break in their stride, Evan had no doubt that they would see nothing amiss. They would believe that Ni-Cio and the others faithfully stood guarding the perimeters.

Evan looked at Juan, whose expression had immediately changed. Blank-faced, the interpreter waited to follow any order issued by Ni-Cio or Evan.

Ni-Cio finally cracked a smile. "What a talent you have!"

Evan grimaced. "Yeah, lucky me. Who knows what other abilities lurk inside me that I'm not aware of." He jerked his chin toward the path they had just marched. "Aris, it's time to see if your plan really works." Aris grinned at Evan as Evan addressed the group, "Let's move!"

Chapter 65

FULL TO BURSTING, and with the remains of her meal gone, Daria once again stared out the window, muttering, "If I was the heroine in a romance novel, I would be wringing my hands by now." To keep from doing just that, she had retrieved a scarf from her closet, which she now clutched tightly in both hands.

She had recently heard from Ni-Cio. They had been taken to the rear of the complex where they were supposed to be guarding the perimeter wall. Evan had compelled the watchtower guards to believe the new recruits still manned their posts; however, Ni-Cio and his men were making their way back towards the entrance. They would come through the front gate. Masked completely, they were no longer visible to the naked eye. Nevertheless, Daria didn't feel any better.

Her hands ached, and when she looked for the reason as to why they should hurt, she realized that she was squeezing the scarf so hard it looked as though she was trying to strangle it. Prying her fingers loose, the material trickled to the floor in a cascading pool of scarlet. Spreading around her feet, Daria shuddered. "Please don't let that be an omen." The scarf resembled spilled blood.

She kicked the fabric away from her feet and resumed her surveillance. Her eyes narrowed and her focus sharpened as she looked for any indication that Ni-Cio had entered the grounds. The gates, while open during the day to admit military personnel, still remained closely guarded. The soldiers never wavered in the inspection or care with which they checked vehicles before admitting people inside.

The sun's rays had just touched the jungle canopy, and inside the walled complex, shadows were drifting to the ground. Night would come soon.

"Please hurry." Daria stroked her belly. The baby had pummeled her all day. Daria knew that she was restless too. She tried to sing a song, but her throat was parched and her voice cracked. She crossed to the bedside pitcher and poured a big glass of water. She drank it quickly and then went back to the window. With a sudden gasp, she craned her neck. She wished she had a pair of binoculars.

A lone man approached the entrance. Swarmed by soldiers, he was patted down and searched thoroughly. He exchanged words with two of the guards, but Daria couldn't detect anybody else near him. Pulling up the desk chair to relieve her aching back, she sat down and studied the man.

Having been checked and cleared, the guards allowed the soldier to enter the grounds and walk up the brick drive. When he arrived at the house, he stopped at the base of the stairs and stood without moving. Was that a distortion or was it her imagination? No! There was something apart from the scenery right behind him! Could it be?

Daria stood, barely breathing, eyes riveted to the Columbian. She braced her body against the back of the chair. There it was again!

Gulping air, she went to the windowsill. With both hands on the glass, she placed her forehead against the pane and stared, unblinking, at the space just behind the man. An unmistakable shimmer moved the air. "They're here!"

She spun the chair out of her way. At the desk, she pulled the lamp as close to the window as the plug would allow and she clicked the light on and off several times hoping to catch Ni-Cio's attention. She dared not send a thought for fear Travlor would know.

She returned the lamp to the desk and hurried back to the window. The wait was interminable and she was starting to sweat. She strained her vision for a glimpse of any distortion. It took forever, but the man finally began to ascend the stairs. He looked up and saw her. Startled, she lifted her head from the glass and noticed just the smallest nod of his head. They were inside!

She hurried to the door and placed her ear against it. Closing her eyes, she listened with every cell in her body. Nothing. She tried to hear any sound that would indicate what was happening or where they were. She held her breath. Was that a rustle of movement outside the door? Were her guards repositioning themselves? She hesitated. If she opened the door would it help or hinder?

Deciding it could divert the guard's attention, she cracked the door. Her groupies stood in various bored positions. Distracting themselves with games, they tapped their phones or rested lazily against the walls. Just another tedious day.

With a bravado she didn't feel, she swung the door wide. She boldly stepped into the corridor and signaled one of the men. He hurried to her side with an inquiring gaze but she hadn't thought that far ahead. She didn't know what to say. She opened her mouth to ask for more food when a quiet demand from Ni-Cio flowed into her mind.

"Show us the way to your quarters..."

Stammering apologies, she backed into her room and slammed the door in the guard's incredulous face. Marshalling her racing thoughts, she sent Ni-Cio a picture indicating where she was.

"We are coming..."

Her stomach roiled and she wished with all her heart that she hadn't eaten anything. Her heart beat like a frightened hummingbird and the blood pulsed through her ears so that she could no longer hear anything. She tried to pace, but her legs suddenly felt like jelly. Her fine muscle coordination departed. She knew if she dared a step now, she would collapse on the tile in a massive, elephantine heap. She ordered her spine to stiffen and commanded her blood to slow. She took one slow deep breath, then exhaled, controlling her breathing.

She took one step and then another until she was back at the door. Putting her ear against the wood, she heard footsteps. Were her guards on the move? She angled away from the door and watched the knob turn. Her heart hammered and the baby spun crazily. Her breathing escalated and she felt lightheaded, dizzy. The door pushed open and Travlor stepped into the room.

Daria fainted.

Chapter 66

HER HEAD FELT LIKE it had been used for a drum. Daria surfaced slowly. When she opened her eyes, she realized that her guards had carried her to Travlor's rooms. Laid out on his bed, she held back a sob as the hot sting of tears pricked her eyelids. She coughed to dislodge the lump that had risen in her throat and swallowed hard to keep from crying.

"Ah, you're awake." Travlor came to the bed and took her hand, a look of true concern on his face. "I have scanned you and you seem all right. How are you feeling?"

She tried to sit up, but he gently placed a hand on her shoulder. "No, you need to rest. I can find no reason that you should have fainted, but I'm not ready to release you under your own recognizance."

She tried to talk, but her voice came out as a croak. "Wa—" She cleared her throat and tried again. "Water, please."

Travlor motioned to his major-domo. The man, standing ready, filled a glass with iced water and added a slice of lemon, then brought it to Daria. She accepted it gratefully and Travlor helped her sit up. She drank half the glass then set it down on the bedside table. "I'm okay. I don't know what happened." She glanced at Travlor. "Maybe I ate too much."

The man actually chuckled. "I doubt that's the cause. Rest yourself; I have work to do. When you're ready, I'll have the men carry you back to your room."

"I'm ready."

Travlor's features settled into a look that brooked no argument. Daria didn't know what to do, so with a shrug, she gave up and slid back onto the pillows. Travlor patted her hand like she was a good little girl and then went back to the outer office and his desk.

It was at that moment that a clamor erupted outside Travlor's door. Shouted orders and the sounds of rapid footsteps could be heard retreating down the hall. It seemed that some of the men were vacating their posts. Daria pushed up and glanced anxiously at the door. Travlor rose from his desk extremely perturbed and perplexed, and rushed to help Daria as she strained to stand.

He searched her eyes with animal ferocity and the snarl of his voice almost made her heart stop. "You know what's happening." He grabbed her wrist and yanked her into the office. "Tell me!"

Daria refused to shrink away anymore and a triumphant smile spread across her face. She started to retort when the door crashed inward. Ni-Cio, with Evan on his heels, burst into the room. Daria fought to free herself, but Travlor easily dragged her behind his back. Eyes blazing like an inferno, Travlor started to address Ni-Cio until his gaze took in his son. Confused, he stammered, "Evan? I—I thought you ... were dead." Travlor glanced around the room, dazed, then back at his son. "How did you find us?"

Unable to hide his disdain any longer, Evan slowly looked his father up and down. "We followed the madness. It wasn't difficult."

Travlor blinked hard and shook his head but his mind had stalled. The only audible sound inside the room was the gentle rake of palm fronds against the windows. No one moved. Without warning, the frozen tableau was shattered when the report of rapid-fire gunshots brought with it the sounds of agonized, guttural screams.

Evan and Ni-Cio simultaneously broke and ran to the door, ramming it shut. Engaging the lock, Ni-Cio yelled, "Barricade it!"

While the men piled as much furniture as they could in front of the door, Daria tried to break free of Travlor's hold, but it was useless. It was like her entire arm was frozen in cement.

Turning back into the room, Evan took one look at the shocked face of Travlor's assistant and sent a compulsion, *"To the bedroom, now! Lie face-down on the bed and don't move!"*

The angry shouts of Travlor's elite soldier's echoed through the hallway. Hammering against the door, they battered the wood, screaming orders as they tried to gain entrance.

Ni-Cio dropped the chair he had been carrying and raced to Daria's side. Wresting her from Travlor's grip, he grabbed her to his chest shouting over the din. "Are you and the baby all right?"

Daria clung to him with all her might, but fear galvanized her to action; she dropped her arms and sent a desperate thought to her beloved, *"We are well, Ni-Cio! But Travlor's men are heavily armed!"*

Ni-Cio left her side and went to the huge desk. He quickly flipped it on its side and signaled Daria, "Get behind this!" When she came around, Ni-Cio lowered her to the floor, then he joined Evan.

Evan ran to Travlor's side and screamed into his father's slack features, "Tell your men to stand down!"

Travlor raised a trembling hand to Evan's face, wonder filling his eyes. His broken whisper could be heard even above the sounds of gunfire. "You look so much like your mother." Travlor looked around as though he couldn't remember where he was.

Wood began to splinter as Travlor's men wielded a battering ram against the office door. Gunfire rang throughout the house and men everywhere shouted for reinforcements.

Evan seized his father by the shoulders and shook hard in an effort to rouse the man. Still dazed, Travlor didn't respond. He continued to peer at Evan in loving wonder. Evan sent a compulsion for the soldiers to stand down, but they didn't comply. The door shook harder and started to give. Wildly searching for his friend, Evan yelled, "Ni-Cio! I can't compel them!"

Evan shook his father, shouting, "Travlor! I can't compel them! What have you done?"

Travlor blinked to clear his vision, but continued to stare as he haltingly explained, "My son, they are my elite guard and cannot be compelled. Not even by you." He touched Evan's face again and in a voice filled with awe, admitted, "A failsafe for me should I be located. Which you have done."

Outside, a sharp command issued a warning. "Stand back! We're blowing the door!"

Evan grabbed his father while Ni-Cio ran back to the overturned desk. Picking Daria off the floor and shielding her with his body, he shouted at Evan, "Bathroom, now!"

Evan pushed Travlor ahead of him and followed Ni-Cio and Daria into the bedroom. They scrambled into the bathroom as the explosives detonated. The concussive force blasted inward and nearly blew the bathroom door off its hinges. Evan was thrown against his father and they stumbled into the vanity. He checked Travlor, then yanked himself upright. Ni-Cio shielded Daria and Evan stepped in front of Travlor as they waited for the soldiers to clear the bedroom door. Evan and Ni-Cio pulled their crystals from their pockets and steadied their aim.

Heavy boots pounded the floor and men boiled into the front office, guns blazing. Travlor stood up and roared an order underscored with a strong compulsion. "Cease fire!"

Wielding his crystal, Evan thrust himself toward the sagging bathroom door and would have made it through, but somebody grabbed him from behind. Travlor blew past his son and burst out of the bedroom into his office. He slipped on a spray of shattered glass and started to fall. Grabbing at an overturned chair in an effort to steady himself, he watched in horror as his men mistakenly opened fire. Bullets ripped into his body.

The soldiers immediately ceased firing and stared in horror as their Messiah sank to the floor, blood pouring from his body. The compulsion with which Travlor had surrounded his men disappeared and he uttered his last command. "Do not fire. Leave us ... alone ..."

Evan raced into the office. Seeing his father lying in a pool of blood, he sank to his side and grabbed his hand. "Travlor!"

Looking for help, Evan screamed a fierce compulsion at the staring elite, *"Leave at once!"* Travlor's men scrambled out of the bullet-riddled room as Ni-Cio led Daria out of the bedroom. They stood over Evan.

Evan's attention was riveted on his father. He shook his shoulders and tried a command, "Travlor!" His father didn't stir. He shouted louder, "Travlor!"

From a great distance, Travlor heard his son's voice. His eyes fluttered open but he couldn't seem to focus. He ordered his fingers to squeeze the hand that held his, yet they refused to move. He opened his mouth to talk and coughed up blood. His chest gurgled as he fought for his next breath.

Travlor tried to talk. He had to tell his son ... something. Evan leaned over bringing his ear next to his father's lips. Travlor forced the words from his throat. "You ... are the man ... I should have been."

His father's eyes rolled back into his head. Evan didn't know what to do until he noticed Daria. He begged, "Do something!"

Ni-Cio helped Daria to Evan's side. She began the healing tones, but as her hands passed over Travlor, her stomach seized in a massive contraction. Unable to stop herself, she pitched forward, falling on the Atlantean. Racked with pain, Daria clutched her stomach and screamed, "Ni-Cio, the baby is coming!"

Ni-Cio tried to lift her off Travlor's body, but her agonized shriek stopped him. Looking helplessly at Evan, Ni-Cio's coloring reflected his abject horror.

Evan pulled Daria from Travlor's inert body. Without thinking, he gently placed her next to his father, then knelt between them and took both their hands in his. He sent a compulsion and from the deepest recesses of his mind the healing tones surfaced.

Evan closed his eyes and opened his mouth, the notes poured forth. Daria's pain immediately ceased. She heaved a sigh of relief and closed her eyes. No longer moving, it was as though she was sealed in a type of stasis, her breathing slowed so that Ni-Cio couldn't even see the rise of her chest. He threw himself at Evan, "No! You are killing her!"

The topsider opened his eyes, issuing a dire order, *"Do not break my hold! You must let me try…"*

Shaking with fear, Ni-Cio did as his friend commanded and settled next to Daria. He carefully lifted her head into his lap and stroked her long strands of hair.

Evan had seen the terror in Ni-Cio's eyes, but there was nothing he could do. If he stopped now, Daria, the baby, and Travlor would die. He closed his eyes, lowered his head, and let the healing tones take over.

Evan scanned Daria and the baby. He had induced a very deep state of sleep and as far as he could tell, they were both fine.

Then he scanned Travlor. His father's heartbeat was thready indicating shock. The tenuous hold Travlor maintained on life was quickly leaching away. Evan sharpened his concentration and with single-minded intensity, deepened the healing tones. Tuning his mind to Travlor's, he sank into his father's thoughts in order to sense any change. Travlor's mind opened to Evan and it was as though he *became* Travlor. He felt his father's heartbeat elevate a millimeter and witnessed the beat incrementally strengthen.

Evan gripped Daria's and his father's hands with savage tenacity as the healing tones gathered strength and force. At last, his father slipped toward the same stasis in which Daria had been placed. Evan as Travlor, approached the edge of darkness, but as he slipped toward death, Travlor roused himself to touch his son's thoughts one last time.

"Must take us ... back ... to ... Atlantis ..."

Holding Daria and his father in a state of suspended animation, Evan knew that it was safe to stop the atonal notes. As he loosened his control, he delivered a fervid thought to his frightened friend. *"Ni-Cio, I cannot let go or we will lose them both ... get us back to Atlantis!"*

Ni-Cio gently pried himself from beneath Daria then bolted for the door. Rushing into the hallway, he ran into Travlor's elite and skidded to a stop, expecting bullets to fly. They all heard Evan's shouted command. "You have mortally wounded *your Savior!* Tell your men to stand down! We have to get him to a hospital, now!"

The guards rushed back into the room, one of them running to Evan's side. "We will take care of everything." The soldier grabbed his walkie-talkie and barked orders. The rest of the men raced from the room to see that his commands were executed without hesitation.

The mercenary, eyes pinned on his Messiah, edged closer to Evan and cleared his throat. Fear and awe filled his voice. "Will our Messiah live?"

Evan hesitated, "We will do everything we can. We need a chopper, *now*."

The captain grabbed his cell and stabbed a button. "Send a chopper to the front entrance of the house, immediately." He pocketed the phone, still unable to take his eyes off Travlor.

Evan jerked his head, "Ni-Cio, get the rest of our men and meet us at the front entrance." When Ni-Cio looked at Daria and hesitated, Evan yelled, "Hurry!"

Ni-Cio sprinted from the room issuing orders to his men, *"Aris! Rogert! Get everybody to the front lawn, now!"*

Evan's gaze locked on the captain, "Make sure that all your men know to stand down. And get another chopper for the rest of our crew!" The man sprang to life and ran from the room, phone in hand.

Alone, Evan stared at his two—three—patients. He had no idea how or why the healing rites had come to him. His mind rocked with the sudden turn of events, but his thoughts were captured by his father. Puzzled, he saw Travlor's rapid eye movements behind closed lids. Was his father dreaming? Evan let his mind sink, once again, into Travlor's. His thoughts became Travlor's and it was then that Evan realized that his father wasn't dreaming. He was reliving his life. The moment unfolded in real-time and faint echoes wound through Evan's mind as though someone was calling him from a great distance. Losing any sense of his own identity, Evan as Travlor, turned toward the source of the sound and listened intently.

Someone drew closer. Travlor recognized the lyrical, loving tones and he grinned. He knew the woman well.

Evan started and let his thoughts diverge. Confused, he tried to make sense of what was happening and saw his father's body twitch. Evan realized that his father was responding to the woman. He let himself submerge, once again, into Travlor's memories.

The woman finally walked into view and Travlor's heart skipped several beats. The overpowering security of his mother's loving presence always brought him immense joy.

Travlor stood, appreciating the strength, power, and grace that flooded his youthful body. On the verge of becoming a man, he still felt childishly happy at the sight of his beautiful mother.

A rapturous smile lifted the corners of her mouth belying her exasperated sigh. With one hand on her hip, the other swiping at errant strands of hair, her voice washed over him with love, "Atlas! I have been looking all over for you! Do you forget yourself? Poseidon … your father awaits your presence!"

END

COMING SUMMER 2018!

DEPTHS *of* REMEMBRANCE

Book Three of the Atlantis Chronicles

Chapter 1

TRAVLOR WAS DEEP into his vision. His mother was as beautiful as he remembered. He didn't quite know how he had gotten here but it was incredible to feel young again and have his whole life stretching before him.

He studied his mother, both hands on her hips. The sun created a corona around her figure and to his young mind, she seemed like a goddess from Mt. Olympus. But he loved the fact that she was human. One glimpse at her blonde hair, fair skin and voluptuous figure and Travlor could see why his father, Poseidon, had taken her to wife. Clieto was the dream by which every man judged beauty.

"Atlas! Are you daydreaming again? Poseidon is waiting for you! Run and rinse your face and hands. Your father needs to speak with you."

Travlor shook himself from his reverie, taller than his mother, at five feet eleven inches, he towered over her slender frame. He brushed the dirt from his pants and reached into a pocket. His sixteen year old eyes burned with delight as he showed his treasure to his mother. "Look, mother, the ultimate crystal for my collection!"

He held the opaque crystal up to the light. A thin striation – no bigger than the width of a hair – gleamed clear and bright. Sunlight winked at him.

Clieto grabbed his hand, bringing the crystal closer to her eyes. "It is beautiful son. Is it the one you have searched for?"

Travlor grinned, "It is exactly the type I was trying to find! Do you think father will be proud?"

Cleito nodded and started toward home. "I have no doubt that he will be very proud. However, if you keep him waiting much longer, it will not be your crystal that draws his attention. Now, go! And clean up!"

Travlor hugged his mother, thrust the crystal into her hand, turned and ran. He felt incredible! He pumped his legs effortlessly and pushed his arms like pistons. Air whipped through his long dark hair and blood thrummed in his veins. He was proud that his breath remained deep and steady.

As he topped the hill leading to his home, the grandeur of Atlantis unveiled herself before him. What beauty, what architecture and color and design! He could hardly wait to become one of the designers of the great city. He wanted to grow up so fast and yet part of him still yearned for the security of his parents.

He ran even faster as his father's thought-form demanded, *"Atlas! Where are you? I will not wait all day!"*

"I am coming, father! I am almost home..."

His home, on a bluff overlooking Atlantis, was the highest home of the city and had a commanding view of the surrounding area. Enclosed by a protective wall, the courtyard was lush and adorned with gardens and trees and meandering streams.

A fountain, in honor of his father, stood in the heart of the courtyard. The music of the falling water lent a magical note to the glorious surroundings.

Travlor loved his home; built from marble so white, it gleamed like another crystal. It was well known by everyone in Atlantis that this was where Poseidon stayed when he visited. Travlor's thoughts focused on the god that had sired him.

Standing six feet eleven inches, the man was commanding even without the god aspect. Travlor smiled remembering his father's laughter; he could laugh so loud and so long that other's joined in the laughter just to share in Poseidon's release of pure joy.

However, Atlas had also witnessed the lightning and thunder that could strike when his father was displeased. It was frightening and awesome in its majesty. That his father controlled the land and the oceans was a concept that he still had trouble grasping. He didn't know, being half-human, half-god, what role his father had planned for him, but he hoped with all his heart that it had to do with his loves and passions; design and architecture. At his sixteenth birthday, his father was to divulge his mission.

His breath came harder but he was almost there. He sent his father a quick thought. *"I am home father!"*

Travlor raced to the front door. A servant held the immense, golden doors open. Travlor barely glanced at the man as he halted his run long enough to grab the nearest pitcher of water. Splashing the liquid into a bowl, he ran his hands through the cool water and doused his face. Travlor hurriedly grabbed the proffered linen, swiped the wet areas and thrust the towel back into waiting hands.

Currents of Will

Running the lengthy hallway, another servant opened the door to the library. "Your father awaits within."

Travlor nodded, took a deep breath and composed himself. He knew his father didn't want to meet him when he looked like a wild thing. He held out his arms. "Father! How good it is to see you!" Travlor hurried to the seated figure.

Poseidon stood, opening his thick, muscular arms. "Ahh, at last. Why do you persist in keeping me waiting?"

He laughed and Travlor fell into his embrace. They held each other tightly until his father released the warm hug. Poseidon reacquired his seat and motioned for Travlor to sit next to him. "So, tell me what have you been up to?"

Travlor excitedly revealed the result of his adventure. "I found one father! I found the exact crystal you told me about!"

Poseidon's face split into a huge grin and his laughter boomed through the house. He slapped his son's knee. "Do you have it with you?"

"No, mother is holding it for me. She did not want me to keep you waiting any longer, so I ran ahead."

Poseidon's dark, blue-black eyes sparkled. "No matter, I will inspect it when she arrives." The huge man settled back into his chair. "We must discuss your upcoming birthday. It is not every day a boy becomes a man and I have many friends who plan on attending the celebration."

The preparations for this momentous occasion had started over two years ago. The Temple of Poseidon, at the very center of Atlantis, had been adorned for the festival. An esteemed list of attendees was expected to come from all directions. Travlor had even heard a rumor that Zeus, Poseidon's brother, would make a special appearance. Travlor had never met him and he was filled with anticipation. "It will be incredible. I can hardly wait!"

Poseidon loved his son almost more than the other children he had sired. Atlas's enthusiasm was infectious and he admired the young boy's sense of adventure, curiosity, and intelligence. These attributes shone from Atlas like a beacon. "You will be honored fully as befits a son of Poseidon.

"But tell me, how far afield did you roam today? I am worried that your wanderings should take you out of the bounds I have set for Atlantis. You become so immersed in your adventures that I fear you do not keep an eye as to our borders."

Travlor shook his head in earnest. "Do not worry, I am careful. I have been close to our western border, but I am aware, father. I promise I will never cross our lines. I know it is for our safety."

"Remember Atlas, it is not only for safety that we keep ourselves apart. The newly struggling tribes and emerging groups that are learning to survive as more than savages must not be tainted by our knowledge or ways. We have granted them the freedom to determine their own course. That is a sacred commitment and so it must be."

Travlor furrowed his brow, "I am aware of the specific Canon father and I am careful, I give you my word."

Poseidon glanced up as Cleito entered the room, his great countenance broke into a huge, love-filled smile. He rose from his chair and crossed the distance quickly. He stood before his wife and let his eyes drink in her pale beauty. His heart quickened, filling his loins with desire. Poseidon embraced her and stroked her radiant face. "My love, I am overjoyed to have you in my arms again."

He kissed her deeply, then looked into her sparkling eyes, "I understand you have a treasure to show me."

Proudly, Clieto took Atlas's crystal from her shift and gave it to her handsome husband. "He has done as you requested."

Poseidon closed his large fist around the crystal and went to one of the windows. The sun was slipping below the horizon, but clearly defined in the last light of day was the singular hairline striation. Glacial in its beauty, Poseidon could see an entire rainbow locked inside. He turned it all around, gazing at the crystal with delight. "You have done remarkably well Atlas. It is truly a new type of striation. I will teach you how to harness its power."

He gazed at his beloved wife and held out his hand. "But now, let us retire to the garden and enjoy the repast that has been set."

Travlor joined his mother and father as they departed. "When will you show me father? You know I have searched for this crystal from the time my birthday celebrations began. Will you be staying with us tonight?"

Poseidon's explosive laughter rang out. "Atlas! Slow down, my son! All in good time. Before your birthday, I will teach you the ways of this particular crystal. That is my promise to you." He ruffled his son's hair. "As for staying, I must decline. I have business elsewhere and I expect to be away for a while."

"But my birthday is only a few months away! How long will you be gone?"

His father's large hand lifted from his head and with it, the comforting warmth. "I will return before the new moon." He saw his son's look of disappointment. "Do not worry! Enjoy the time you have left. As you step into manhood, responsibilities invariably arise. With the little time left, be a boy with an excellent sense of adventure and no responsibilities!"

Poseidon placed an arm around Clieto and Atlas and guided them out of the house and into the gardens.

Lit like fireflies, candles hung suspended in the trees and graced the low marble wall surrounding the veranda.

Servants stood, holding out the chairs. When they were seated, a signal from the butler indicated that the meal was to be served. The doors connecting the kitchen flew open and a line of men and women proceeded outside with every kind of food imaginable. The smell was intoxicating. Travlor felt his stomach awaken and he was ravenous!

Twinkling with the last rays of a dusky-gold sunset, candlelight filled the veranda with warmth and serenity as a gentle night breeze wrapped the small family in a loving caress. Atlas was home and he felt marvelous!

About the Athor

SUSAN MACIVER GREW up in Roswell, New Mexico. She has stated, emphatically, that she knows nothing about *The UFO Crash*. However, since she claims that she never wanted to be a writer, it is curious as to where she got the idea for The Atlantis Chronicles Trilogy.

She attended The University of Texas in Austin, where she enrolled in dance and acting. Her acting career was brought to a screeching halt when, at her first student audition, she was informed that she had quite a strong accent. She claims her accent was a by-product of southeastern NM, but it sounds suspiciously Texan.

Intervening years occurred and time passed. She was blessed with a son, Eric, who has been an entrepreneur since the ripe old age of three. He now resides in Los Angeles and, of course, has his own company.

Married to Duke Ayers, Susan says, "Duke has taught me more about unconditional love than any other human I've met." Sharing their love and their adventures in Arizona, she credits Duke with the fact that she is writing again.

If you would like to learn more, please visit her website at
WWW.SUSANMACIVER.COM

or

FACEBOOK.COM/SUSANMACIVERAUTHOR
INSTAGRAM@SUSAN.MACIVER

and

TWITTER@SUSANMACIVER

Made in the USA
Middletown, DE
15 July 2024